The Younges

Mara Kay

Margin Notes Books

Published by Margin Notes Books, 2015
First published by Macmillan, 1969

Every effort has been made to trace the copyright holders and to obtain their permission for the use of copyright material. The publisher apologises for any errors or omissions and would be grateful if notified of any corrections that should be incorporated in future reprints or editions of this book.

Margin Notes Books have been unable to trace the heirs to the estate of Mara Kay. Royalties have been set aside and the publishers would be pleased to hear from the heir.

Design and layout © Margin Notes Books 2015

All rights reserved. No part of this publication may be reproduced, stored in or introduced into a retrieval system, or transmitted, by any means (electronic, mechanical, photocopying, recording or otherwise) without the prior written permission of the copyright owner and publisher.

A CIP record for this book is available from the British Library

ISBN 978-0-9564626-5-7

www.marginnotesbooks.com
info@marginnotesbooks.com

Published by Margin Notes Books
5 White Oak Square
London Road
Swanley
Kent BR8 7AG

CONTENTS

1	Remembrances	5
2	Good-byes	14
3	The world outside	21
4	In the Winter Palace	33
5	In the Summer Garden	45
6	The Peterhoff Fête	56
7	The flood	71
8	The rescue	85
9	Winter weather	90
10	Aunt Daria	105
11	In the woods	119
12	Pushkin	127
13	Anna Wulff	133
14	Sophie's wedding	144
15	Otrada	152
16	High Summer	164
17	The legend of the cross	171
18	The news from Taganrogue	177
19	The new emperor	187
20	December fourteenth	195

21	In Senate Square	210
22	Afterwards	217
23	Smolni again	225
24	By Peter and Paul Fortress	230
25	For ever and ever	237
26	The reunion	247
27	Home	259

1

Remembrances

It was very early in the morning. St. Petersburg was just beginning to wake up to a new day: April seventeenth, 1824.

The immense building of the Smolni Institute for Noble Girls, with its majestic porticos and pillars, stood wrapped in the fog creeping up from the river Neva. Behind the building, where the school garden gently sloped down to the high stone wall built on the water's edge, the fog was even thicker, veiling the trees and hanging low over the grass. In front, on the vast cobbled place, the oil lamps shone dimly, flickered and went out one by one.

In the dormitory of the White form, on the second floor, Masha Fredericks watched the pale outline of the windows, and listened with growing impatience to the quiet breathing and light snores coming from the other beds.

'How can they all sleep so soundly?' she wondered. 'This is our last morning in Smolni. Nine years of classrooms and dormitories! And now, in just a few hours, we will be leaving for ever.'

The windows were becoming faintly pink. Masha moved restlessly on her pillow and glanced around. No one was stirring. She threw off her blanket and pattered across the polished floor to the nearest window. Hitching up her nightgown, she climbed on the sill and looked out.

Below, the garden was slowly emerging from the fog. It looked strange and lonely without the crowd of pupils in their brown, blue and white uniforms, swarming over the sanded paths, or sitting on the old stone benches. The flower-beds were still bare, but the trees and the big group of lilac bushes were sprinkled with green buds. Further away, just barely visible behind some tall pines, a silvery birch tree stretched itself towards the rising sun.

Masha smiled and blew a kiss in the direction of the birch tree. 'Good morning,' she whispered, 'good morning. Do you realise that it is the last? We will not meet tomorrow. I wish I could take you with me; we have been friends for so long. From my first day in Smolni…'

She leaned her forehead against the cold glass. As she looked out on the silent garden she had an almost eerie feeling that if she sat still enough and kept remembering, she would see little Masha appear from behind the lilac bushes.

In another moment, there she was: a short sturdy child in the brown uniform of the youngest forms, blonde hair cut short and strained back with a round comb. The round freckled face was tear-stained, the light brows puckered. She pushed through the shrubbery and vanished among the trees.

Crouched on her perch, the eighteen-year-old Masha smiled dreamily. She could remember so clearly what happened next. Little Masha would go up another path, turn to the left and come to a small round lawn with a scrawny newly-planted birch tree in the middle, looking just as scared and uncomfortable as the small new girl. They would become friends…friends for life.

The bells of the Smolni monastery nearby began to ring. Nine years. For nine years those familiar bells had ushered in each day: happy days, and days of grief…all shared with the birch tree. Little Masha had exchanged her brown uniform for the blue one of the middle school, then put on the coveted white of the seniors. The birch tree grew taller; its twigs became proud branches. The date, 1815, little Masha had scratched on its bark to mark their first meeting, had become blurred and was now far above her head. It did not matter, not as long as she could put her arms around the trunk and whisper some special secret she would not confide to anyone else, not even to Sophie.

At the thought of Sophie, Masha glanced over her shoulder at the rows of beds stretching across the dormitory. Twenty-three of her classmates were sleeping in strict obedience to the rules: on their right side, arms rigid on the blanket. Only Sophie lay on her back, her arms flung wide, her nightcap off, bronze curls all over the pillow.

Sophie…always different from the others, with unpredictable moods. Her face looked vivacious even in sleep, lips curled up in mischievous smile.

'My two dearest friends,' Masha whispered to herself, looking from Sophie to the distant silhouette of the birch tree, then again at Sophie.

As though she felt Masha's eyes on her, Sophie suddenly yawned and sat up in bed. 'What are you doing up there?' she asked sleepily.

'Hush!' Masha jumped lightly off the windowsill. 'I woke up at dawn and I was too excited and anxious to sleep.'

'Excited, I can understand, but why *anxious*?' Sophie asked.

'I don't know myself,' Masha answered truthfully. Only…it seems so unreal. It all happened so suddenly. I've never dreamed I would become a lady-in-waiting. When Mamma died, and I realised I had no home and no money, nobody but myself in all the world, there seemed no alternative to becoming a governess, or a companion, or even maybe a nursery maid. If I hadn't been so shy and awkward at the interviews, that's where I would be going today! But when nobody wanted me, I began to feel desperate. And then came the graduation ball and my whole life changed. Oh, Sophie, when I think that if you hadn't forced me, I wouldn't have gone!'

Sophie giggled. 'You mean if I had not dragged you from under the bed?'

Masha flushed. 'Wasn't I silly? But I was terrified at the idea of talking to strange men and dancing with them, and then, when we were in the ballroom and you went dancing off, with so many partners and no one invited me, I became resentful and miserable. And yet it was because of that, because Grand Duke Nicholas noticed me sitting by the wall dance after dance that he invited me to waltz. Then, when he said that he wanted to present me to his wife, I was terrified. Everyone knows that Princess Charlotte likes girls to be pretty and graceful. I felt all thumbs and my hair was becoming uncurled. But we talked…I can't understand it even now. Sophie, why do you think that Princess Charlotte chose me to be her lady-in-waiting? There are many girls in the White form who are much prettier than I and have graduated with higher marks.'

'That is not the point,' said Sophie. 'Take Sashette, for instance. She certainly *is* a beauty and she graduated with top honours, but what does she talk about when she is telling us of her brilliant future as a lady-in-waiting?' Sophie started to count on her fingers. 'She is going to live in a palace and dance at the court balls; she is going to have her own money; she will be able to meet young men from the best families and this means a rich marriage. It is 'I…I…I…' all the time. Now, I am sure that Princess Charlotte just looked into those blue eyes of yours and realised that all *you* would care about would be serving *her* to the best of your ability. And she is right! She could not possibly have a more devoted lady-in-waiting. You would give up your life for her, wouldn't you?'

'Life…' Masha repeated pensively. 'That should be easy enough. There must be something more precious than life.'

'I…' Sophie began and stopped.

Masha looked up. 'Yes?'

'Nothing. I just felt very solemn all at once.'

Masha nodded. 'I felt the same. Isn't it strange?'

'It's because we are leaving school,' Sophie decided. 'We are taking everything seriously now. Well, what I was going to say? Oh, yes! You simply must stop calling Her Highness 'Princess Charlotte'. She became the Grand Duchess Alexandra Feodorovna when she married the Grand Duke Nicholas and that was six years ago.'

Masha sighed. 'I know. I will try not to forget, but it will not be easy. I think of her as Princess Charlotte. I suppose it is because of everyone calling her that when she came from Germany as a bride. I am afraid I am going to make many silly mistakes, Sophie. Sometimes I wish Sashette and I were going to be together. Sashette is always so sure of herself. But I don't suppose the suites of the empress and the grand duchess meet very often.'

'Sh...don't wake her up.' Sophie glanced at the bed where Sasha Rossett's dark head was resting on the pillow. 'Goodness, Masha, you must be really scared if you want Sashette's company. She has always been nasty to you and now she is vexed because she is not the only one in the form to become a lady-in-waiting. The less you see of her, the better. You ought to be glad that she will be in the Winter Palace and you at Anichkov.'

'But I don't know anyone at court,' Masha protested. 'And I *am* scared. It is easy for you, Sophie, you are just going home to your father.'

'Easy?' Sophie's tone had a note of uncertainty in it, and her blue-green eyes clouded. 'Yes, I am going home, but I am not at all sure Papa is happy about my coming. He may be wondering what to do with a grown-up daughter. After all, we don't know each other very well. He has seen me once or twice a month on visiting days. We try to talk for half an hour, then he kisses me on the forehead, gives me a box of bonbons and leaves. I don't remember what the house is like inside. I know it is very impressive outside because I've seen it a couple of times when we were taken out in the carriages. But is it home-like, cosy? I was barely eight when I was sent to Smolni, I know as much about my home as you know about Anichkov Palace.'

'I never thought of it like that,' Masha said soberly. 'It is the life that we have led at Smolni.'

'But what about…' Sophie hesitated. 'What about *your* home? Was it sold after your mother's death?'

'Yes, to pay the mortgage.' Masha spoke with an effort. 'There were other debts as well. It has been torn down. There is a brick factory in its place.'

'Do you remember it at all?' Sophie's voice was very soft.

Masha nodded. 'It was old,' she said dreamily, 'but I loved every stone of it. If Papa had not been killed at Borodino, I would never have been sent away to Smolni. But he left no money and Mamma wanted me to have a good education so I could earn my living later on. I can remember the day I left. The peasants came to say goodbye, the terrace was full of them. Niania Akulina, my old nurse, was wailing on the steps. I knelt on the back seat of the carriage and looked, and looked. Oh, no, I could never forget, never…'

Masha's voice trailed off. She swallowed hard and looked away.

Sophie waited for several minutes, then touched her friend's hand. 'Masha, are you asleep?'

'What?' Masha seemed startled. 'No, I was just thinking… When I first came to Smolni and was told to call the principal 'Maman' I could hardly get the word out. You lost your mother when you were a baby, Sophie, so maybe it did not matter that much to you…'

Before Sophie had time to answer, a bell clanged loudly just outside the dormitory door.

'Seven o'clock!' Masha exclaimed, sliding off Sophie's

bed. 'I never realised it was so late.'

In another moment, tumult had broken out. Girls were hastily scrambling out of beds, tearing off their nightcaps, racing to the lavatory and calling to each other from one end of the dormitory to the other.

'Our last day at school! Just think!'

'Look at the weather. It is beautiful.'

'My parents arrived only yesterday. The roads were so flooded, they had to change horses at every station.'

'I haven't seen my parents in all these nine years. I am afraid they won't recognise me,' Natasha Meller, a slim dark-haired girl told Masha wistfully.

Several voices answered, 'I haven't seen my parents either since I came to school.'

Masha pretended to be very busy making her bed. 'Mamma would have been coming to fetch me too,' she thought, holding the pillow so that it hid her face.

Katish Muffle, whose bed was next to Masha's, looked up from lacing her stays, her pink face radiant. 'When I think that in just a few hours I will be sitting in the carriage between my parents, I could scream with joy,' she said. 'And yet I cried my eyes out during that speech Maman made last night, after church.'

'We all cried,' Nadia Maslova mumbled through hair pins in her mouth. She took them out and shook her mop of brown hair, 'Bother! Why doesn't it stay neat like the rest of you? Well, believe it or not, I am really sorry to leave. After all, Smolni is almost my home, I was only three when I was sent here.'

'Never mind. Just wait until you start on that foreign trip of yours. You will forget Smolni and all of us soon enough,' Katish teased.

'Never!' Nadia cried beginning to hug whoever happened to be near.

'And why is our future lady-in-waiting so pale today?'

Katish asked Masha good-naturedly.

Sasha Rossett, sitting on a stool and brushing her dark hair in front of a hand-mirror, turned around. 'Do I look pale? I don't think so.'

'I was talking to Masha,' Katish answered coldly.

'How nice it will be to wear our own clothes,' Marie Divova, Sashette's friend, remarked, struggling into her uniform. 'Mother ordered my going-away frock at the best dressmaker in St. Petersburg. Wait until you see it! It is a lovely colour, *fraise ecrasée*, and it really *is* just like a crushed strawberry.'

Sashette interrupted her. 'No matter how beautiful your gown may be,' she said sweetly to Marie, 'It is going to look like a rag beside Masha's. She will have the most ravishing gown of us all, suitable for a lady-in-waiting to Grand Duchess Alexandra Feodorovna. The grand duchess cares about fashion.'

Masha felt her hands grow moist. She had dreaded the subject of clothes, and now Sashette of all people... 'I don't...' she began.

But Katish gave her a slight poke in the ribs and said sharply, 'Be quiet, Sashette. Masha is going to be dressed properly and that is all. Do you want her to wear a ball-dress in the morning?'

Sashette shrugged her shoulders and started to say something, but Natasha Meller pleaded, 'Now, girls, please. Let's have no quarrels. Remember that we are all about to part in a few hours.'

Katish pulled Masha aside. 'What were you going to say?' she whispered. 'The school always provides clothes for those who have no family. You are being taken care of, aren't you?'

'I...I don't know.' Masha stood embarrassed, twisting a button on her petticoat. 'Emilia Agte is getting a going-away dress from the school. She is not an orphan, but her parents have very little money. She has been called to the linen-room several times to be fitted. I wasn't. I suppose they have something they know will fit. I only hope it will not be too bad.'

'Of course not. After all you are not just going home like Emilia; you are going to Anichkov Palace. I am sure you will get something very nice,' said Katish encouragingly.

'Please don't tell Sophie,' Masha begged. 'You know how easily she flares up. She is quite capable of making a big fuss, even going to Maman.'

'Why don't you go to Maman yourself? There *could* have been some confusion about your clothes,' Katish suggested.

Masha shrank back. 'Me? Go to Maman? I never could!'

Katish laughed. 'Better stop being so shy, or you will find it hard at court. Now, let's hurry and get dressed. The bell for prayers may ring any minute.'

Masha put on her low-necked, white wool uniform with its tight bodice and bunchy skirt almost touching the floor. She smoothed her green apron, rolled her hair into a neat knot, leaving a curling wave at the temples, and laced the ribbons of her shoes. She was ready just as Madame Legarpe, the form mistress of the Whites appeared in the door with a '*Bonjour, Mesdemoiselles.*'

2

Good-byes

'Never again,' Sophie declared, putting down her cup as the girls were finishing their breakfast in the big refectory.

Katish giggled. 'Meaning that this is your last breakfast in Smolni, or that you will never drink such weak tea again?'

'Both,' Sophie answered with feeling.

'At what time are the parents supposed to arrive?' Katish asked. 'About ten, isn't it?'

'About eleven,' Nadia answered. 'My future chaperone is coming for me. I still haven't decided what to call her. She is something between a third cousin and a great-aunt. We are going to stay in a hotel to buy a few things I need and set off for France next week. Who is coming for you, Sashette?'

Sashette drew herself up. 'Maman told me last night that one of the court ladies is coming to fetch me, and…'

She had not finished when her neighbour and best friend, tiny Stephanie Radzivill, burst into tears.

'I don't w…want Sashette to…to leave me,' she sobbed.

'Oh, my goodness, here she is crying again!' Sophie exclaimed, while Natasha said gently, 'But you and Sashette can visit each other often, Stephanie. You are staying in St. Petersburg, aren't you?'

'My g…guardian wants me to go to Poland and see my…my castles,' Stephanie managed to bring out through her tears, 'I own many c…castles.'

'Two months isn't long and then you will be back,' Sashette said, stroking Stephanie's golden hair.

Masha leaned over the table. 'Do you think that court

lady is to take me too?' she asked Sashette, 'No one has told me anything.'

Sashette's tone instantly became icy. '*I* am going to the Winter Palace, Her Majesty the Empress Elizaveta's residence. *You* are going to Anichkov Palace. I really have no idea who is going to escort you there.'

'Another court lady probably,' Katish said airily, but Masha was not reassured.

'Could it...could it be that the grand duchess has changed her mind about having me for a lady-in-waiting?' She spoke aloud, without realising it.

'One never knows,' Stephanie said spitefully.

'What nonsense! Of course you are going to be a lady-in-waiting,' Nadia cried hotly, and several girls glanced at Sophie, expecting her to fly in Masha's defence.

But Sophie was sitting quietly, staring at the crumbs on her plate.

'Sophie, are you all right?' Katish asked anxiously.

'What did you say?' Sophie looked up with a languid air. 'No, I am quite well. I was just worrying about Stephanie. She hardly knows her guardian. Suppose, mind I only say *suppose*, he locked her up in one of her castles and let her starve to death while he grabbed all her money.'

Stephanie blanched, and Sashette said crossly, 'Sophie is only joking. A very silly joke too!'

A few girls murmured, 'Come, Sophie, don't tease her,' but the majority whispered, 'Go on. She deserves it.'

Natasha diverted everyone's attention by saying wonderingly, 'Has the refectory really become smaller since yesterday, or am I just imagining it?'

Masha looked around. Yes, the refectory with its green-topped, black-legged tables did seem smaller and somehow unfamiliar. 'This is the last time, the very last time,' she thought with a half-excited, half-frightened quiver in her heart.

Breakfast over, the Browns and the Blues rushed to the Whites for a last frantic good-bye.

Masha did not wait for the assault. Slipping out of the refectory she hurried along the familiar corridors until she came to the door into the garden. As she opened it, the chilly air of early spring rushed in but she had no time to look for her Smolni cloak. She sped down the path, past the lilac bushes, the pine trees, the fountains, still dry and silent, waiting to be turned on any day now, towards the little round lawn with the birch tree.

'Good-bye, good-bye, don't forget me,' Masha murmured, hugging the trunk. 'And thank you again, and again, and again. I have put a small spray of your summer leaves into my prayer-book. I will be thinking about you every time I pray. You are my friend forever.'

She whispered 'Good-bye' once more, dropped a last kiss on the bark and ran blindly across the lawn and back into the building, her eyes full of tears.

Back in the dormitory, two maids in blue and white striped uniforms were just bringing in the hampers of clothes and pink hat-boxes.

'Where did you disappear to?' Sophie called as soon as she saw Masha. 'I've been looking everywhere for you.'

'Just saying good-bye,' Masha replied evasively, and stepped aside to make way for the two maids carrying an imposing-looking hamper.

'Oh, it must be mine!' Marie Divova exclaimed, hurrying forward. 'Put it over there, please.'

There was no hamper beside Masha's bed, nor any sign of new clothes whatsoever. She sat down on a stool and tried to look indifferent, but her eyes anxiously followed the two maids as they kept bringing in more hampers.

All around her, the girls were examining their dresses, trying them on, comparing, admiring.

'It's so pretty, so pretty! Mother made it herself.' Natasha

Meller stroked the folds of her pale-blue muslin.

'What a beautiful hat! I love feathers!'

'Look at Sophie! Doesn't that green suit her? And that silver braid!'

Masha was glad that Sophie was too absorbed in her own garments to look in her direction. She forced herself to talk, and admired Nadia's bright orange gown.

'I chose the colour myself,' Nadia said placidly. 'Maman was shocked but I know it suits my colouring.' She added in a carefully off-hand voice, 'Your clothes will probably arrive any moment now.'

'Of course,' Masha tried to match Nadia's tone. Out of a corner of her eye she watched Emilia Agte put on the dress provided by the school. It was a pretty dark blue gown trimmed with lace. 'If only mine could be as nice,' she prayed inwardly, and realised with a shock that every girl except herself had a hamper already.

To make matters worse, Sophie was running up, holding a wide-brimmed green hat in her hand. 'Look! Aren't those white roses better than feathers? I never imagined Papa could choose a hat so well!' She broke off and stared at Masha's bed. 'Where are your clothes?'

Masha shook her head, close to tears, 'I haven't any.'

'You haven't...' Sophie remained speechless for a second but promptly recovered her voice. 'Oh, but that is ridiculous! I am going to Maman. Yes, right now, and don't try to prevent me.'

Other girls were looking up from their hampers, and asking, 'What has happened? Why is Sophie going to Maman?'

Suddenly, a loud wail from Marie Divova silenced the comments, 'Why, this hamper is not mine after all! There's mine, by the door. The big one is for Masha. It says "M. Fredericks" on the tag.'

'For me?' Masha could hardly believe her ears. Two girls

were already dragging the hamper towards her. Another girl followed with a hat box.

'Open it! Open it!' several voices cried.

Masha knelt down and lifted the lid. The scent of white lilac rose from the neatly-folded undergarments. 'Princess Charlotte's perfume!' she exclaimed, glancing up at the eager ring of girls that had already formed around her. 'Look at the lace! And the blue ribbons. The ruffles!' they cried, pushing each other to get a better look.

Feeling dazed, Masha lifted out a white muslin gown with a wide lace collar and short puffed sleeves. A row of dainty blue velvet bows ran from the waist down to the ruches edging the skirt. The sash was of matching blue velvet.

'You see! You see! You have the most ravishing gown of all, just as Sashette predicted!' Sophie cried triumphantly.

'The collar is of Brussels lace!' Katish touched it reverently.

'It is the latest fashion!' Marie Divova's voice was grudging but admiring.

The girls were still crowding around Masha, when Madame Legarpe appeared, and promptly ordered everyone to get dressed and not waste time chattering.

Having sent the girls scampering to their own hampers, Madame Legarpe addressed Masha. 'My dear child,' she said graciously, 'I wish to congratulate you on receiving such kind attention from Her Highness. She chose the pattern of the gown herself and the…er lingerie is made by her own hand. I hope you appreciate it as you should.'

Masha curtsied dutifully, pressing the gown to her heart. 'She put her perfume on it too,' she exclaimed, burying her face in the soft folds.

Madame Legarpe looked disapproving. 'My dear, please try to show more restraint. Also, never say 'she'. Say 'Her Highness'.' She nodded and sailed out of the dormitory.

Sophie helped Masha to unpack the rest of the hamper. One by one, they took out a lacy petticoat, whalebone stays, flat shoes of soft cream leather with long white ribbons, white stockings, a blue velvet cape, and at the very bottom a reticule, matching the shoes, with a gold clasp and silk lining.

Masha packed all her belongings in the reticule. They were few: the silver medal she had received at the prize-giving, her volume of the New Testament and her prayer-book, a packet of her mother's letters, tied with a ribbon, a pincushion. There was nothing else to take with her. Her uniform, her underclothes, her shoes, her cake of soap in the lavatory, would be used by some other pupil coming up from the Blue form.

Sophie helped Masha to dress. As each school garment was added to the small pile on the bed, Masha felt that one more thread tying her to Smolni was breaking.

Soon everyone was ready. Hand-mirrors flashed, throwing bright spots of light on the dormitory walls, new petticoats crackled with starch, gowns swished.

'How different we all look!' Nadia exclaimed, 'I did not recognise Lena Mandrika in that pink hat. You are a beauty, Lena! Aren't you glad you have decided not to enter a convent after all?'

Lena Mandrika, a slim, frail looking girl, answered quietly, 'I promised Maman to find out first what life is like. I am going to keep my promise.'

'Ellie and Mary Vuich look sweet too,' Katish said, looking at the inseparable brunette sisters in their white *broderie-anglaise* gowns.

'My dress is nice but I feel so uncomfortable in new shoes,' Stephanie complained.

Natasha Meller began to laugh. 'Isn't it funny how we are all accustomed to wearing hand-me down shoes and clothes. My petticoat is pricking me already.'

Sashette, in an exquisite frock of pale yellow, shrugged her shoulders, but several other girls cried, 'Yes! Yes! I feel uncomfortable too!'

'*Mesdemoiselles*,' Madame Legarpe's voice brought sudden silence, 'Are you ready? Your parents are waiting.'

Faces flushed and paled in turn. Someone began to cry. Masha hastily took her new bonnet out of its box. It was of white straw with a big bunch of blue corn-flowers nestled in the crown. She tied the ribbons with shaking hands and threw the blue cape over her shoulders.

The dormitory was now a chaos of frantic good-byes, kisses and a desperate scramble for bonnets and gloves. Natasha whispered, 'Don't forget me, Masha, even if we never see each other again.'

Sophie said with fierce determination, 'We will be together as much as possible.'

'Come, *Mesdemoiselles*, come,' Madame Legarpe called and everyone moved towards the door.

On the threshold, the girls stopped as if by command, and every head turned back to give the last look to the rows of beds, the bare walls, the narrow white cambric curtains framing the windows.

For one more generation of girls, life in Smolni was over.

3

The world outside

It was a new experience to descend the stairway in a chattering crowd instead of a solemn 'no talking' procession. 'Mother promised to bring my little brother along. I am so thrilled,' Natasha was telling everybody. 'Just think, he is three years old and I have never seen him.'

'And there will be a court lady waiting for Sashette, and probably another one for you, Masha. Aren't you excited?' Katish asked.

Masha answered, 'Yes, of course,' adding inwardly, 'but it will be a stranger, not Mamma.'

Absorbed in her thoughts, she never noticed that they had reached the ballroom and was quite unprepared for a sudden surge forward and the almost agonised cries of 'Mother!' as soon as they were inside. Carried away, she made a dash herself, stopped short, then went on again. Someone *was* waiting for her and it was not a stranger. Standing among the parents, clad in a modest grey gown, was Grand Duchess Alexandra herself. With a gay, 'Ah, here is Masha, all ready to face the world,' Alexandra caught up the girl just before she had time to sink into a curtsey, kissed her, smoothed her collar and stuck a stray hairpin in place. 'Just as a mother would have done,' Masha thought gratefully.

'Your Highness,' she began breathlessly, 'How…how can I thank you enough. First those lovely garments and now…' she blushed, stammered and stopped.

'I thought I might take your mother's place for today,'

the grand duchess said gently, her blue eyes smiling at Masha, 'and I am so glad you liked the clothes. I wanted them to be a surprise. And now say good-bye to kind Maman and your form mistresses, and thank them for taking such good care of you.'

Masha started a little as she realised that Madame Adlerberg, the Smolni principal, was standing behind the grand duchess. Maman was smiling, but her sharp eyes scrutinised Masha keenly from under her enormous lace bonnet. A Smolni pupil must never let her emotions show, no matter how great the excitement. There was a hint of disapproval in Maman's slightly-raised eyebrows.

Beside Maman stood Mademoiselle Neigardt, the inspectress, her thin, cold face expressionless as usual.

Fraulein Knappe, the Whites second form mistress was there too: kind Fraulein with her ruddy cheeks and grey hair. Though not on duty, she had come to say good-bye to her girls.

A deep curtsey to Maman, another one to the inspectress, to the form mistresses, murmured words of thanks, gracious nods in return, a hearty kiss from Fraulein Knappe, and Masha's good-byes were over. The grand duchess said simply, 'Come, my dear, we are going home,' and they started to walk across the big white and gold ballroom, Maman and the rest of the staff following behind, groups of girls and their parents stepping aside with bows and curtsies.

Masha saw Sophie hanging on the arm of a tall man with general's epaulettes. A little further on Natasha was kneeling in front of a small boy, coaxing him to 'kiss the big sister'. Sashette went by, accompanied by a small elderly lady almost hidden by a big feathered hat.

Masha knew it was customary for the wealthy parents to use rented carriages when fetching their daughters from Smolni, out of consideration for the girls whose parents could not afford to keep horses. Still it was a shock to see a modest rented carriage waiting for them and to realise that the grand duchess had come without a single attendant. The uniformed doorman, his chest full of decorations, wished Masha good luck and opened the carriage door. Another moment, and the white pillars of Smolni began to slip away further and further...into the past.

Rigid with shyness, Masha sat beside the grand duchess; the fresh spring air coming through the slightly-opened carriage window made her dizzy. She wondered why it seemed to taste different from the air in the Smolni garden. It was a sunny day and the wooden pavements were crowded, it reminded Masha of her first day in St. Petersburg, when she arrived to enter Smolni. But people looked different now, especially the ladies. Instead of plain gowns falling straight from high waists, the dresses now were sashed and waisted and much ornamented with laces and embroideries. Men looked much the same, except that she could not see a single one in knee breeches.

Alexandra watched Masha's face with an amused smile. 'Fascinating, isn't it?' she asked nodding at the throngs beyond the window. She spoke in French, with a slight German accent.

Masha murmured shyly, 'Yes, your Highness. We were not taken out often in Smolni. It is all so new.' She gathered her courage and went on hurriedly, 'I am afraid, Your Highness, I may be very awkward and do something wrong. I never expected to be a lady-in- waiting and...'

Alexandra patted Masha's hand. 'There is no need to be afraid,' she said. 'We lead very simple life in Anichkov Palace, and you will be with me a great deal. Don't forget that you are going to be my very special lady-in-waiting.'

She hesitated for a moment and then looked at Masha, smiled and went on, 'I think you may have been wondering, my dear, just why you have been chosen, and why you will be special—to me. Perhaps I should explain. When I first saw you at the graduation ball, Masha, so shy and grave, so unlike your gay companions, I became interested. Then I heard your story…'

Alexandra paused, and Masha sat up, alarmed, 'I am afraid I was not restrained enough, Your Highness. Maman said…'

The grand duchess stopped her with a gesture, 'Never mind what Maman said. You were right to be frank with me, and what you told me wrung my heart. I thought, 'Here is a young girl with nothing behind her but a childhood spent in poverty and the cold discipline of Smolni, and nothing ahead but the bleak prospect of some lowly position among strangers'. I decided I would not let it happen!' Alexandra threw back her head defiantly and tapped the floor of the carriage with her slim foot. 'Yes, I decided you were not going to be anyone's nursery governess or companion. I talked to Madame Adlerberg and here you are with me! Are you happy?' She peered under Masha's bonnet.

'Oh, yes!' Masha breathed, forgetting to add, 'Your Highness'. But her 'Yes', came from the bottom of her heart and the grand duchess did not seem to mind the breach in etiquette.

'That is exactly as it should be,' she said warmly. 'You are young and should be enjoying life. I am going to see that you do! I want you to keep in touch with your friends, accept their invitations and invite them to visit you. And I hope you will share your joys and fears with me and look on me as your most loving friend and counsellor, almost a Godmother.'

She began to ask Masha what books she had read, whether she liked music, about her life in Smolni, and was amused to hear that Masha had been among the pupils who were present at her arrival from Prussia as Grand Duke Nicolas's bride.

'So you even remember what hat I had on that day!' she exclaimed laughing, then became serious again. 'But it is strange I never happened to speak to you when I visited Smolni,' she said. 'I know several girls in your form by their first names, but *you* never came near me. I wonder why.'

Masha flushed painfully. 'Because...I...' she stammered unhappily, 'I happened to overhear once that...that Your Highness preferred people who are attractive, and...I...'

Alexandra interrupted her. 'Dear Masha,' she said gravely, 'the princess who thought like that was very young. She has learned better since and often at her own expense.'

Masha sat silent, not knowing what to say. There was a little pause and then the grand duchess continued, her gaze suddenly sombre, 'Perhaps I should admit that there is something more, too, in my desire to...to alter your fate. You have some growing-up to do still; you must now meet a world outside Smolni. Dear child, be thankful that you are not royalty. You will be able to grow naturally, unhampered by politics and tradition. The kind of life I plan for you I never knew myself. It was not allowed. Protocol and intrigue ruled my existence at the Prussian Court. It may be that what I really want is to re-live that time in you.'

She looked up and smiled at Masha with great sweetness. 'But you mustn't look so solemn about it. Think about the good times ahead of you. Your duties will not be strenuous, no more than I would require of an older daughter. You are going to accompany me to our summer residence in Pavlovsk sometime in July. There will be picnics, riding, dancing. I am sure you will like my children. I have told them about you and you are expected with impatience.'

Masha was just beginning to be a little more at ease when the pinkish-red walls of Anichkov Palace loomed into sight. It did not look very big or imposing, but the long rows of windows made her heart sink again. She felt as if strange eyes were watching her from behind every curtain.

The sentries saluted and the carriage rolled into the courtyard. Livened footmen helped Alexandra and Masha out. For the next ten minutes, Masha hardly dared to look up, so that all she could later remember of her arrival at Anichkov was a confused jumble of footmen's silk stockings, carved legs of furniture, and soft rugs that seemed endless. Every time she ventured to glance around, her own frightened face stared back from the mirrors.

On the second floor, the grand duchess turned into a room, gay with blue chintzes and light furniture. 'This is the room of my youngest lady-in-waiting!' she announced.

'For me?' Masha stared at the blue-canopied bed, the small writing-desk, the pretty dressing-table. 'I . . . I have only had my bed in the dormitory in all these years,' she said shakily, 'I . . .' But the grand duchess did not let her finish. 'What you have said just now is quite enough,' she said. 'Leave your cloak and hat here and come to the nursery with me. I want to introduce you to the children.'

As they entered the nursery, Masha wondered desperately how one should address the royal children. Before she could decide whether to curtsey or not, the six-year-old Alexander had rushed to her and grabbed her hand. 'This is Anichkov bridge,' he explained, dragging her to a pile of wooden blocks in the middle of the floor. 'See how it opens up in the middle. Do all bridges open up?'

The grand duchess smiled and slipped away.

Masha did not know much about bridges, but she told a story about the lead soldiers who escaped from their box one night, built a castle of blocks and made one of the dolls their queen.

As the story went on, Alexander's younger sister Mary crept nearer, leading the two-year-old Ollie by the hand, and asked which of the dolls was the queen.

Masha thought the sisters looked like dolls themselves with their long corkscrew curls and white dresses with puffed sleeves. She told several more stories and was delighted when the grand duchess came back and allowed her to have lunch in the nursery with the children and Mimi, their English nurse.

It was late in the afternoon by the time she returned to her own room. She was surprised to find a buxom, round faced, white-aproned girl carefully arranging a white silk gown on the bed.

At the sight of Masha, the girl curtsied. 'The name is Nastia, Miss,' she murmured, 'I am to be your personal maid.'

Stunned at the idea of having her personal maid, Masha was desperately thinking what to say, when her eyes fell on the dress. 'What is that?' she asked.

The maid looked guilty. 'I took the liberty of laying out the white for you to wear at dinner tonight, Miss,' she stammered, 'but if it is the pink one that…'

Masha did not listen further. She ran to the clothes press and flung it open. Several dresses were hanging inside. Powder and perfume stood on the dressing-table.

'It is like a fairytale,' Masha thought. 'Still…I wish I could have all my meals in the nursery. How I dread the dinner tonight!'

After Nastia had left, she tried to rest, grateful for those few hours alone, but she felt too excited to keep still. Walking around the room, she touched each object, murmuring, '*My* mirror, *my* screen, *my* chair.' Coming to the window, overlooking the courtyard, she thought, 'If I wanted to, I could go down there. I could even walk out into the street. There is no form mistress to forbid me.' Alarmed by her own daring, she sprang away from the window.

It was dusk when Nastia came to help her dress for dinner. She was barely ready, when there was a knock at the door and Nastia admitted a tall elderly woman with elaborately-arranged white hair and traces of great beauty on her faded, somewhat haughty face.

Masha recognised Princess Volkonska, a court lady who often accompanied the grand duchess to Smolni. She gave Masha a keen look that travelled from the girl's face down to the bottom of her frock.

'Her Highness has ordered me to act as your chaperone this evening, Mademoiselle,' Princess Volkonska explained, and added a few polite words about being glad to welcome Masha as a member of the grand duchess's suite.

Masha thanked her in a voice that was almost a whisper and curtsied as low as she could.

They were about to leave the room, when Princess Volkonska stopped Masha with a brisk, 'Your gloves, Mademoiselle.'

Scarlet, Masha snatched at the gloves Nastia hurriedly presented to her and pulled them on. 'Suppose I do something silly at dinner?' she thought frantically as she walked beside the princess down the long corridor. 'Suppose I forget or mix up people's names?'

To her relief, only a very small group was gathered in the gold and yellow room, waiting for the grand duke and his wife to appear. Princess Volkonska dutifully introduced Masha to everyone present. A few minutes later their highnesses made their entrance.

Grand Duke Nicholas welcomed Masha with a cordial, 'We are glad to have you with us, my dear,' but as usual she felt ill at ease under the severe gaze of his pale blue eyes. The grand duchess smiled her kind smile and told Masha the children were hoping for more stories tomorrow. She was accompanied by a young woman who looked like a baby put into a grown-up dress by mistake. Soft blonde curls waved around a plump pink face with a rosebud mouth, and an upturned nose.

'This is Mademoiselle Ayler, your fellow lady-in-waiting,'

the grand duchess said as the two girls were being introduced. 'She will tell you a little about our life here, later on.'

'She will have to tell me a great deal; I need it,' Masha thought, watching Mademoiselle Ayler chat with two elderly officers of the Chevaliers of the Guards, who were teasing her about something. She seemed to be enjoying it.

But once seated in the oak-panelled dining-room, Masha felt better. After the austerity of Smolni refectory, the crystal and silver vases, the hothouse roses, the footmen in powdered wigs, everything seemed like a dream and one cannot be shy in a dream.

Princess Volkonska sat beside Masha, keeping up light conversation but at the same time observing her movements. Masha realised she was being examined and almost froze again, but her right-hand neighbour, the poet Zhukovski, came to her rescue. Masha was glad to see him. All the Smolni girls liked the soft-faced, soft-voiced man who lectured to them about literature and had once helped them to stage a play.

Leaning towards Masha, he whispered mysteriously, 'Be careful when you unfold your napkin, Mademoiselle Fredericks.'

Surprised, Masha picked up her napkin. A carved ivory fan and a leather case slid onto her plate. She opened the case. Inside was a beautiful gold bracelet with the date of her graduation engraved on the inside.

Alexandra, who had been watching Masha, said, 'These are your graduation gifts, my dear. Something to help you remember this important year in your life.'

Masha stammered her thanks as best she could and tried to put on the bracelet, but her hands shook so that M. Zhukovski had to help with the clasp.

The Grand Duke Nicholas, who was talking to a general with a hearing aid, interrupted himself and looked at his wife. His eyes were no longer severe, Masha noticed; they were full of infinite tenderness. Alexandra returned the look with a smile.

'They love each other!' Masha thought. The discovery surprised her but somehow made her feel less tense. She began to enjoy the fine food and interesting sights like the massive gold plates in front of the grand duke and his wife. In fairytales, princes and princesses always ate off gold. It was a disappointment to see china plates put on top of the gold ones.

Grand Duke Nicholas did not touch any of the dishes served, but dined instead on some potato soup and boiled vegetables.

'That is His Highness' usual fare,' Zhukovski explained to Masha in a low voice. 'He is a real spartan. Travels even in winter in an open carriage, and if it happens to break down, he simply borrows a peasant cart in the nearest village.'

Princess Volkonski had apparently been satisfied with the results of her inspection. She was talking to her other neighbour, but now turned back to her charge. 'Do you know when you are going to be presented, Mademoiselle?' she asked.

'Presented?' Masha echoed in dismay, 'But I thought…'

Across the table the grand duchess began to laugh. 'Poor Masha!' she said, 'There is really no end to her ordeals. Of course you have to be presented to Her Majesty the Empress Elizaveta Feodorovna. But it is a very simple little ceremony. All you will have to do is to wear your prettiest gown and make a graceful curtsey.'

'And no running away this time,' the grand duke said pointedly, though he smiled, too.

Masha's ears flamed. She *had* run away from the grand duke when she was a small Brown because she thought he was an ogre. 'How could he remember it was *me* after all these years!' she thought in despair.

Coffee was served in a small candle-lit drawing-room. Mademoiselle Ayler drew Masha to a sofa and began pouring into her ears endless stories about palace life. Most of it was just a jumble of names to Masha. Still, she gathered that there were five ladies-in-waiting including herself. Sophie Moder was the oldest, in her late thirties and had a beautiful contralto voice. Lily Dubois was half French and a painter; that landscape on the wall was her work. Mademoiselle Kochetova was nice but a little strange, dressed in front of open windows in winter and had ice put into her bath-tub.

As to Mademoiselle Ayler herself, she was twenty-two, younger than all the other ladies-in-waiting—except, now, Masha—and engaged to be married. Her fiancé was in London with the Russian embassy. 'We were planning to be married in the autumn,' she told Masha, 'but then these terrible things appeared on my face. Now, I don't know what to do. The wedding may have to be postponed.'

'Terrible things?' Masha asked in wonder, looking at the fresh pink face in front of her.

'Yes. Just look. I hoped they would disappear in winter, but they didn't.' Mademoiselle Ayler pointed to a few freckles barely visible under the layer of powder. 'I've tried everything,' she went on, 'donkey's milk, almond milk, all kinds of herbal brews. Nothing helps. How can I be married looking like this?'

The tragic revelation put an end to Masha's hopes of learning something more about her future companions and about court etiquette. No matter how hard she tried to turn the conversation away from freckles, Ally, as she asked Masha to call her, always came back to the subject of her 'disfigurement'. 'What will Anatole say when he sees me?' she lamented. 'And he is due back next month.'

Secretly, Masha thought it all very silly, but otherwise she found Ally pleasant and good-natured. When she mentioned where her room was, Ally said simply, 'You are the only one who is so near Her Highness. The rest of us have rooms in the opposite wing. It looks to me as if you are going to be more like an adopted daughter than a lady-in-waiting.'

But there was no malice in her voice and Masha was grateful for it.

At last, the evening was over. Masha returned to her room so full of new impressions, her head was swimming. She felt tired too, as if she had lived through several days instead of one. Standing by the window she thought about Smolni. The pupils would be all in bed now. The form mistress on night duty would be making her round. Suddenly, she longed to be back in the Whites dormitory.

Nastia came in, bringing hot water. Her cheerful air chased Masha's loneliness away. 'Does the palace always go to sleep so late?' she asked, listening to the steps passing her door and to the distant sound of doors opening and closing.

'Her Highness takes a long time getting ready for bed,' Nastia explained. 'Almond milk is made fresh for her face every night and she chooses her gowns for the next day. The last thing she does before retiring is visit the nursery. But His Highness retires early.' Nastia lowered her voice. 'He sleeps on a mattress stuffed with straw, like a soldier's,' she whispered. 'Grum—he is His Highness's personal valet —told me.'

Masha let Nastia help her off with her gown, then sent the girl away. 'I can undress myself,' she said firmly, and thought again of the familiar discipline of Smolni.

Folding each garment and putting it neatly on a chair just as she had in the dormitory, made Masha feel calmer. She slipped into her bed and blew out the candle.

Her first day in Anichkov Palace was over.

4

In the Winter Palace

'Masha, my dear, there is really no need to be so nervous. I am sure that other young ladies who are to be presented this afternoon are looking forward to it,' the grand duchess said patiently as the carriage rolled towards the Winter Palace.

Masha murmured, 'Yes, Your Highness,' and heaved a sigh that fluttered the ribbons of her bonnet.

'Your old classmate, Mademoiselle Rossett is going to be presented too,' the grand duchess went on, 'even though she is already the empress's lady-in-waiting. I have told you before, it is purely a formality.'

Masha tried to look calm, but she was far from reassured. The prospect of meeting the Empress Elizaveta, whom she had only seen once at a distance, was overwhelming.

As she mounted the white marble steps of the Jordan Staircase, she could feel the last remnants of her courage ebbing away. She followed the grand duchess through spacious rooms, their high ceilings painted with frescoes, past priceless tapestries and paintings, feeling smaller and more frightened than ever.

In the Malachite Drawing-room a dozen young girls stood in groups, talking, while their parents hovered discreetly in the background. The grand duchess introduced Masha to the master of ceremonies, whispered in French, '*Voyons, du courage!*' and disappeared.

Most of the girls were in white and looked as nervous as Masha herself. She noticed another classmate, Marie

Divova, at the other end of the room and timidly moved in that direction. Marie had never been friendly, but at least she was a familiar face. Masha was only a few steps away, when she heard Marie whisper loudly, 'A real country girl and quite penniless. None of us can understand why she was made lady-in-waiting. A whim of the grand duchess, I suppose.'

Colour flooded Masha's face. She turned abruptly, almost colliding with a girl behind her. The girl accepted Masha's apologies with a curt nod and looked wrathfully at the toe of her white shoe bearing the dark imprint of Masha's heel.

Utterly embarrassed, Masha pretended to admire an oil painting on the wall. 'I shouldn't pay attention. It is only Marie. What does it matter?' she tried to calm herself, but her face burned, and she felt as if everyone's eyes were on her.

A small page in green and red appeared in the door and announced that Her Majesty could be expected soon.

All conversations stopped. The girls hastily smoothed their gowns and patted their hair in place.

'Mesdemoiselles, may I have your attention, please!' the master of ceremonies lifted his hand. 'Kindly form a semi-circle. A little more to the back of the room. You, Mademoiselle, please move to the right. You too, Mademoiselle, please.'

Masha did not realise immediately that the last order was meant for her. She stepped forward just too late for the place was already taken by another girl and narrowly escaped another collision. There were several titters.

Scarlet, Masha allowed the master of ceremonies to take her elbow and conduct her to the other end of the semi-circle. 'Here, please, Mademoiselle,' he announced, placing Masha between two girls who moved aside with bad grace. One, a pert-looking brunette, even drew back a little as if protecting her lace skirts from Masha's clumsiness.

The master of ceremonies began, 'Mesdemoiselles, you will all...' stopped and looked with a frown over his shoulder.

A late arrival was ushered in. Masha stared, not daring to believe her eyes. Tripping lightly across the inlaid floor, surrounded by a cloud of white gauze, was Sophie.

Something tight and cold inside Masha gave way. With a joyful cry, 'Sophie!' she rushed to her friend.

The two girls were in each other's arms, when the doors were flung open and the page announced, 'Her Imperial Majesty'.

The master of ceremonies swayed in despair, but Sophie did not lose her head. Masha felt herself gently pulled aside and before she knew it, they were both standing with the other girls.

The presentation began. Girl after girl plunged into a deep curtsey as the master of ceremonies announced her name... The empress murmured, '*Charmée de faire votre connaissance, Mademoiselle*'; the grand duchess added some cordial remark, and they moved on.

Masha dared a glance at Sophie. Her friend was shaking with suppressed laughter. 'I...I don't know how I am going to speak,' she whispered. 'It was so funny!'

'Sophie, *please*,' Masha whispered, horrified. She had no time to say anything else. Her name was announced and she sank into a curtsey. When she rose, the Empress Elizaveta stood in front of her. From the vague rumours that penetrated into Smolni, Masha knew that the empress was not popular. People found her cold and haughty. She seldom appeared in public. It was usually the Dowager Empress, *debonnaire* Marie Feodorovna, who did the honours at big events.

Masha saw no haughtiness on the pale thin face with its finely-chiselled features, only resigned sadness. The grey eyes gave Masha a weary look. The polite smile was tinged with bitterness.

The grand duchess spoke to Masha as if they were meeting for the first time. 'How do you do, Mademoiselle?'

It was all over in two minutes. The empress and Alexandra moved on to Sophie, who had recovered sufficiently to speak demurely though her eyes danced.

Empress Elizaveta left as soon as the last girl had made her curtsey but the grand duchess stayed. The drawing-room became filled with voices and laughter. Excited girls talked to their parents and to each other. Footmen were passing trays with refreshments.

Sophie seized Masha's arm. 'How glad I am you are here. I hoped you would be. Just imagine, we haven't seen each other for almost a week! Wasn't it terrible my being late? There was a fire near the Palace Square and the police wouldn't let our carriage through. Never mind, you are coming to visit me tomorrow. Papa has arranged it already with Her Highness. See them talking together?'

'How, how wonderful!' Masha squeezed Sophie's hand. 'I shall be counting every minute till tomorrow.'

'So will I. Wait here. I must introduce you to Papa,' and Sophie darted away.

Masha waited, happy again. Even when Marie Divova passed her, she only thought indifferently how unimportant Marie's unkind remark seemed now.

'Ah, here you are!' a voice said behind Masha. She turned around and saw Sashette, looking very elegant in palest pink. 'You probably wonder why I didn't come to you sooner.' Sashette's tone was slightly defensive. 'I was entertaining two elderly ladies who brought their granddaughters to be presented, and from the distance... Well, the truth is I didn't recognise you until you threw yourself into Sophie's arms.' She added briskly, 'You can't imagine how much you have changed just in these few days since we left Smolni.'

Without realising why, Masha felt guilty. 'It is the clothes,' she murmured.

Her head on one side, Sashette studied Masha. 'You *are* well dressed,' she admitted, 'I suppose the grand duchess chose that gown. But that is not all. You look...happy. Are you?'

'Yes,' Masha confessed, 'I love being a lady-in-waiting.'

Sashette shrugged her shoulders. 'Sorry, but I can't say the same about myself. But don't let us discuss it here. Come to my room. We can talk there.'

'Her Highness is probably leaving soon. I don't know if I should,' Masha said evasively, flattered by the invitation but not quite sure whether she really wanted to accept it.

Sashette bit her lip. 'Listen. I realise we have never been friends in Smolni. I know I've been nasty to you many a time. But surely we can forget it now. Do come. It will give me real pleasure.'

'Oh, I would like to come!' Masha exclaimed, contrite. 'But Her Highness...'

'I will see what I can do,' and Sashette went to meet the grand duchess who was coming towards the girls, General Brozin and Sophie at her side.

The grand duchess listened attentively while Sashette made her request and gave a kindly nod.

'You seem to be in great demand,' Alexandra said laughingly, coming to Masha and giving her a pat on the cheek. 'I have accepted two invitations for you in the last few minutes.' Turning to Sashette, she said, 'I am going to have tea with Her Majesty. Send Masha there at six. This will give you two girls almost an hour to chat.'

'And don't forget that I am expecting you tomorrow at two,' Sophie said, kissing Masha good-bye. She gave a cold nod to Sashette, who responded with an even colder one.

'Be prepared for a long climb,' Sashette warned Masha, leading her through several rooms and corridors until they reached the foot of a long stairway.

'I don't mind,' Masha assured her, but she drew a long breath when they finally reached the top landing. 'Eighty steps!' she exclaimed.

'You have counted right,' Sashette answered grimly. 'Now, this is called "Ladies-in-waiting Corridor". Here is my room. Come in.' She opened a door and ushered Masha into a large but rather dark room.

'How different it is from mine in Anichkov,' Masha thought, looking at an uninviting pink sofa and some heavy straight-backed chairs. At the back of the room, behind an embroidered screen, loomed an old-fashioned bed with dark green curtains gathered at the top and held by a somewhat battered gilded cherub.

'All the cast-off odds and ends of furniture find their way into the ladies-in-waiting rooms,' Sashette said crossly, kicking aside a footstool and seating Masha on the sofa. 'And it is always draughty in here, no matter what the weather. How I look forward to the day I will be out of this nunnery!'

'Are you planning to go home?' Masha asked in astonishment.

'Home!' Sashette almost choked. 'To live with my stepfather? Never! Do you know that he had the arrogance to visit me? Yes, two days ago. He said he wanted to see how I was doing, but I didn't believe a word of it and I was right. Five minutes later he asked me if I could talk to the Emperor Alexander about him. It seems he wouldn't mind moving to St. Petersburg if only he could get a nice wellpaid position. I did not give him time to explain what kind of a position. I just *looked* at him. He understood!'

'Perhaps you could have...' Masha tried to put in, but Sashette cut her short. 'Perhaps nonsense! Besides I haven't told you everything yet. Mother sent me some jewellery to wear at the court balls. Would you believe that it took me almost two hours to persuade my step-father to part with it? He simply sat clutching at the casket with both hands and pleading with me to share the jewels with my step-sister, "who doesn't have your good fortune, my dear",' Sashette mimicked the last words. 'Of course I wouldn't hear of it; the jewels were left to me. They are mine. I simply took the casket away from him. But he played the fond father to the end. Even tried to kiss me good-bye. I hope I never see him again.'

'How is Stephanie?' Masha asked quickly, thinking this would be a safer subject.

Sashette's face cleared 'Stephanie is enjoying herself. She has discovered she is rich and she buys a new pair of satin shoes every day. Her guardian wanted her to buy leather shoes, but she won't listen. She is lucky and happy. I wish I had her good fortune.'

'But you said you were hoping to leave,' Masha reminded her. 'How?'

Sashette answered simply, 'By getting married of course. What else?' She met Masha's eyes and went on with an unnaturally indifferent air, 'At the last reception, a gentleman was introduced to me. He is not handsome and he likes to laugh at his own jokes which are not funny, but he has plenty of money. He seemed interested in me. Well, why not?'

'Because you couldn't possibly love him!' Masha cried. She was immediately sorry, knowing from her Smolni days that it was always best not to contradict Sashette.

'Love?' Sashette repeated, as if Masha had suggested something preposterous. 'Don't wish that calamity on me! Oh, yes, I know what I am talking about. I have an example, right here in the palace. Empress Elizaveta married the Emperor Alexander when she was fourteen years old and he only a year older. Everyone thought it was such an idyllic marriage. And what has happened? She still loves him, blushes and trembles like a young girl when she hears his voice. And he? He hardly notices her. Oh, there may be moments. Last spring when he was sick, something wrong with his leg, he wanted her at his side all the time because she knew how to make him comfortable, but now…'

'Sashette,' Masha interrupted gently, 'Are you sure you are not imagining it all?'

Sashette gave her a disdainful glance. 'Certainly not. I have eyes and ears. Besides, the other ladies-in-waiting like to gossip. After all, that is all we have to do when we are not on duty. Life is not gay in the Winter Palace. The empress is constantly ill. The emperor shuts himself up in his study and broods or reads the bible. Do you know something?' She moved closer to Masha and her tone became mysterious, 'People say that the emperor behaves so strangely because he feels guilty of his father's death. He knew that there was a conspiracy, he even took part in it. It is true that the other conspirators promised him that his father would not be hurt, only made to abdicate, but they did not keep their word.'

Masha shivered. 'We shouldn't talk about it really,' she whispered.

Sashette shrugged her shoulders. 'Why not? We are not in Smolni now.' She moved closer to Masha. 'You know,' she said in a low voice, 'in my opinion the emperor should feel guilty. He may have thought it better for the country if his father were forced to abdicate. Emperor Paul was going out of his mind, that is no secret. Still, that does not justify murder. No wonder he fainted when someone addressed him as "Your Majesty" for the first time.'

'Do you think the Grand Duke Nicholas knew about the conspiracy?' Masha asked anxiously.

Sashette laughed. 'Of course not, Alexander's younger brothers were children at the time, and even if they had been adults, they wouldn't be very important.'

Masha felt annoyed at Sashette's dismissive tone and it was with relief that she heard the bells begin to chime six o'clock. 'It is time for me to join Her Highness,' she said, rising. 'It has been nice to see you, Sashette.'

Sashette rose too. 'And I am happy to see *you*,' she said with unexpected warmth. 'I...I am lonely here, Masha. The other ladies-in-waiting don't like me. Stephanie is leaving for Poland in a few days. Marie Divova is busy with balls and admirers. Every letter I receive from home has something unpleasant in it. You look so happy, it is restful to be with you.'

Masha felt touched and at the same time slightly embarrassed. This was so unlike Sashette. 'Let's try and meet again soon,' she suggested. 'But now I really must go.'

'Yes, now you must go.' Sashette laughed without mirth. 'I must direct you to Her Majesty's boudoir. Shall I tell you what you will find? The empress and the grand duchess will be sitting by the fire, the curtains will be down though it is still daylight and the air will be stuffy. No, don't try to find it by yourself. I will send a footman to show you the way.'

Sashette had guessed right. The empress and Alexandra were talking by the fire. The room was half-dark, lighted only by a big oil lamp under a pink shade. Near the lamp, an elderly man with a long face and deeply sunken eyes was sitting in an armchair, a manuscript in his hand. Masha recognised Karamzin, one of the Smolni trustees and a great historian.

At Masha's entrance, the empress lifted her blonde head streaked with silver and said cordially, 'I have just been told what a charming companion you make, Mademoiselle Fredericks.'

'We call her Masha,' the grand duchess said, 'She is one of the family. And a great admirer of yours, Monsieur Karamzin.'

Masha, who had barely enough time to rise after her curtsey to the empress, promptly plunged into a curtsey again.

'It is pleasant to see a young lady so interested in history,' the old gentleman said kindly, looking at Masha from under his grey eyebrows.

Alexandra began to laugh. 'I was talking about your novel, *Poor Lisa*,' she explained. 'I found Masha crying over it in her room yesterday. She had a wet handkerchief in her hand and two clean ones all ready beside her.'

Before Masha could answer, a lady-in-waiting appeared at the door and announced, 'His Majesty'.

Masha caught her breath, then saw the expression on Elizaveta's face and forgot everything else. Instead of a sickly, middle-aged woman, a young girl was watching the door with eager eyes.

Alexander was already entering. Masha thought that the emperor had changed considerably since his last visit to Smolni almost a year ago. The clean-shaven face looked older, the rounded chin sharper, the shoulders sagged slightly under the green uniform.

'Just a flying visit, Elizabeth, my dear,' he said, kissing his wife's hand. 'Alex, what a pleasant surprise!' He passed on to the grand duchess.

Masha was presented and the emperor addressed a few polite words to her. It seemed strange and rather frightening to be so near him, instead of worshipping from afar, or running after him with an excited crowd of Smolni girls.

'Monsieur Karamzin was reading the newest chapter of Pushkin's *Eugene Onegin* to us,' the grand duchess said. 'What a talent! There are copies all over St. Petersburg. He is a genius.'

The emperor frowned. 'Please, Alex, don't let us become over-enthusiastic. I admit that Pushkin is a great poet, but I have no admiration for him as a person. He is always in some trouble, has no respect for anyone. He wastes his talent writing poems mocking his elders and betters.'

'Aren't you being too severe, Alexander?' his wife protested, but the emperor did not soften.

'Not enough,' he said shortly, 'If I receive one more report about Pushkin being mixed up in a duel, or if he permits himself one more disrespectful remark about the government in his verses, I will order him to stay in his father's country estate and forbid him to enter St. Petersburg.'

The irrepressible grand duchess murmured, 'Oh, Alexander!' but Karamzin coughed as if apologising for taking sides and voiced his opinion that Pushkin was a real libertine, 'ni foi, ni loi', though his poetry was certainly beautiful.

'Speaking about poetry,' the empress said, 'I have received a new book today. It contains poems of that French poet, Victor Hugo. Maybe your Masha could read to us for a little while. You should be a very good reader, child, with your soft voice. The book is on the shelf, that brown volume.'

Masha whispered, 'Yes, Your Majesty' and went to the small rosewood bookshelf near the fireplace. Her unsteady fingers found the brown volume somehow. She sat down on the nearest chair and opened it. A sentence underlined in pencil caught her eye, '...for I acknowledge my transgressions and my sin is ever before me.'

'I am sorry,' Masha apologised, hastily closing the book. 'I've made a mistake. It is the *Psalms*.'

'May I?' The emperor held out his hand. 'I must have left this book behind a few days ago,' he told the empress. 'I have been looking for it.'

After a hesitant start, Masha found herself carried away by Victor Hugo's beautiful ballads; the nervousness left her voice and she read clearly and easily. Yet she found herself always conscious of the emperor's tired face, pale against the purple silk of the armchair.

Was it weariness from too much glory? Payment for his victory over Napoleon, the triumphant entrance in Paris? The fatigue of a warrior? Or was it the unbearable burden of guilty conscience?

The visit was over at last. Masha and Alexandra were again in the carriage, driving back to Anichkov Palace.

'You made a very good impression on Her Majesty,' the grand duchess told Masha, looking pleased. 'She even suggested...' Alexandra stopped for a moment, 'I don't know if you are really going to like it, my dear. Her Majesty has asked that you stay with her for the three months while my husband and I are in Germany, visiting my family. We are planning to leave in September and we will be back for Christmas. I had looked forward to having you with us, but in view of the empress's request...'

Masha straightened up, not sure whether to be glad or sorry. 'To stay in the Winter Palace?'

Alexandra nodded, 'Yes. As Her Majesty's personal lady-in-waiting. You have seen the lady-in-waiting, Mademoiselle Valuyeva, who was on duty today? She is not young and suffers dreadfully from rheumatism. It would do her a world of good to visit one of those mineral-spring resorts in Germany. I have long wanted to take her with us, but knowing how my sister-in-law depends on her, I hesitated. However, if you agree to stay, it might be possible.' She smiled at Masha. 'I am not forcing you, my dear. But it would be a good deed on your part and you can come with me next time. We travel abroad almost every year.'

Masha clasped her hands hard. It was difficult to decide. The possibility of seeing new places was tempting, but she remembered the empress's sad eyes. 'I will stay, Your Highness,' he said.

5

In the Summer Garden

Sophie's house, on the English Quay, turned out to be a somewhat gloomy-looking building of grey stone, with deep-set windows heavily ornamented with sculptures. Wide stone steps led up to a massive front door guarded by two squat grey pillars.

The court carriage delivered Masha promptly at two. Sophie must have been counting the minutes for she came running down the carpeted stairway as soon as Masha was inside the hall. 'At last! At last!' she cried…'I was so afraid you might not come after all.'

'Sophie, dearest,' Masha kissed her friend several times, 'It is so wonderful to be with you! But you look different from yesterday! What have you done to yourself?'

'Oh, it is a new hairdo,' Sophie turned her head aside to let Masha have a better look. 'It is the latest fashion. Do you like it?'

'I don't know,' Masha answered cautiously looking at Sophie's hair piled on the top of her head, and leaving only two long curls falling down her cheeks. 'It is just…a little strange.'

Sophie sighed. 'That's what Papa said. I suppose I will have to go back to my old style. But don't let us stand here. I have a guest I want you to meet.'

'A guest? Who?' Masha asked, while the footman took her cloak.

'A cousin of mine. Come on. I can't leave him alone so long.'

'Sophie, wait!' Masha protested as Sophie was pulling her up the stairs. 'I can't keep up with you.'

'Can't you indeed! Why don't you simply say you are still not accustomed to walking in new shoes?' Sophie teased, throwing open the door of the drawing-room. Her sleeve caught on the doorknob. There was a rending sound and the sleeve tore almost in two.

'Oh, how aggravating! Now I must go and change,' Sophie cried wrathfully, looking at the tatters of green silk hanging from her arm.

'Gracious, Sophie! Did you hurt yourself?' a masculine voice exclaimed. A young man jumped from an armchair and hurried to the girls.

'Of course not,' Sophie said, laughing. 'Masha, this is my cousin Sergei Davidov. He has just graduated from Heidelberg University. Sergei, this is my dearest friend, Masha Fredericks. We have spent nine years together behind the Smolni walls. You two keep each other company while I change.'

She pushed Masha into a chair and vanished.

For the first time in her life, Masha was left *alone with a man*. She sat on the edge of her chair, her eyes lowered, her hands folded primly on the lap of her blue muslin. At last, she dared to take a swift look at Sergei sitting opposite her. He reminded her of someone. She dared another glance. His dark hair brushed off the high fore head and his straight nose made him look like a poet, she thought, but that was not where the strange elusive resemblance lay.

Sergei's clean-shaven face looked amused as he watched the door through which Sophie had just disappeared. 'I simply can't imagine Cousin Sophie locked up in a boarding school,' he said chuckling. 'I understand you were her classmate, Mademoiselle Fredericks?'

'We were in the same form,' Masha answered primly, thinking that this was an excellent conversational opener, only she was too tongue-tied to take advantage of it.

Sergei glanced at her quizzically. She saw that he had very vivid grey eyes. It was something about his eyes that was familiar. She blushed and lowered her own for she realised he had caught her staring at him.

There was a rather long silence and then with slightly ironic formality he enquired if Masha had seen Scrib's *Valerie* that was causing such a furore at the Bolshoi theatre.

'No I have not seen it,' Masha hoped her tone was casual enough and at the same time not bold. She made an effort and got out, 'But I did see *El Cid* when the White form was taken to the theatre last Christmas.'

Sergei made a grimace, '*El Cid*? With those dreadfully long monologues? Did you enjoy it, Mademoiselle?'

'Enjoy it?' Masha opened her eyes wide. 'Naturally! It was the *theatre*.'

'Really?' The quizzical look had returned. 'You mean that the Smolni pupils don't go to the theatre very often?'

'I've been only once,' Masha answered simply.

This time, Sergei looked sympathetic. 'I can remember the first time I was taken to the theatre,' he said pensively. 'It was a ballet. I think I enjoyed the audience as much as the ballet itself. It was all so new.'

'Oh, yes!' Masha exclaimed, forgetting to be shy. 'I did too. Our box was just above the front ranks of the orchestra. It was so interesting to watch. There were mostly young men, and those in military uniforms spoke French, and the ones in civilian clothes spoke English. I wondered why.'

'The Imperial Guard is made up of young aristocrats to whom French is more familiar than Russian,' Sergei explained. 'Many of them are educated in France. But the rich merchants send their sons to England to get a good education and to learn a trade.'

'Really?' Masha said with astonishment. 'I never knew

merchants went to the theatre. I thought they just stood behind the counters.'

'Many of them are richer than our richest aristocrats,' Sergei said, looking at Masha with a half-humorous, half-rueful smile.

She asked in a small voice, 'It is ridiculous, isn't it that I don't know so many things?'

'I think it is rather wonderful,' he said thoughtfully. 'You are out to discover the world, a fascinating venture. First you will find out something about your own country, and then one day...' His voice became dreamy, 'One day someone will take you abroad. You will see the sun rise on the Alpine peaks, the pines of the Black Forest in Germany, Rome, Venice... How you will love it all!'

He broke off and asked, 'Does it alarm you: the thought of all the world? You mustn't be afraid. It will all come little by little, in its time.'

Masha was silent. Unbidden, a sudden brief vision flashed through her mind—of two people walking arm in arm up a mountain path, herself and Sergei. The picture faded out as soon as it came, leaving her with burning cheeks.

To her relief, Sergei said in a completely different voice, 'I suppose you spoke mostly French in Smolni.'

'French one day, German the other,' Masha corrected. 'If we spoke Russian to a form mistress, she wouldn't answer.'

Talking of Smolni made Masha think again about someone who was like Sergei. Where *had* she seen those grey eyes with a curious dark edging around the iris?

Suddenly, she knew: the young cadet, also Sophie's cousin, who danced with her at the graduation ball and counted 'One, two, one, two,' under his breath. 'Michael!' she cried. 'That's who you remind me of! You're like Michael.'

'You must mean my brother,' said Sergei. 'Do you know

him?'

'I met him at the graduation ball in Smolni,' Masha explained. 'I am afraid I could not remember his last name, but when I saw you…'

'But we are not at all alike,' Sergei protested.

'Yes, you are in a way,' Masha insisted timidly. 'You are dark, and much older, but there is a resemblance.'

'Not so very much older,' Sergei looked amused. 'Michael is going to be nineteen next month, and I am twenty-three. He is graduating in a few months.'

'Is he going to study in Germany too?'

To her surprise, Sergei's face clouded. 'No,' he answered drily, 'Michael's heart is set on a military career. He wants to serve his country.'

The last words were spoken with such biting irony that Masha was quite disconcerted. 'What is wrong with that?' she asked, puzzled. 'Doesn't Russia need soldiers?'

Sergei said slowly, 'Russia needs freedom, freedom of word and deed for everyone. I would like to see Michael help prepare a new life for the Russian people.'

'I don't understand,' Masha murmured, completely at a loss, but at that moment, Sophie came skipping into the room and soon afterwards Sergei left.

'How did you like him?' Sophie asked.

Masha hesitated. 'Very much at first, but then he began to talk in such a strange way, I don't know what he meant really.'

'All men talk in a strange way sometimes,' Sophie said airily. 'I never listen. Come to my rooms. Papa had them done over especially for me. I think you will like them.'

'It is charming!' Masha exclaimed as they entered Sophie's pale green and white boudoir, gay with flowers everywhere, knick-knacks, low settees and soft light-coloured rugs.

Sophie swept a pile of *Journal de Dames* and *Wiener Mode*

off the deepest armchair, pushed Masha into it, and curled on the rug at her feet. 'Tell me everything,' she said, 'but first of all this: is Anichkov Palace a *home* to you?'

'Home?' Masha thought it over for a minute. She hardly knew her way around the palace yet, had no idea where some of the corridors led, most of the faces were still not familiar to her, and yet...the small writing desk in Alexandra's study was now called 'Masha's desk', she sat there every morning answering some of the grand duchess' personal mail, she knew every doll and toy horse in the nursery by name and the children clamoured for her to spend her afternoons with them. In the evenings she sat in 'Masha's chair' reading a Walter Scott novel aloud. Walter Scott was the grand duke's favourite writer and Masha felt proud when her reading was praised. 'Yes, it is home' she told Sophie firmly. 'I will tell you about it.'

Sophie listened attentively. 'I am glad you are happy,' she said at last, 'but I am a little disappointed. I thought you would be going to the theatre or to a ball every night. Instead you tell me how the grand duke plays with the children and how he and his wife sit together and talk. It doesn't sound very exciting.'

'But I've been in Anichkov for only a week,' Masha protested. 'There are balls and receptions but not every day.'

'And you don't feel shy any more with the grand duke and duchess?' said Sophie.

'Never with her,' said Masha. 'But I think I will always be a little afraid of Grand Duke Nicholas. He is always formal and restrained, even when he is trying to be pleasant. It is only with his family that he unbends. He leads a life of great austerity and we all have to be very punctual in anything that concerns him. One cannot feel at ease with him. But Alexandra Feodorovna is an angel. I really am happy, Sophie. What about you?'

Sophie's eyes sparkled. 'About me? Well, first of all I was

wrong thinking Papa wouldn't want me. He spoils me dreadfully...I think he is proud to show me to all his friends. I've been to two big dinners and a ball already. That reminds me! I want to show you something an aunt sent me from Vienna as a graduation gift.'

Sophie jumped up and ran to her dressing-table which was loaded with bottles of perfume, powder-boxes and hand-mirrors. 'Look!' she announced, returning.

It was a small oval tray of gold filigree. Three gold monkeys were sitting in the centre, one with a violin, the second with a trumpet and the third with a drum. A crystal flask of perfume stood in front of each monkey.

'Now watch!' Sophie took a bottle off the tray. Immediately a hidden music-box started to play. It sounded just as if the monkey orchestra was performing.

'Isn't it lovely!' Sophie clapped her hands in delight. My aunt says no one will try to steal my perfume with my monkeys on guard.'

But for some reason Masha found the toy unattractive. She listened to the little tinkling melody, wondering why it sounded so ugly to her. 'Oh, shut it off!' she cried, so sharply Sophie nearly dropped the bottle.

'What is the matter with you?' Sophie asked. 'You really startled me! Is anything wrong?'

'Nothing,' Masha confessed. 'I...just don't like that tune. It...frightens me.'

'Frightens you? Masha you must be out of your mind! You need some fresh air.' She looked at Masha with a hint of mischief. 'I did have a plan, to go to the Summer Garden this afternoon. What do you think?'

'I'd love to,' Masha agreed with alacrity. 'I haven't seen the Summer Garden yet. Oh, Sophie, isn't it extraordinary to be able to go wherever we want? I can't get used to it.'

'I'm beginning to,' Sophie said. 'But there's always Miss Alice.'

'Miss Alice?'

Sophie pouted. 'She's my companion, governess, call her what you want. Papa found her somewhere—at the bottom of grandmother's trunk, I believe. She is supposed to look after my morals and improve my English. I don't mind English, but I hate to be chaperoned.'

'What is this sudden rebellion?' Sophie's father, General Brozin, had come into the room unnoticed. He bowed to Masha and then said jokingly, 'I never expected such a wayward daughter. Already there's not a trace of Smolni discipline left.'

'I am afraid Sophie never had much respect for discipline,' Masha answered, laughing.

'Well, she has no choice,' General Brozin said firmly, 'It is either Miss Alice, Sophie, or you will have to entertain your friend at home.'

Miss Alice appeared, wrapped in grey silk cape. She had a small withered face made even smaller by an enormous grey and silver turban. She greeted Masha politely in French and told her that she was afraid it might rain. One never knew with St. Petersburg's damp weather.

'It is a beautiful day, Miss Alice. We've had no rain for the whole week. You are confusing St. Petersburg with London,' Sophie argued, while a maid was adjusting on her head a hat that looked like an oversized bunch of white and orange-striped ribbons. 'It is the latest thing in hats, called *a la giraffe*,' Sophie explained to Masha.

When the party got out of the carriage at the entrance to the Summer Garden, Miss Alice laid her mittened hand on Masha's arm. 'Look at the grille work, my dear,' she said, 'Isn't it beautiful?'

'It is,' Masha murmured, looking at the airy grille with golden spikes joining the pink granite pillars crowned with vases and urns. Behind the grille gleamed the green depths of the garden.

'Let's go inside. You have admired that iron thing long enough,' Sophie urged.

'That Sophie, there is no poetry in her!' Miss Alice sighed, following the girls into the garden.

To Masha the garden seemed like something in a dream. The afternoon sun lit up long avenues bordered with trees and made the many statues stand out white against the dark pines. It was very warm, more like June than the end of April. Miss Alice started to explain the meaning of the statues, pointing out Night with an owl on her shoulder, and Architecture with an unrolled plan in her hand, but Sophie wouldn't listen. 'Who cares about those marble people?' she protested. 'I want to see the living ones.' Taking Masha's arm, she dragged her into the midst of a gay throng walking along the central avenue.

After taking a few steps, Masha realised there was something strange about the crowd around them. As far as she could see it was entirely composed of young girls, each accompanied by an older woman. Every girl was dressed to outshine the others. Silk gowns, embroidered ruffles, lacy capes and Persian shawls, made Masha almost ashamed of her simple muslin and white silk shawl. Even Sophie's hat *a la giraffe* paled in comparison with beribboned and beflowered bonnets of every shape and colour.

'Are we caught in some kind of a procession?' Masha asked Sophie in a low voice.

Sophie giggled. 'It *is* a procession, or a parade rather. Keep quiet,' she whispered back, with a glance at Miss Alice's direction.

'But what does it all mean?' Masha insisted. 'Just look at all those men.' She indicated several men lining the avenue. Most of them looked like prosperous merchants with tall hats on their heads, massive gold watch chains shining against their velvet vests, and carrying silver-topped canes. They were staring at the passing girls, who blushed, lowered their eyes and took short mincing steps.

'See that man on the right, the one with fat red face?' Masha whispered. 'He is looking at that girl in yellow as if he were going to buy her! And that old woman beside him is pointing at her too.'

Sophie's shoulders shook and she pressed a handkerchief to her lips. 'Hush,' she whispered, 'that old woman is a 'svakha'. She goes from house to house to arrange marriages. It is not always convenient for her to bring the man to the girl's home, so once or twice a year girls parade in the Summer Garden. Svakha points out the particular girl, so the man can decide if he likes her.'

'Suppose the girl doesn't like *him*?'

'I don't believe it matters really. It is the parents who decide for her. Svakha arranges everything, bargains about the dowry, makes sure the girl has enough pillows and mattresses for her new house, and…'

'How do you know all this?' Masha interrupted. 'From my maid,' Sophie confessed. 'And it is she who told me this is the day to go to the Summer Garden to see the svakhas at work. Isn't it fun to watch? I never knew there were so many men anxious to get married. Of course a few are here just for the sake of seeing a pretty face. Those officers, for instance. Over there; a Moscow regiment, I believe.'

'They are looking at you,' Masha warned. 'Especially that tall blond one.'

'Which? Which one?' Sophie looked up quickly.

'Oh, Sophie! Miss Alice may notice,' Masha pleaded, glancing over her shoulder at the merry-faced young lieutenant.

At the sound of her name, Miss Alice peered near-sightedly from under her turban. 'What is it?' she asked suspiciously. 'Who are these gentlemen?'

The next moment, her eyes fell on Sophie, blushing prettily, her head on one side.

With unexpected energy, Miss Alice took her charge by the arm and marched her into the nearest side avenue. Masha followed, doing her best not to laugh.

Miss Alice's long lecture on suitable behaviour in public lasted for the greater part of their ride home. As soon as the governess began to doze, lulled by the movement of the carriage, Sophie pressed her lips to Masha's ear.

'His eyes are blue, aren't they?' she whispered. 'He has no moustache. Never mind; I think I like it. One can see the corners of his mouth turn up when he smiles. Did you notice that birthmark on his neck, just above the collar? Masha, is this what people call "love at first sight"?'

'Sophie!' Masha was shocked, 'You are simply being silly.'

'But didn't you notice the way he threw back his head when he laughed?' Sophie went on, ignoring Masha's remark.

'I didn't notice anything special about him,' Masha answered firmly.

Sophie made a face. 'Oh, well, if you prefer the serious, cold type like my cousin Sergei…'

'He is not at all cold!' Masha suddenly found herself roused up, 'You don't know what you are talking about.'

'Oh! Oh!' Sophie exclaimed laughing.

6

The Peterhoff Fête

July twenty-second, the day of St Mary of Magdala, patron saint of the Dowager Empress Maria Feodorovna, was always marked by a fête in Peterhoff palace. The entire court drove out from the city to the fairy-tale castle standing above the Finnsky Bay, surrounded by a magnificent park with famous fountains. To Masha's delight the grand duchess told her that Sophie was being invited to join the court for the outing.

'You may forget all about being a lady-in-waiting for a day,' Alexandra added. 'Just enjoy yourself and be ready to leave at ten. I will be driving in a closed carriage with the French Ambassador's wife, but you young things will have more fun in an open landau. At your age dust doesn't matter.'

'Who would worry about a few specks of dust anyway?' cried Sophie as the girls took their places in the landau, in company with Ally Ayler, all swathed in veils against the possibility of more freckles.

The rest of the suite were also getting into landaus and carriages. Anichkov courtyard was filled with gay voices and the thumping of hoofs. Already it was getting hot. Ladies opened parasols and fanned themselves; Masha carefully spread out the folds of her sprigged muslin and hoped that the heat wouldn't uncurl her hair.

The landau was about to start, when a carriage rolled into the courtyard and stopped abruptly, the coachman shouting something. The door opened and Sasha Rossett jumped out. 'Wait, wait for me!' she called to the girls.

A footman ran to help Sashette into the landau. Another footman followed with an enormous carton that was put beside the coachman. Sashette collapsed on the seat opposite Masha, her pink straw bonnet askew on her dark ringlets..

'I was so afraid you would be gone,' she said, fanning herself.

'We imagined you would be going with the Winter Palace suite,' Ally said wonderingly, peering at Sashette from behind her veils.

'They...they've already gone,' Sashette said.

'And left you behind!' Masha exclaimed.

'Not exactly.' Sashette seemed a little evasive. 'She, I mean Her Majesty, was feeling poorly and decided at the last minute not to be present at the celebration. Of course it had to be *my* day on duty and...'

Sophie suddenly leaned forward and touched Sashette's knee. 'You don't have to tell us anything more,' she said in a sympathetic voice. 'I can imagine what happened. Devoted as you are, you felt privileged to stay and take care of Her Majesty. But your brave smile could not hide your disappointment. You just couldn't help shedding a few tears and maybe you tore a handkerchief or two in sheer despair. Her Majesty noticed it and insisted you should join us at Anichkov. Now, isn't it all true?'

'Sophie!' Masha said helplessly, doing her best not to laugh, but Ally took it all quite seriously.

'How touching! And how clever of you to know. You must be a wonderful reader of character, Mademoiselle Brozina!' she exclaimed beaming at Sophie.

'Well, you see the three of us lived together in Smolni for many years. We know each other,' Sophie answered sweetly.

'Do you think it will take us long to reach Peterhoff?' Masha asked Ally, to divert her attention from Sashette.

'It is hard to say,' Ally answered. 'It is not very far but the highway will probably be crowded. The Peterhoff park is open to the public today. Everyone is anxious to see the fountains and the fireworks in the evening.'

When the landaus left the city and the highway came in sight, Masha understood what Ally meant. The whole population of St. Petersburg seemed to be on the road. Carriages and buggies, carts and gigs rolled in an endless stream, raising dust with every turn of their wheels.

Masha and her companions looked at each other and started to laugh. Their faces were grey and flakes of dust were clinging to their dresses.

'Never mind. We will wash and change as soon as we arrive,' Ally said reassuringly.

'Are you sure Nastia packed my dresses with yours?' Sophie asked Masha anxiously.

'She packed them as soon as they were brought from your house last night,' Masha reassured her. 'Nastia is probably waiting for us in Peterhoff already. She and several other servants left at dawn. By the way, Sashette, what about your dresses?'

'They are there, by the coachman,' Sashette answered curtly, apparently still smarting from Sophie's teasing.

Masha tried to think of some tactful remark to remedy the situation, but gave up. It was too hot for any effort. The sun was becoming scorching. Thin frilly parasols did not offer much protection.

'I am so thirsty!' Ally complained.

'I am too,' Sophie declared. 'Look! There is a boy selling kvas. Let's have some. Hey you! Come here!' She waved a copper at the urchin pushing a cart with a small barrel on it.

'Sophie, it is not proper,' Masha admonished, but Sophie was already leaning out of the landau and accepting a brimming glass.

'To the health of all present!' Sophie announced, raising

the glass. Abruptly, she broke off, her face scarlet. Following her friend's gaze, Masha saw a bony finger menacing Sophie from behind the window of a passing carriage. With dismay the three Smolni girls recognised the thin face and keen eyes of their former principal, Madame Adlerberg.

'Well now!' Sophie exclaimed, watching the carriage disappear in a cloud of dust. 'Do you think Maman is going to write to my father and advise him to send me back to Smolni for a few more years of discipline?'

'I shouldn't wonder. Better get used to the idea of wearing the brown uniform again. Maman is sure to start you from the very beginning,' Masha said, so seriously, everyone laughed. Even Sashette seemed to be in a better mood.

'I can't wait for the ball tonight. Everyone says it is marvellous,' she remarked, studying her face in a small mirror framed into her fan.

'I am counting the minutes too,' Ally answered. 'My fiancé will be there.'

'Sergei said he might be at the ball,' Sophie remembered. 'Did I tell you about it, Masha?'

'No,' Masha replied, wondering why the small bunch of faded flowers pinned to Sophie's shoulder suddenly seemed so beautiful. 'I didn't know he was invited.'

'Oh, he is something-or-other in the diplomatic corps now. They are always invited,' Sophie answered negligently. 'Won't we enjoy ourselves tonight!'

'If we ever get to Peterhoff,' Sashette grumbled. 'Look at all those people.'

'Make way! Make way!' the coachman cried as the landau slowly trundled its way among throngs of vehicles and people making the trip on foot.

Masha had just closed her eyes to rest them from the glaring sun, when there was a sound of galloping hooves.

She hastily blinked the dust from her lashes and saw a group of young men in military uniforms flash past on horseback. At the same moment, something white flew through the air.

'I thought they threw something at us, but I don't see anything. How strange!' Ally exclaimed, looking around.

'Yes, isn't it. I am sure I saw something too,' Sophie said with an innocent look.

Sashette kept silent, but her dark eyes darted suspiciously from Sophie to the cavalcade disappearing behind the next bend of the road.

Masha felt thankful no one noticed the white rose that Sophie had deftly thrust up one of her wide elbow-length sleeves. She blushed instead of her friend and was only too glad when a strange structure alongside the road caught everyone's attention. It was a landau surmounted by a makeshift screen of shawls and open parasols.

The old coachman turned around in answer to the girls' surprised exclamations. 'Some young ladies are changing in there,' he explained. 'It is difficult to find a room in these parts today. All the inns are full. Their dresses are all dusty and they want to look nice and fresh.'

He was still speaking, when a group of young university students came along. They were on foot and carried their jackets hung on canes over their shoulders. As they passed the improvised dressing-room, one of them caught at a shawl with the crooked end of his cane. In a moment, the whole fragile structure collapsed, exposing two young ladies in petticoats who screamed and tried to hide behind the parasols. There were answering squeals from a similarly equipped landau standing across the road and laughter from passers-by.

Another ten minutes of dusty roads and Peterhoff's palace came in sight, towering above the green park with gilded statues, and fountains playing on the terraced slopes. Below, the blue bay was full of white sails, scattering and assembling again like a flock of giant seagulls.

'It is a paradise!' Sophie exclaimed as the landau stopped at the front entrance. Other landaus and carriages were rolling up and discharging their passengers, all laughing and shaking their dusty clothes.

Sashette, anxiously supervising the unloading of her box of finery, touched Masha's shoulder. 'I just want you to know that it is not just for the sake of having fun that I wanted so badly to come,' she whispered. 'It is because *he* is going to be at the ball tonight.'

Meeting Masha's blank gaze, she said crossly, 'I mean the gentleman I told you about. The one I hope to marry. Don't you remember?'

'Yes, yes, of course I do,' Masha assured her quickly and the girls parted to go to their rooms.

Masha found that she and Sophie had been put together. Nastia was waiting for them. Fresh dresses were laid on the beds. The jugs on the washstands were filled with hot water.

Sophie immediately produced the white rose from her sleeve and put it into a vase on the table. 'Did you recognise him?' she asked Masha with a mischievous smile. 'Remember the Summer Garden?'

'Oh, Sophie! You don't even know him!' Masha protested.

'No, but I trust fate to bring us together somehow,' Sophie answered gaily.

Arrayed in pale muslins, wide-brimmed straw hats on their heads, the girls left their room to take a walk in the park. Though it was not quite noon yet, it was already full of people. Girls in light summer dresses, old ladies in stiff gowns dating back to Catherine the Great, elegant young men in tight-fitting jackets and billowing neckties, simple folks dressed in their best, all milled around the fountains. A delegation from some oriental land passed in full splendour of bejewelled turbans and bright silks.

Masha wondered whether it was proper for her and Sophie to wander around unchaperoned, but the fountains were so enchanting, she soon forgot her misgivings. The girls stood spellbound in front of the giant statue of Samson fighting the lion. A powerful spray of water came from the animal's throat and rose high against the dark background of a grotto. Masha liked the Sun Fountain, throwing light sprays of water, like beams, all around. But Sophie declared that the Shepherd's Fountain was the best of all. A young shepherd sat on a rock in the middle of a small pond, watching his dog swim around after the ducks. Every few minutes the dog barked, the ducks quacked and water spurted above the charming group.

'Oh, how lovely!' Sophie clasped her hands. 'Here they go again! They must be alive. I am sure the little dog climbs out of the pond at night and shakes itself.'

'It is only the pressure of the water which puts them all in motion,' a gruff voice said behind Masha.

'Michael!' Sophie cried, whirling around.

It was Michael Davidov, in his cadets' uniform and behind him Sergei, very elegant in a striped waistcoat of the latest fashion.

Masha blushed, wondering whether Sergei would recognise her. After all, they had only met that once, at Sophie's. But Sergei was already bowing, and something in his eyes told Masha he had not forgotten her. She curtsied to him and did her best to look indifferent.

'Don't let Michael's mechanical information disenchant you, Cousin,' Sergei told Sophie. 'If these figures look alive to you, enjoy them and forget what puts them in motion.' He turned to Masha, saying, 'My brother is not imaginative. He considers it unmanly.'

The tone was so biting, Masha felt sorry for the boy. 'Are you attending the ball tonight?' she asked Michael.

It was Sergei, however, who answered. 'I have been

honoured with an invitation,' he said, 'but Michael must wait until he is an officer. He has passed all his examinations and is waiting to be commissioned.'

'What regiment are you joining?' Sophie asked.

Michael squared his shoulders. 'His Majesty's Preobrazhenski regiment.'

'Well, I am sure you will make a good soldier,' Sophie said, 'but in the meantime it seems we are reduced to only one partner for the ball tonight.'

'Two,' Sergei corrected. 'For I would like to introduce a friend of mine, Mark Panov. He is a lieutenant in the Moscow regiment and one of the best dancers in St. Petersburg. There he is, admiring a fountain. Mark!'

'But...but...it is *he*!' Masha gasped, staring at the slim, uniformed figure swinging down the avenue, while Sophie crimsoned.

'May I...' Sergei began and stopped as Sophie and Mark looked at each other, both trying not to laugh.

'I really should tell your father,' Sergei threatened after Sophie told him about the scene in the Summer Garden. 'He would lock you up on bread and water for a week!'

'I had not one but *two* chaperones in attendance, Miss Alice and Masha,' Sophie defended herself.

At the mention of Miss Alice's name, Mark made a frightened face and looked around as if expecting a box on the ear.

'Is Miss Alice the lady I saw with you in the Summer Garden?' he asked. 'She's already tried to kill me with a look; this time she may use her green umbrella!'

Masha liked Mark. His handsome face was gay and open, but it was a strong face too, and kind. 'Miss Alice is not here,' she told him laughing. 'If she were, Sophie and I would be wearing cloaks in case of a breeze from the sea and galoshes so as not to get wet from the fountains.'

'And have you seen the Mushroom Fountain?' Mark said

rapidly to Sophie. 'It is very fine. It really looks exactly like a mushroom and it is imperative that you see it. May I show you?' He offered her his arm which she promptly accepted and the two of them ran up the avenue, laughing, with Sergei striding behind, calling, 'Stop! Wait! You have not asked my permission, Sophie!'

Masha and Michael followed more slowly.

'Your brother doesn't seem to like the idea of a military career for you,' Masha remarked.

The minute the words were out, she was sorry, for Michael's face changed. It became older, bitter and stubborn.

'I do not have to ask my brother's permission,' he answered, 'Let him study his German and French philosophers and try to order his life by their impractical ideals. I like things better than theories. Have you ever watched the faces of simple soldiers when they look at the flag? They have promised to give their lives for their emperor and for their country and they are ready to keep their promise. I learn from them, no need to go to Heidelberg University.'

Masha listened with surprise to Michael's long speech, but before she had a chance to answer, Sophie came running back, the hem of her dress dripping wet.

'I went too close,' she explained.

Behind her, Mark Panov raised his hands in a comic gesture of despair. 'The Mushroom proved treacherous,' he said apologetically. 'We were so busy talking, we forgot how far the spray reaches. It is all my fault.'

'We'll have to go back to the palace then. You can't stay in this wet frock,' Masha decided.

Mark bowed to Sophie, suddenly formal. 'May I beg you, Mademoiselle, not to forget the dances you promised me?'

Sergei bowed too, 'May I have the first waltz?'

It took Masha a moment to realise that Sergei was

speaking to her. She blushed and her heart beat so loudly she felt sure Sergei could hear it.

Keeping her eyes demurely downcast, she curtsied, murmuring, 'Certainly, with pleasure,' and hoped her ears were not too red.

More bows and curtsies, and at last Masha and Sophie were back in their room.

'Isn't it wonderful that Mark has turned out to be Sergei's friend. I told you fate would arrange it! I knew it! I knew it!' Sophie rejoiced.

The rest of the day passed quickly. First there was a gay meal in company with other ladies-in-waiting and courtiers. Then the girls and other guests were taken in open carriages all over the beautiful grounds.

A short rest and it was time to get ready for the ball. Wearing her ball gown, her hair expertly arranged by Nastia, Masha sat down at her toilet table and studied herself in the mirror. The pale lavender of the dress made her skin look very white and there was a becoming pink on her cheeks. She flicked open her fan. 'Sergei asked me to dance with him tonight,' she whispered to herself.

From the mirror, her eyes smiled back at her over the fan. There was a new expression in them, something that had never been there before. Masha held her breath. She had seen many a girl look over a fan, but whenever she tried it herself, it always looked as though she were hiding. Now it was different, but then everything was different...

Sophie said nothing for once, but sitting in an armchair, her azure gown spread out around her, she watched Masha with deep interest, mingled with surprise.

'Shall we go now?' she asked as Masha reached out for her long white gloves.

Masha only nodded. 'I feel really pretty for the first time,' she thought, following Sophie out of the room.

They were just in time. They had barely entered the

immense ballroom when the strains of a polonaise signalled the entrance of the royal family.

The Emperor Alexander with his mother, the dowager empress, led the slow tour around the ballroom. It seemed to Masha that the polonaise would never end, but it was over at last. The orchestra began a waltz and Masha saw Sergei threading his way towards her.

'I shouldn't show I am watching for him. It just won't do,' Masha admonished herself. 'I should sit and look indifferent.' But she was on her feet as soon as Sergei approached her, a smile already breaking through.

'It is our waltz,' Sergei said. She put a slim hand on his shoulder, and they glided into the stream of dancers.

From under lowered lashes, Masha could see Sergei's necktie, billowy and dazzlingly white against his black tight-fitting coat with tails. She did not dare to look higher, afraid he might read the thoughts in her eyes. Sergei deftly turned her around and drew her a little closer. 'You are so light, I am afraid you might fly away,' he said, as they passed an open window, a starry sky behind it. A quiver ran through Masha as she caught the undertone of tenderness in his voice.

They had made a full round of the ballroom now. Gold epaulettes, ribbons, decorations, jewels shimmering on ladies' bare shoulders and arms, flashed past Masha and floated away. From time to time, she noticed old Smolni classmates among the dancers. Stephanie was there, in the latest Paris fashion, ruffles edged with fur; Ellie and Mary Vuich, looking shy as usual; Katish Muffle, her round face smiling happily; Marie Divova.

The music flowed on, the magic light of hundreds of candles streamed from the gold and crystal chandeliers. 'May it never stop,' Masha prayed. But the waltz ended and Sergei led her to a seat where they were joined by Sophie and Mark. 'Look,' Sophie whispered to Masha. 'Here is

Sashette and her beau coming.'

Sashette, coldly beautiful in white, a diamond aigrette in her dark hair, was advancing with a proud air, accompanied by a young man, tall and thin, with such a sharp profile it seemed cut out of cardboard.

'Monsieur Smirnov,' Sashette presented him. The young man blinked and bowed somewhere between the girls.

'He is very near-sighted,' Sashette whispered to Masha, 'but as you know, it is against etiquette to wear spectacles in court.'

It turned out that M. Smirnov knew Mark. He talked to him in a slightly patronising manner that made Sophie's eyes blaze. Mark only grinned. Masha hoped Sashette's admirer would leave quickly, so that they could dance, but instead he began a long story about 'something really funny' that had happened to him during his last trip abroad. 'I was staying in an inn in Naples,' he was saying, 'no, it was in Germany... Let me think... Well, anyway, it was so amusing!'

Sashette stood by with a stony face while the young man rambled on. At last he ended with a triumphant, 'Voila!' and gave a thin high laugh.

The girls smiled politely. Sergei pretended to cough, and Mark exclaimed, 'Wonderful, *mon cher*! You should write it down.'

Sashette bit her lip and took Smirnov's arm. 'I am afraid we must leave you now,' she said with a brief nod.

'Oh, how can she?' Masha whispered to Sophie when the pair was out of earshot.

'He must be a trial,' Sophie agreed. 'Sashette is intelligent, I admit it, and he seems so stupid.'

Mark had overheard Sophie's remark. 'Oh, no,' he said. 'Smirnov is not at all stupid in spite of his weakness for telling these so-called funny stories. He is intelligent enough and very shrewd. Wouldn't stop at anything to make a career. He has a good position now and will probably end as a governor of some province.'

'Never mind him,' Sophie interrupted impatiently. 'We have missed the gavotte because of him, but I am not going to miss this quadrille.'

Masha's lavender slippers were almost worn out long before the ball was over. She knew it was considered improper to dance more than twice with the same partner, but threw caution to the winds and had four dances with Sergei. In between she had other partners. The court was beginning to know and like the youngest lady-in-waiting. Grand Duchess Alexandra, all in pink, pom-pom roses in her hair, and dancing every dance, smiled at Masha from a distance. 'How nice everyone is! How wonderful everything is!' Masha's heart was singing as she flew from one end of the ballroom to the other in the lively 'galope'.

After the third quadrille, Sergei drew her away from the ballroom into a small, booklined room overlooking a quiet corner of the park.

'I wanted to show you this,' he said, leading her to a window. Outside, in the garden, stood a giant bush of jasmine in full bloom, bathed by moonlight.

'It is like something in music,' Masha murmured. 'How peaceful it is here. Everyone must be in front by the fountains. I think…. Oh! …' she broke off and stepped back from the window.

A tall figure with slightly stooping shoulders had come from behind the jasmine bush. Masha could see the golden epaulettes gleam in the moonlight. She recognised the sparse blonde hair and clean-shaven round face. Emperor Alexander was escaping the noise and heat of the ball.

At the same moment, Masha noticed another figure. It was just a vague outline of a man standing under an elm tree, a few feet away from the tsar. Suddenly the man lifted his right hand, then slowly lowered it again and vanished into the dark depths of the park. A few seconds later,

Alexander also moved away.

Masha caught Sergei's arm. 'Did you see that man? He had something in his hand. What do you think he was doing?'

As Sergei turned his face to her, Masha saw with surprise that he was very pale and his voice sounded breathless as he answered. 'His name is Kahovski.'

'Kahovski?' Masha repeated. 'Who is he? A friend of yours?'

There was a pause and then Sergei said, 'A friend? Yes, yes, I suppose you could call him that.'

'But what was he doing?' Masha insisted, completely baffled.

'How do I know?' Sergei sounded irritated, 'It may not have been Kahovski at all. I could have been mistaken. Maybe someone of the public was being curious.'

Unconvinced, Masha would have liked to ask more, but Sophie and Mark burst into the room, Katish Muffle and several other young people at their heels.

'Why are you hiding in here?'

'The supper is to be served on small tables. We want you to sit with us.'

'The fireworks are about to begin. Come on the terrace!'

As they were all leaving the room, Masha noticed that Sergei drew Mark aside and said something to him in a low voice, nodding at the window.

Straining her ears, Masha heard Mark answer, 'Yes, I know, Kahovski boasted he could do it, but of course he wouldn't really. Just his big words.'

'What does it all mean?' Masha wondered standing beside Sophie on the terrace. Then Sergei and Mark joined them and the fireworks began.

Giant golden flowers unfurled against the dark night sky, formed flaming bouquets and fell down in a shower of stars. Shimmering arches rose high above the trees. Immense silver fans opened, became two halves of a pearly shell and exploded into blue flames. Hundreds of golden darts flashed, while Catherine wheels spun dazzlingly around and around. Fountains spouted molten gold, emeralds and rubies.

At the stroke of one, the dowager empress appeared, handsome and smiling, seated in an open carriage beside her son the Emperor Alexander. The carriage slowly rolled along the wide avenues of the park. Immediately, giant initials M.F. flamed in the sky. The cannons boomed, people shouted hurray.

On the terrace, Sophie cheered and waved her handkerchief. Katish Muffle jumped up and down like a little girl. But Masha stood still, her eyes shining, hands clasped. The sound of cheering was all around her, but she was conscious only that Sergei, at her side, was looking down steadfastly at her, rather than up at the spangled heavens above them.

7

The flood

Autumn had come, and with it Masha's move to the Winter Palace for the three months while the grand duke and duchess were in Germany. Outside in the November dusk the rain fell ceaselessly. It seemed to Masha that it had been raining for weeks on end, but tonight, alarmingly, the cannons of St Peter and St Paul's fortress had begun to boom in sullen warning that the waters of the Neva were rising.

Wild winds caught the salvos and carried them across the river. Every time a deep boo-oom came, the windows of the Winter Palace facing the water trembled and the crystal pendants of the chandeliers tinkled against each other.

Alone in the empress's bedroom, Masha tried to ignore the ominous sound and concentrate on the various small duties she had performed every night for the last two months as the empress's personal lady-in-waiting. She put a bible on the night table, and arranged beside it a glass of sugared water and a candle under a green shade. Having made sure the maid had drawn back the bed curtains just as the empress liked it and that the dressing table was in order, she crossed the room to see if the right clothes were laid out for the empress to wear tomorrow.

The highwaisted, long-sleeved gown of brown wool, laid on the back of a big blue velvet armchair, looked very drab, especially when compared to Grand Duchess Alexandra's gay, fashionable dresses.

Masha chased the thought away. It was better not to

think about Alexandra, or about Anichkov Palace, she decided firmly, it would only add to the lonely homesick feeling that had been haunting her for the last few weeks. After all, she reminded herself, it was by her own free will that she had agreed to stay with Empress Elizaveta. She was not regretting her decision. The empress was kind to her, and she was getting used to the Winter Palace. Sashette had been unexpectedly pleasant, and always sending notes and small gifts. If only… But here was another thought that Masha did not want.

'I must pay attention to what I am doing,' she reminded herself, bending over the empress' gown. The white ruching at the neck had been sewn on crooked. That silly new maid! Masha was about to ring the bell, but changed her mind and decided to re-sew the ruching herself.

There was a small sewing-table in a corner of the bedroom, always ready for small last-minute repairs. Masha took a needle from the big scarlet pincushion, threaded it and was just beginning her task, when the guns sounded again. She started and pricked her finger. The waters must be getting even higher. She remembered uneasily Nastia's story of the German pharmacist living in Palace Place, who said he could read the stars and predicted a flood, 'the greatest in centuries'. Nastia had also reported that one of the palace cats was constantly dragging her kittens to the highest step of the back stairway, and that many people noticed that ants were crawling upwards on fences and walls, 'A sure sign of a flood,' Nastia said.

Sewing diligently, Masha tried to assure herself that all this was nonsense. One expected rains in November, especially after such a dry autumn. She had accompanied the grand duchess to Pavlovsk in August and though they had expected to stay only two weeks, the weather was so unusually radiant they had stayed all through September.

Sophie had gone to Finland with her father and Sergei.

'I am enjoying myself,' she wrote to Masha, 'but I am longing to be back and see you. It is getting chilly here and I suppose we will return soon, all three of us.'

Masha read and reread that last sentence and at the end of September, when they returned to St. Petersburg she hastened to the house on the English Quay the very day they got back. Sophie was home and smothered Masha with her embraces, but Sergei had not returned. He was travelling in Switzerland and was later to join the Russian embassy in Sweden, Sophie said. All through the visit, Masha hoped to be told that Sergei had sent a word to her, just something about being sorry he couldn't see her, something…anything. And she had cried a little sitting in the carriage on her way to Anichkov Palace.

But there was no word and it was really not important, Masha thought finishing her sewing and replacing the gown on the chair. Sergei was still away and as far as she was concerned he could stay away. She threw back her head and walked to the window to look at the weather. The wind must be really strong, to shake the heavy blue velvet curtains. She drew them apart and recoiled. For a moment it seemed to her that the torrents of rain were going to hit her in the face. The glass shook under the onslaught of the wind. She could not see the sky, only a black void.

She shuddered and dropped the curtains just as the empress appeared in the door. 'We haven't had such a storm in years,' Empress Elizaveta said, rubbing her hands with a chilly gesture. 'I won't need you any more tonight, my dear. Remind me to sign the letters on my desk tomorrow morning.'

Climbing the steps leading to Ladies-in-waiting Corridor, with the wind screaming round the palace walls, Masha was seized with such a fit of loneliness, she decided not to go straight to her room. Instead, she knocked at Sashette's door.

A rather cross voice called, 'Come in.'

Masha hesitated. Sashette in one of her black moods was not a pleasant companion, but it was too late to back out.

Sashette was curled up in a corner of the sofa polishing her nails. 'Oh, it is you,' she said when Masha entered. Sorry I sounded so disagreeable. I was thinking about my family.'

'Has your step-father been. . .unpleasant?' Masha asked, choosing her words carefully.

Sashette snorted. 'Unpleasant? He wouldn't dare! Not now that I am at court. No, it's worse. He keeps whining all the time about being hard up, how he's lost a great deal of money in some law-suit and how expensive it is to educate the children. I have two younger brothers and a step-sister, you know. And just imagine his audacity! He's suggested that I ask Empress Maria Feodorovna if my step-sister, *his* daughter, could be educated in Smolni at the government's expense.'

'And have you...' Masha began, but Sashette answered sharply, 'I have *not*. There are private boarding schools in Odessa, and if they are too expensive, let her stay at home and knit.'

Masha remained silent, not knowing what to say.

Sashette did not seem to care. She rushed on, tears in her voice. 'I have not told you yet about the awful thing my step-father is trying to do. He wants to send my youngest brother to a trade school because he is not as good a student as the older one. The boys have a tutor now. I won't let it happen! Mother is on my step-father's side as usual, but I've told her to send my brother to St. Petersburg next month. I will take care of him. He has always dreamed of becoming a sailor. He can enter the Naval Academy here, and I will pay. Later, if his marks improve, it might be possible to get a scholarship for him.'

'*You* are going to pay for him?' Masha exclaimed, thinking of the ladies-in-waiting's modest salary.

Sashette nodded. 'I shall manage somehow. I won't have my brother turned into a carpenter or a shoemaker.'

'It is wonderful of you,' Masha said warmly. Sashette never changed. She was just like this in Smolni: moody, often cross and disagreeable, yet sometimes one could not help admiring her.

Still, it was wiser not to linger. The flashes in the dark eyes predicted a scene. Masha began to rise from her chair. 'I am going to bed,' she murmured, 'It is getting late.'

Sashette glanced at the small china clock on her writing desk. 'It is not really late, just a few minutes past ten. But you do look pale. Has *she* tired you out today?'

'I am not really tired,' Masha protested. 'Only this wind and rain make me feel out of sorts.'

'Oh, don't bother to make excuses,' Sashette snapped. 'I understand you. No one could possibly expect you to like Her Majesty's sad airs and long silences.'

'It is not airs, the empress *is* unhappy. The emperor hardly ever comes to see her. It breaks my heart to see her constantly watching the door.'

Sashette's eyes narrowed. 'That is *your* point of view. I don't agree with it. She may be unhappy as you say, but why make everyone else around her unhappy too? I was to go with her to the theatre last night. It was that new play and I longed to see it. She was all dressed, the maid was finishing her hair. Suddenly, she puts her head down on the dressing-table and declares she is sick and can't go. I really think she did it on purpose!'

'Don't say that!' Masha cried indignantly, 'Nobody can help being sick.'

'Then stay with her forever, nurse her, bear her whims!' Sashette snatched a piece of chamois cloth she was using on her nails and began to tear it into bits. 'What are you doing here? Go and sleep at her door if you are so devoted.'

Sashette's rage frightened Masha. She made a step

towards the door. 'I'd better leave. I'm sorry I upset you, Sashette. I didn't mean to. I realise you have a lot of troubles…'

'*What* do you realise?' Sashette's eyes glittered. 'You mean my step-father, don't you? Well, let me tell you that dealing with him is a pleasure compared to the humiliation of planning and contriving to get a man I don't love to marry me.'

'But you said once…' Masha faltered.

'Be quiet!' Sashette cried violently. 'You don't know what you are talking about. All *you* have to do is to throw a few more adoring glances and that cousin of Sophie's will be at your feet.'

Masha felt her cheeks burn. 'It is *you* who don't know what you are talking about,' she retorted. 'I am going. Good night.'

'Yes, go away! Do!' Sashette screamed, tears streaming down her face.

Masha's shaking feet carried her somehow to the door. She closed it thankfully behind her.

It was comforting to be back in her own room and to see Nastia's buxom figure noiselessly moving around, opening the bed and snuffing the candle. Masha felt grateful to the grand duchess for sending Nastia with her to the Winter Palace. 'There are many little things she can do for you,' Alexandra had said, 'and you won't have to depend on strange servants.'

Masha hoped that Nastia's cheerful smile would help her to forget the scene with Sashette, but the girl did not look gay. She jumped at every gust of the wind.

'Is anything wrong, Nastia?' Masha asked.

The maid started and it seemed to Masha that she looked guilty. 'No, Miss, it is just the wind. Hear how it is blowing.'

The wind *was* blowing hard. It kept Masha awake long after Nastia had gone. The nightlight flickered, the papers on the desk near the window rustled, even the bed-curtains moved.

Turning her face to the wall, Masha tried to forget the darkness outside. 'The storm will be over in the morning,' she kept telling herself, 'It will be bright and sunny.'

But there was no sunshine when she woke up. The wind was still howling and whistling, but now it was accompanied by another sound, a steadily mounting grumbling roar.

'It sounds like a waterfall,' Masha thought. Getting out of bed, she went to the window, but it was impossible to see anything through the rain-streaked pane.

The small clock on the bedside table said nine. She stared at it unbelievingly and tilted it towards the feeble nightlight. Outside it seemed as dark as midnight.

Steps passed her door and then there was a strange noise, as if something heavy was being dragged across the floor.

Masha rang the bell for Nastia but the maid did not appear. After waiting for a while, Masha started to dress, seizing wrong garments and fumbling with hooks and buttonholes. Wrapping a warm shawl over her shoulders, she opened the door and almost fell over a big roll of bedding on the floor. Her 'Ah!' of surprise passed unnoticed in the noise and bustle filling Ladies-in-waiting Corridor. Bundles of clothing, boxes with pots and pans, even babies' cradles, filled every inch of space. Two little boys sitting on a mattress looked at her with frightened eyes. Beside them, a yellow cat was making frantic efforts to get out of a basket., An old woman was squatting down and trying to push a small wooden trunk out of the way.

An elderly footman hurrying by paused as he saw Masha. 'I am sorry, Miss,' he mumbled, 'The servants quarters are flooded. People are trying to save what they can. The water won't rise this high.'

'Yes, yes, I see.' Masha felt so bewildered, she did not

know what to say. 'Please just help me to get through. I must go to Her Majesty.'

'Certainly, Miss. All the other young ladies are downstairs. This way, please.'

It took Masha several minutes to walk down the stairway. She had constantly to flatten herself against the wall as people passed her, loaded with their belongings, men looking grim, women crying, many of them with babies in their arms and older children close behind.

She darted down the few remaining steps, shivering in spite of her shawl. It was bitterly cold and piercingly damp. Her feet slipped on the wet floor and she kept colliding with distraught-looking courtiers, all exchanging the latest news. 'Two-thirds of the city is under water,' 'It is the wind blowing against the current that's made the Neva overflow,' 'The empress is on the ground floor,' 'No, she is in the corner room, watching.'

Masha turned and ran to the corner room, slipped through the door and stood, transfixed with horror, in front of the big window overlooking the Palace Quay. As far as she could see there was nothing but a whirling, raging expanse of water, merging with the dark sky. Bodies of cattle, overturned carriages, lumber, uprooted trees, even coffins from the cemetery, swept past, went down, appeared again and vanished in the foaming waves. An overturned boat, people clinging to its sides, emerged from the chaos. Masha thought she could hear the screams. In another moment, the boat spun out of sight and there was nothing but the raging water.

She was aware that someone had called her name. With an effort, she turned from the window and saw the Empress Elizaveta sitting in an armchair. Several ladies-in-waiting were bustling around. One was rubbing the empress' forehead with vinegar, the other was holding smelling-salts. Sashette hovered nearby, repeating, 'I begged Her Majesty not to leave her rooms to look for the emperor. She slipped and fell. I knew it would happen.'

The empress spoke in a weak voice, 'Masha, please go and try to find His Majesty. Ask him to come here. I am told he is on the cutter with General Benkendorf. But I don't think so. I believe I heard his voice. Please go quickly.'

'Yes, Your Majesty,' Masha was already at the door. But once out of the room, she stood uncertain what to do next. A young officer of the palace guard passed by and she ran after him, asking if he had seen the emperor.

'His Majesty is not on the cutter,' he told her. 'General Benkendorf persuaded him not to risk his life. The chief of police has just arrived with the latest report on the calamities. His Majesty should be on the ground floor with him.'

Masha ran to the stairway. She was half-way down when a sudden gust of wind whipped her skirts and almost made her lose her balance. She clutched at the bannisters and realised that one of the big plate-glass windows below had shattered in the wind. The flapping curtains had swept the china figurines off a small table; their fragments littered the mud-tracked floor.

Hugging her shawl around her shoulders, Masha picked her way through the crowd of servants who were taking paintings off the walls and moving furniture away from the broken windows. At the end of the long row of rooms she caught a glimpse of a green and silver uniform and thought, 'The emperor!'

She was right. Alexander stood surrounded by a group of men, giving orders. 'The cutter to the Gallernaya Bay,' he was saying, 'That is the worst place.' At the sight of Masha, he stopped and raised his eyebrows. When she told him that the empress was ill with anxiety, his face became serious and displeased. 'I will come at once,' he said. 'You too, please, Mademoiselle. It is not safe for you to stay on this floor.'

Trying to keep up with the emperor's long strides, Masha followed him. They were passing through a deserted drawing-room when she heard a low chuckle.

An old woman, dressed in a purple brocade with panniers, her powdered hair piled high above her elaborately-painted face, sat at a small table, a game of cards spread in front of her. Masha knew her only by sight. She was a pensioner who had once been lady-in-waiting to the Empress Catherine, and now lived in a remote corner of the palace. Pointing at the cards, the woman cackled crazily. 'Two aces, the king of hearts and the king of spades. Yes, that is right. Danger! Death!'

Alexander was going to pass, but the old lady rose and barred his way. 'The city is doomed, Your Majesty,' she screamed. 'This is the time to pray and repent. The blood of the Emperor Paul is upon us!'

Terrified, Masha watched Alexander shrink back. 'Not all of us,' she heard him murmur.

There was a rustle of silk and the Dowager Empress Maria Feodorovna burst into the salon. Always very German when excited, she ran to her son, waving her hands. '*Mein Gott*, Alexander! Where have you been? Poor Lise is so worried about you. It is terrible, terrible! We will all die if the waters continue to rise.'

They hurried out together, leaving Masha with the ancient lady who tapped the cards and gestured menacingly. 'This is the last hour. We must pray!' she screamed.

Masha's nerves snapped. She turned and fled, running blindly through the rooms, just to get away from the strident voice and wild eyes. At last she stopped, breathing in gasps, her hair falling on her shoulders. She pinned it up somehow while looking around. She was in a narrow passage, lined on both sides with low arched doors. The doors looked heavy and several were padlocked. Masha opened one of those which were not locked and peeped inside. She saw big wooden chests, rolled up rugs, a few armchairs covered with sheets. She opened another door. More wooden chests, dusty china washbasins, a dim mirror. Masha realised that she was in the 'storage corridor'. Nastia had mentioned it once, but Masha had never seen it before. She was about to turn back the way she came, when she saw another door at the very end of the passage and decided to try it. Anything rather than return through the salon.

Behind the door was a narrow carpetless stairway disappearing into blackness. The smell of water was so strong, Masha almost expected to see waves lapping out of the dark. She was about to close the door and retreat, when she heard muffled crying, and a voice lamenting below her.

'It is Nastia!' Masha exclaimed. Gathering up her skirt she went down, feeling every step before putting her foot down.

It *was* Nastia. Seated on the wet steps, her face buried in her apron, she was sobbing hopelessly.

Masha bent over the girl, 'Nastia, what is it?' she asked.

The girl lifted her head, stared at Masha, and burst into fresh sobs. 'My older sister's children, Miss. Two girls and a boy. Her husband is in the army and she was taken to the hospital yesterday morning. Dropped a kettle of boiling water and scalded her leg something terrible. I promised to spend the night with the children. but with that wind and rain... I didn't go. The older girl is seven and she takes good care of the younger ones. I stoked the stove and left them plenty of food. I thought they wouldn't need me. They will be drowned, and what can I say? Oh, why didn't I go!'

For a moment Masha felt like sitting down beside Nastia and crying too, but she restrained herself and said firmly, 'You don't really know the children are drowned.'

'They are drowned,' wept Nastia, 'dead and drowned.'

'Nonsense,' said Masha. Faced with Nastia's tragedy, her

own fears seemed nothing. 'We will get a boat and go and see.'

'A boat?' Nastia sniffed and wiped her eyes on her shawl. 'I begged and begged for a boat, Miss. No one will listen.'

'We will try anyway,' Masha insisted, helping Nastia to her feet. 'Where does this staircase lead to?'

'It is all water down there, Miss,' Nastia said hopelessly.

'But I can hear voices!' Masha cried. 'Maybe there are people who could help us. Come!' She dragged Nastia after her.

The two girls descended the last few steps to the place where the stairway made a turn. There was a loud splash and Masha plunged almost knee-deep into the dark muddy water smelling of manure.

'Look, Miss! Horses!' Nastia exclaimed.

Feeling she must be in a nightmare, Masha saw several horses tethered at the end of a long dark room with a vaulted ceiling, dimly lighted by a few horn lanterns hanging on the walls. 'Are we in the stables?' she said to Nastia.

The horses snorted and rolled frightened eyes at the water swishing around their feet.

Before Nastia could answer, a man came splashing out of the shadows, holding up a lantern. 'What are you doing here?' he shouted, 'Go back. The water is mounting.'

Masha ignored him, her eyes on the tall bareheaded figure in a long leather cloak, wading behind him. 'Sergei!' she cried.

Sergei exclaimed, 'You! Why…' He had no time to finish, because just then Masha slipped and almost went down into the water. He caught both her hands and held them fast, while their eyes met and smiled into each other.

Sergei said in a low voice, as if confiding a secret, 'Be careful. The floor is covered with ooze. You can hurt yourself.'

Masha only nodded. She felt tired and happy as if she

came to the end of a long voyage. They stood quietly, her hands in his, the lanterns throwing a reddish glow on their faces and reflecting in the dark water around them.

A sob from Nastia made Masha come to herself. 'Did you come in a boat?' she asked Sergei hopefully, 'This is Nastia, my maid. Her sister's children are all alone in their home. We must save them.'

Sergei smiled grimly. 'I came by water, but not by boat. I was crossing the Palace Square in a carriage, and before my coachman or myself realised it, we were surrounded by water. We unharnessed the horses and waded in here, holding on to their manes.' He glanced at a small group of people whom Masha could now see, standing beside the horses, 'We were not the only ones.'

'But there must be a boat somewhere!' Masha cried, and before Sergei could stop her she was splashing across the floor, her dress trailing in the water, stumbling, splashing and running again.

Reaching a narrow, shuttered window, she tugged at the fastenings. It opened unexpectedly, letting in a blast of wind that sent her tottering backwards into Sergei's arms. Gasping for breath, she stared at the white-crested waves rolling across the vast expanse of the Palace Square. Someone pushed past her. She saw Nastia clinging to the window-frame and frantically waving her apron in the direction of a passing boat that seemed to emerge from the low-hanging black clouds.

A man looked up from the oars and shouted, 'Hey, there!'

'Help!' Nastia called back, 'Three children are drowning. Help!' The words were carried away by the gale, but the man must have heard. He waved and bent over the oars again. The boat skipped from wave to wave, sometimes disappearing in the foam, sometimes riding the crest. There was a short lull in the wind and the boat stopped abreast of the little group at the window.

A rope uncoiled in the air. Sergei caught it. The other men came to his help and made it secure.

'Step aside,' Sergei told Masha, 'I will help the girl out.'

She answered firmly, 'I am going too.'

Sergei started to say something, then looked at Masha's face and silently helped her onto the ledge. The waves swept the boat perilously close to the stone walls. The stranger was fighting to keep the oars in his hands. Masha felt herself lifted and heard Sergei shout into her ear, 'Jump! Jump!' She sprang forward, the wind cutting her face, and hit the bottom of the boat, making it rock. In another moment, Nastia collapsed beside her. Sergei followed, and the boat bounced away from the wall just as the rope snapped.

8

The rescue

'Where to?' the owner of the boat shouted above the wind. Nastia shouted back the name of the street and he looked doubtful. 'We will try anyhow,' he called, leaning on the oars.

Something dark obscured Masha's vision. She looked up and saw that Sergei was wrapping his leather cloak around her and Nastia. She started to protest, but he paid no attention. Rolling up his sleeves he picked up another pair of oars from the bottom of the boat. Steadied by two pairs of rowers, the boat rocked less, and Masha eased her grip on the wet planks. Beside her, Nastia kept crossing herself, mumbling prayers and glancing fearfully at the threatening waves.

The muddy-yellow water foamed past. Beams, doors torn off the hinges, carriage wheels, parts of fences floated dangerously near the boat, tossed by the waves. A wooden garden gate passed, with an elderly couple huddled on it, he holding a speckled hen and she a small white dog. Hoisting herself up, Masha managed to look back. She saw with relief that the wind was chasing the gate towards the Winter Palace and people were leaning out of the storeroom window, ready to catch it as it passed by.

Masha had no time to see more.

'Hold tight!' Sergei cried as the boat emerged into the Senate Square, exposed to the full force of the raging wind. The little craft swerved perilously, then somehow straightened up again as both men bent to their oars. The monument of Peter the Great flashed past, barely seen through the net of foam. The rider on the rearing horse, silhouetted against the dark sky, seemed to move.

Masha was trying to catch her breath, when the bow of the boat suddenly rose in the air. Nastia screamed and the stranger called frantically, 'To the right, to the right!' Something heavy grazed the boat and for a moment it seemed to Masha that they would be swamped. She closed her eyes tightly, whispering, 'God, please, please…' No other words came, but Sergei cried, 'Saved!' and she dared to look again. A heavy carriage roof was dancing on the waves to the left of the boat. Masha realised they had been almost overturned by it and echoed thankfully, 'Saved!'

The boat turned into a narrow side street. The roar of the wind diminished and the water became less deep. Still, the porches of the houses and the stoops were below the surface. Through the open door of a narrow, two storeyed house, a man's voice could be heard, pleading 'The piano! Save the piano first. Never mind the other furniture.'

The voice was so young and anxious. Masha sympathised with the owner and hoped the piano would be saved.

An older voice answered, 'For goodness sake, Glinka, can't you keep quiet? The piano would be upstairs already if you weren't under foot all the time. Get out of the way!'

The boat turned around the next corner and Nastia exclaimed pointing at a house some distance away, 'There! In the basement. It is not under yet. They may be alive.'

The stranger attached the boat to a lamp-post. 'It is getting shallow,' he told Sergei. 'I am afraid of damaging the bottom. You can walk from here. I will wait for you.'

Sergei helped Masha out of the boat. Nastia jumped out by herself. The stranger remained seated in the boat, trying to keep it clear of the pavement.

Clinging to Sergei's arm, Masha struggled along, knee deep in water, feeling as if each of her shoes weighed several pounds. Nastia splashed on in front, her wet hair plastered over her head.

'I hope we are not too late,' Sergei murmured as they reached the house. Water was pouring down the basement steps.

Nastia's shaking hand could not fit the key into the lock. Sergei took it from her and opened the door. Masha hung back, afraid of what she might see, but Nastia gave a convulsive sob, and dashed inside.

In the dimly-lighted room, two small girls and a baby boy were huddled together on a kitchen table. The floor was covered with water several inches deep. Overturned chairs, pots and pans were floating around.

Nastia seized the boy and cradled him in her arms, kissing him and crying.

'Stay on the steps,' Sergei told Masha. 'The faster we all get out of here, the better.' Wading to the table, he picked up the older girl, handed her up to Masha and returned for the younger one.

'It was cold,' the child said, 'I couldn't light the stove because of the water. It kept coming in. That's why we all climbed on the table.'

'You've been very brave,' Masha said. 'But now you must come away. See the gentleman is bringing your little sister.'

They were half-way up the stairs when the girl wrenched her hand out of Masha's and ran down again. Masha promptly rushed after her, in spite of Sergei's urgent, 'It is dangerous! Wait for me!'

Splashing her way through the room, the child snatched something from the bed and darted back. 'You really shouldn't have...' Masha started to say, and checked herself. The girl was pressing to her heart a pitiful little wooden doll in a red calico dress. Without a word, Masha took her hand again.

It was difficult to struggle up the stairs against the water, but Sergei's hand was firm and soon they reached the street.

Going back was easier. The wind seemed to have died down a little and the waves not so high. Other boats began to appear, all filled with people, wet and haggard, clutching at the few belongings they had managed to salvage. Pale faces looked from the upper windows of the houses. Several dead bodies slowly floated by. Masha set her teeth and looked aside.

Sergei said reproachfully, 'Why did you let that child run back and then went after her, instead of letting me do it? You risked your life for a doll.'

Masha smiled. 'I didn't know it at that time, but anyway I am not sorry. I know how a little girl can treasure her doll. When I was a small Brown in Smolni, an older girl gave me a doll. I named her Anya and to me she was alive. She slept with me and listened to all my secrets. I am sure I would have gladly risked my life to save her.'

For a moment, Sergei's oars hung motionless over the water. 'You are loyal,' he said, more to himself than to Masha.

In a little while, the palace loomed in sight. This time, the boat could stop at one of the back entrances. Several hands stretched out to help Sergei unload the two girls and the children. The boat pushed off and was gone on another errand of mercy.

Masha drew the ends of her wet shawl around her shoulders, but before she could speak Nastia pushed the children aside, and stepped in front of Masha and Sergei.

'I thank you,' she said, bowing low from the waist and touching the ground with her right hand in the ancient traditional gesture. For a moment, the city ways were forgotten and Nastia had reverted to the centuries-old village custom of her childhood: duty and thanks to barin and barinia. Tears rose in Masha's eyes. For a moment she too was a little girl again. Just so had Mavra bowed before her mother. Yet she was conscious of Sergei's gesture of annoyance. Surely he could not mind?

'It is all over,' she thought. 'We saved them.' She tried to feel glad and couldn't. Only now was she beginning to realise how tired she was, and how cold. Glancing down at her feet, she saw her shoes all swollen with water. The bottom of her skirt torn.

Nastia turned and shepherded the children away.

'You look frozen,' Sergei said. Picking up the trailing end of her shawl, he tried to wrap it around her shoulders with an awkward, tender gesture.

Masha's lips trembled. She stood silent, wondering what made her suddenly long to hide her face on Sergei's breast and burst into tears. Utter weariness, or the bliss of being consoled by him?

She steeled herself. 'I must try and reach my room without attracting too much attention,' she told Sergei. 'I am supposed to be on duty.'

'If you really don't need me any more,' Sergei said reluctantly, 'I will get on the cutter when it comes back with another batch of survivors. They can probably use another pair of hands.'

'Will you try to find out what has happened to Sophie's house?' Masha asked anxiously. 'I know Sophie left for Moscow with her father last week. But what if there is no more house for them to come back to?'

Sergei began to laugh. 'Don't worry,' he told her. 'It would take more than a flood to sweep that away. It's too solidly built. You may be sure it is still standing.'

There were sudden cries, 'The cutter! The cutter!' from people bustling around, and Sergei was caught up in the rush. Going up the nearest stairway, Masha couldn't restrain herself from glancing back. She caught a glimpse of Sergei among the men crowding at the door. He was looking back too... She blushed and turned away.

9

Winter weather

The water went down at the end of the second day. Church bells all over St. Petersburg began to toll for the victims of the flood. Survivors rushed to their homes, often to find only wind-swept ground. Frosts set in. People had no shelter and no clothes. Disease started to spread and the hospitals were overflowing.

The Dowager Empress Maria Feodorovna organised a sewing circle to make clothes for the needy, and invited several opera singers to give a concert at the Winter Palace. After the performance, Masha and Sashette collected the donations, walking slowly between the rows of red velvet chairs, silver trays in their hands. Gold coins rained in. Many ladies were so carried away, they took off their diamond bracelets or rings, and added them to the money.

Towards the end of December, Grand Duke Nicholas and his wife returned from Germany and Masha thankfully went back to Anichkov Palace.

Alexandra's charity was different from her mother-in-law's. She began by talking discreetly to the palace servants and found out that many of them had relatives who needed help.

Masha begged to take part in the grand duchess's good work and at last Alexandra allowed her to deliver baskets of food and bundles of clothing. 'But not alone of course,' Alexandra said firmly. 'Nastia must go with you.'

Early one afternoon, Masha was coming out of a modest little house that had suffered greatly from the flood, when she found herself face to face with Sergei.

'All by yourself?' he exclaimed. 'And in this part of town! We seem to be fated to meet in strange places.'

Pink with pleasure, Masha explained to him about the grand duchess's charity work. 'The carriage is waiting for me around the corner,' she said, 'It upsets people when a court carriage rolls up to their door. Nastia and I take turns going into the houses.'

'Oh, Nastia is with you. That is better.' Sergei looked relieved. 'How are those children?'

'They are doing very well. Their mother is out of the hospital and they are with her. She has turned out to be an excellent seamstress. All the ladies-in-waiting give her work and she makes good money.'

'That is good news. May I accompany you to the carriage?' and Sergei began to walk beside Masha.

It was the first mild day since the flood, so mild it was hard to believe Christmas was not far off. The snow was brown and the wooden pavements were damp. The sound of dripping icicles mingled with the chirping of the sparrows fighting in the gutter. The street was deserted. Only two little girls with skipping ropes were playing in front of a distant house.

Sergei was telling Masha about a barge that was carried by the waters into the garden of the catholic bishop, and how in the Bolshoi theatre the rats came out of the cellars and swarmed all over the boxes. Suddenly, he broke off. 'You should always wear blue,' he remarked unexpectedly, looking at her blue velvet cloak and hood edged with fur.

Masha blushed under his glance. 'I like blue, just as Sophie likes green.'

'Speaking of Sophie,' Sergei said, 'I've visited her several times lately, but you were never there. Why?'

'Because I...' Masha stammered, then decided to be frank. 'Sophie always urges me to visit her, but whenever I do your friend, Mark Panov, is with her. He and Sophie sing duets, he reads poetry to her, or they just banter with each other. I feel...I feel in their way. You know what I mean?'

'Yes, I know,' Sergei frowned. 'So Mark is singing duets with Sophie. That is the first step. The next will be a walk in the moonlight and the third the offer of his heart.'

Masha's eyes opened wide. 'You seem so...bitter about it. Suppose your friend really is...fond of Sophie. Is it wrong?'

Sergei shrugged his shoulders impatiently. 'No, not wrong. Only, it is not the right time.'

It was on the tip of Masha's tongue to ask Sergei to explain what he meant, but she glanced at his closed face and decided not to.

'We must cross here,' Sergei said, stopping. 'No, wait, it is too wet. Let's use that magnificent bridge over there.'

The 'magnificent bridge' proved to be a plank someone had thrown over the slush in the gutter. Masha looked doubtfully at the slippery surface. 'Better go to the corner, the way I came,' she suggested.

Sergei offered his arm. 'Just hold on to me. I won't let you fall.'

They had only made a couple of steps when the plank wobbled. Masha's fur boots slipped. She gasped, 'Sergei!' and clung to him with both hands.

He clasped her around the waist. 'I told you, I won't let you fall. You are safe.'

'I am sorry,' Masha murmured, 'It was silly of me. Let us go on.'

Sergei did not move. His eyes on Masha's upturned face, he said in a low breathless voice, 'This is the second time you have called me by my Christian name. Do you remember the first time? It was in that flooded room of the Winter Palace. I am a fool, I realise it, but please say it again. Just once more.' His voice became even more clipped, his hand held Masha tighter. 'If you only knew how much courage it gives me, how much faith...'

The sparrows chirped something shrill and joyous, sending a sudden wave of reckless happiness through Masha's heart. She swayed towards Sergei, her blue velvet hood almost touching his shoulder. 'Sergei,' she murmured, and watched his face coming closer and closer to hers, the answering kiss already on her lips.

There was a sound of light steps on the wooden pavement, and a young man appeared on the other side of the street. Slim and boyish-looking, he was walking rapidly, his long dark cape flying behind him.

Sergei started and straightened up, his hand dropping off Masha's waist. Instinctively, Masha pulled her hood further over her head.

The young man did not seem to have noticed anything unusual. Lifting his top hat, he bowed in Masha's direction, called to Sergei gaily, 'Don't forget about the meeting tonight. We are expecting you,' and passed on.

Sergei nodded curtly and taking Masha's elbow helped her across the street. She walked blindly through the snow, feeling robbed of something precious that could not be regained.

'Where did you say your carriage was?' Sergei asked.

'Around the corner,' Masha tried to speak naturally, 'The way that young man went.'

As Sergei did not answer, she repeated, 'The young man who had just passed and reminded you of something.'

'Oh, yes. Sorry, I was thinking about something else. He did remind me of...my duty,' Sergei seemed to stumble over the last word.

The next few steps were made in silence. 'Here is your carriage,' Sergei said at last. He helped Masha in, muttered something about it being a pleasure, and closed the door.

Masha was not surprised that by the time she and Nastia

returned to Anichkov Palace, the weather had changed. Clouds rolled up and fine sleet started to fall.

Days wrapped in muddy snow followed each other. Masha did not care. They fitted her mood. Christmas arrived, but though the streets were full of people going to church, the festive note was missing; too many were in mourning. In Anichkov Palace, a tree was lit for each member of the grand duke's family. Masha was touched to find there was a special tree for her too. She looked for a long time at the twinkling candles, tears trembling in her eyes.

It was almost annoying to receive a visit from Sophie, full of gaiety and plans for a New Year's party.

'Father owns a country house on Yelagin Island,' Sophie chattered gaily. 'He seldom uses it, especially in winter. But he is going to have it opened and heated for the party. We are going to have a wonderful time, and I promise you a sled ride you will never forget. The only sad thing is Sergei will not be with us. He has been sent abroad for a few weeks.'

'There is hardly any snow,' Masha objected, ignoring Sergei's name. 'It is wet and slushy.'

'Oh, but there will be. I must have snow. It is important to me,' Sophie put on a mysterious face and moved closer to Masha. 'I am going to tell you a secret,' she whispered, 'Mark is going to propose to me on the New Year's Eve.'

Masha's eyes opened wide. 'But how can you know? Has he said anything?'

Sophie laughed. 'No, and that is just the point. He has come close to saying it several times, but at the last moment the poor man loses his courage and begins to stutter. I don't want a stuttering proposal. I want a nice, passionate one.'

'What makes you think you will get a passionate proposal at the party?'

'You will see. I am not going to tell you now,' and

Sophie pressed her lips together.

'How sure she is of him,' Masha thought, suppressing a sigh.

Sophie must have exerted some magic power over the weather. It snowed all the night of December thirtieth, and New Year's Eve dawned dazzlingly white, clear and frosty.

The grand duchess gave Masha permission to spend the night at Sophie's. The two girls set off for Yelagin early in the morning in a sleigh drawn by four horses. Miss Alice who accompanied them complained of the cold, but Masha enjoyed the ride. 'It was wonderful,' she told Sophie as the sleigh stopped in front of a long, one-storeyed house, with a wide porch and surrounded by a large garden.

'That is nothing. Wait until the ride after lunch,' Sophie answered, 'Let's go inside now. My nose is freezing.'

'I am not going out again today,' Miss Alice declared, as two footmen almost carried her into the house. 'What a climate!'

The house was very simply furnished and had the impersonal look of a seldom-used summer residence, but the stoves were hot and a big open fire flamed in the drawing-room.

General Brozin, who had arrived before the girls, helped Sophie to receive the guests. By noon everyone was gathered around the fire.

After a light meal, young people rushed into the garden, leaving their elders to drink coffee alone. 'A snowman! Let's build a snowman!' Mark cried. Several young men answered with enthusiastic cries and immediately started to roll immense balls of snow. Girls helped, or hindered. Faces were flushed, voices rang in the clear air. 'A broom! He must hold a broom!' Sophie called, and a footman rushed into the house to reappear a moment later with a broom in his hands.

Masha was the last to come out. She stood on the porch,

tying the ribbons of her bonnet and feeling no great desire to join in the fun.

'But I'd better,' she decided, 'I don't want Sophie to notice that I…that I miss Sergei. And I don't miss him,' she assured herself, giving the ribbons a last twist.

She was half-way down the porch steps, when she noticed a group of children gathered around a young man in a green military coat. General Brozin's St Bernard was rushing among the children, barking furiously and wagging his tail.

At the sound of Masha's steps, the young man turned around and looked up. 'Mademoiselle Fredericks!' he exclaimed, a warm pleasure in his voice. Masha had to look twice before she recognised Michael Davidov. Forgetting to return his greeting, she stood staring, wondering how silver epaulettes could turn a boy into a man.

Michael returned her surprised gaze with an amused smile, then bent over the children. 'Now you know how to play that game,' he told them. 'You don't need me any more. Off with you!' He clapped his hands and the children ran, the St Bernard after them.

'When did you arrive? I did not see you at lunch,' Masha asked as Michael held out his hand to her.

'Only about ten minutes ago, and the children got hold of me immediately.'

'I didn't know you liked children,' Masha said, and Michael answered simply, 'I do. Animals too. Horses and dogs especially.'

His tone was so earnest, Masha found herself saying, 'When I was little, I had a dog; his name was Trezor. I loved him very much.'

Masha paused. She had not talked about Trezor for several years now. The name brought back so many remembrances…her mother's death, the old house gone for ever.

Michael looked at her. 'Shall we take a walk to the end of the garden and back?' he asked. 'The paths are cleared. What kind of a dog was Trezor?'

Masha walked slowly at Michael's side, telling him about Trezor, and thinking oddly that she could not have talked to Sergei like that. He wouldn't be interested. Carried away, she began to describe her childhood home to Michael. 'I was barely nine when I was sent to Smolni,' she told him, 'but I can remember every room, every picture on the walls. It was a very old house. The doors sagged, the roof leaked. On windy nights, the floor boards creaked. I liked to imagine it was the Domovoy walking in the attic. No, it was more than just imagining! He seemed real to me. Mother used to be quite annoyed about my being so superstitious. She tried to explain to me that only village folks believed there was a spirit watching over every house, that the Domovoy did not exist. But I could see him so vividly, all dusty and hairy, I just couldn't give him up.'

Michael nodded sympathetically. 'I should think not. When I was very young and we lived in the country, we had a Domovoy too. Only ours lived in the bathhouse in company with a Kikimora.'

Masha's laugh rang out joyously. 'Oh, Michael! How lovely! Do tell me how you imagine your Kikimora. No one had ever been able to describe her to me. Or should I say 'it'?'

'Now, let's see,' Michael assumed a grave air. 'I think a Kikimora looks something like a scarecrow. Only it is very long and thin, like…mm…like a dried-up twig.'

Masha clapped her hands. 'That is it! That is exactly how I see Kikimora! Only I think it has green hair.'

'Oh, it does. I just forgot to mention it,' Michael took Masha's elbow to help her climb over a snowdrift.

They had reached a low stone wall marking the boundary of the garden and stopped, looking at the endless fields covered with snow. 'I hope I haven't tired you out,' Michael said.

Masha shook her head. 'Not at all. How could anyone feel tired in this country air?'

Michael's face glowed. 'Yes, isn't it heavenly? One day I am going to settle down in the country for good.'

'Really? You mean you are not going to stay in the army until you become a general?' Masha teased, feeling perfectly at ease with Michael.

'I am not aiming at high rank,' Michael answered stoutly. 'And I don't intend to stay on active duty forever. If my country needs me, that would be different, but otherwise I have my own plans.'

'Are they very secret?' Masha asked playfully. Putting her hand on Michael's sleeve, she begged, 'Tell me your plans. Please!'

Michael smiled. 'They are not secret at all. I would like to buy a country house, have orchards, flower gardens. Sergei and I lost our parents when we were quite small. Our guardian decided to sell the family estate and to invest the money for us. He did very well. I could buy a good-sized property with my share.'

'Is it going to be an old house?' Masha asked, 'Or would you rather have a new one built?'

He answered with conviction, 'An old house of course. With birds'-nests under the eaves and a greenish pond in the park.'

'The floors will be creaking underfoot?'

'They certainly will.'

'And the paintings on the walls will be dark?'

'So dark, you won't be able to tell whether it is a man, a woman or a battleship.'

'That would be lovely,' Masha walked in silence for a few minutes, then said in a small voice, 'Michael, will there be a Domovoy?'

He laughed. His eyes, so like Sergei's and yet so different, crinkled at the corners. 'How could I live without a Domovoy? Who would look after the house and take care of the stables? I will have the biggest, greyest, dustiest Domovoy I can find.'

'There will be a mistress in that dream house, naturally?'

Michael did not smile this time. 'Maybe,' he answered. 'Shall we go back now? I understand Sophie has organised some special sort of sled ride this afternoon. We don't want to miss it.'

'Yes, let's go. It is too cold to stand still.' Masha stamped her feet and accepted Michael's arm.

They walked slowly, following the paths between snowed-up trees and shrubs. 'Look, we are just on time,' he said.

There was a jingling of bells and a big six-horse sleigh dragging behind a long line of small sleds attached to each other drew up before the house. Sophie's father and a few older guests were sitting in the horse sleigh; the young people were quickly pairing off, a couple for each sled.

'May I be your escort?' Michael asked eagerly. 'This is going to be fun!'

'Do you think so?' Masha eyed the sleds with some misgiving. 'Suppose we fall off? Or another sleigh runs into us all?'

'If we fall, we will simply pick ourselves up. As to another sleigh running into us, there is very little possibility of it. Yelagin is still a wilderness, especially in winter. So don't make up excuses,' and Michael led Masha firmly to the nearest sled.

As they seated themselves, somewhere in the middle of the line, Masha noticed Sophie deftly manoeuvring to get to the very last sled, Mark at her side.

There was a last-minute scramble and the horn announcing departure blew in the frosty air.

The big sleigh moved and the sleds lurched after it. Girls squealed, men laughed. A young woman sitting on the sled in front of Masha's, waved her muff in the air and dropped it. Her escort jumped off, retrieved the muff and had to run full tilt to catch up.

The first bend of the road was passed and a white plain came in sight. The driver gathered the reins and his 'Oh, ho, ho!' echoed in the distant woods. The horses took off, their feet hardly touching the snow. Masha grasped Michael's hand. The icy air cut her breath, her heart was beating, her ears throbbing. At the same time, she felt a wild exhilaration mount in her blood that made her want to shout with delight. Her fright vanished, leaving only the joy of flying in space.

A slight incline made the throng of sleds sway to one side. The ladies screamed. The horses' pace slackened.

Masha turned her head away from the wind and noticed that in the last sled, Sophie was talking animatedly to Mark. At the same time she seemed to be leaning further and further backwards. Michael noticed it too, and called a warning that came just too late. There was a flash of bright green and Sophie rolled off the sled into the snow. Masha caught sight of Mark's desperate face, suddenly replaced by a pair of long legs as he dived after Sophie.

The horse-sleigh drew to a halt; the sleds bumped against each other. Everyone's eyes were on Mark, who was kneeling in the snow, some distance away, Sophie in his arms. 'He is taking a long time saving her,' a girl said, giggling.

General Brozin rose in his seat, shading his eyes from the glare of the snow, smiled and sat down again. Sophie and Mark were coming back, both a little pale, with strange, wondering smiles on their lips. They took their seats accompanied by enthusiastic waving and cheering, and the magic flight started again.

It was dusk when the merry party returned. As soon as they were inside, Masha pulled Sophie into a corner. 'Did he?' she asked breathlessly.

Sophie nodded and looked guilty. 'I thought it would be such fun to tell you all about it,' she confessed, 'but now I find I can't. It is too precious. I want it all for myself,' she whispered the last words and looked down at her cupped hands, as if she were holding happiness between her palms. 'He kissed me,' she went on dreamily, 'That kiss is mine too. He is going to talk to Papa tonight. Masha, I still can't quite believe it. I love him so!'

'I know,' Masha whispered softly.

Sophie gave her a quick look. 'Masha, I don't want to pry, but you and Sergei...I thought...'

'We are good friends,' Masha's tone was distant, 'Please don't start imagining things, Sophie.' She saw with relief several guests bearing down upon Sophie and hurried away to dress for dinner.

It was Michael who took her to the dining-room and seated himself at her right. He was frowning and kept drumming on the table with his fingers. 'Well,' he said, 'I suppose we are going to be invited to a wedding soon.'

Masha started. 'Hush,' she admonished, 'It is not official yet.'

Michael did not seem impressed, 'Do you really imagine no one knows? Just look at Mark.'

Masha looked. Mark's hand was groping for his wine glass without finding it. His eyes were on Sophie, seated across the table from him.

'He will make a wonderful husband,' Masha said firmly.

Michael bit his lip. 'I am sure he will. I have nothing against Mark personally, but in my opinion as long as he is a member of the Freedom Society, he has no right to get married because he doesn't know what may happen to him.'

'Freedom Society? What do you mean?' Masha

whispered.

Michael said calmly, 'You don't have to whisper. No one is listening.'

Glancing around Masha agreed. The long table was buzzing with talk. Her left-hand neighbour, a friend of Sophie's father, was talking to his neighbour. It seemed safe enough. She turned to Michael. 'Go on. Tell me,' she said urgently.

'The Freedom Society is made up of aristocracy, mostly,' Michael explained, 'Their aim is to liberate the serfs, abolish social classes, have equal rights for everybody, and no absolute monarchy any more. They want a parliament. Some members even dream of a republic.'

Masha listened, her fingers tightening on the handle of her fork. Michael smiled. 'Don't feel as if I am burdening you with a terrible secret. Quite a few people know about the existence of the Freedom Society, including Emperor Alexander.'

'He knows!' Masha exclaimed with relief. 'But they are actually plotting against the government? I don't understand…'

'When he was young, he had the same ideals,' Michael told her. 'Do you know what he said when he received a report on the Freedom Society from the secret police? He said, "It is not for me to punish them".'

'Because of his own part in the plot against his father?' Masha thought. 'Michael,' she said, 'Last summer in Peterhoff…' and she told him about the strange man in the palace park. 'Your brother seemed to recognise him. He said the man's name was…Kahovski. Do you think he is…'

'One of the most devoted members of the Society,' Michael finished for her. 'Even fanatic. It is hard to say just what he was planning to do. Maybe plead with the emperor to start the reforms, or maybe…something much worse.'

He glanced at Masha's averted face and said soothingly, 'Well, you know that nothing happened. Whatever it was, he probably lost his courage at the last minute.'

'Your brother is a member,' Masha spoke with deadly certainty. 'I know he is.'

Michael nodded. 'Yes, and a very enthusiastic one too.'

'And you?' Masha could not help asking.

Michael's face became set. 'I do agree with them on certain points, like liberation of the serfs for instance, but plotting behind closed doors is not for me. Besides, I have promised to serve my emperor and I will serve him to my last breath.' He seemed to think for a moment, then said slowly, 'I pray it never happens, but if there is ever a clash of arms, Sergei and I will be in opposite camps.'

Masha suddenly leaned forward, her hand on her chest. 'I...I have never thought about it. But then, if it happens as you say, Sergei...he will be risking his life.'

There was a strange wistful look in Michael's eyes. 'How very concerned you are about it,' he said, and added in a low voice, 'Now, we are attracting attention... Do you not feel well?'

Masha caught a few surprised glances and pulled herself together. 'No, no, I am quite well. It is so hot in here! I just wonder,' she spoke fast, anxious to prevent Michael from mentioning Sergei again, 'shouldn't someone tell Sophie about Mark?'

'Better not,' Michael advised. 'General Brozin is not a member of the society, but he knows about it and sympathises with them. Don't spoil Sophie's happiness. Mark will tell her himself, if he wants to. And don't forget that all this is just talk...so far.'

Michael was very silent for the rest of the dinner. Masha struggled to respond to the dutiful gallantries of General Brozin's friend. They did not speak again until General Brozin rose to his feet and announced that it was a few minutes to the New Year.

The big grandfather clock struck twelve. There was a chorus of voices exchanging good wishes and clinking of glasses.

'Now is the time to make a special wish,' Michael told Masha as she was lifting her glass to her lips.

Masha whispered to herself, 'May Sophie be happy with Mark.' The strange emptiness in her heart made it impossible to wish anything for herself. 'I hope my wish comes true,' she said to Michael.

He answered gravely, 'Mine will not.'

The hands of the clock were moving on, marking the minutes. The year 1825 had begun.

10

Aunt Daria

'An April wedding! Isn't it lovely! We will be able to wear the latest spring fashions,' Katish Muffle exclaimed joyfully.

Sophie's engagement dinner was just over and a group of old Smolni girls were gathered in her room.

'If it is warm enough,' Sashette remarked.

Sophie nudged Masha. 'There she goes! Always pouring cold water over everything. She is simply annoyed at not being a bridesmaid. I did not want to invite her tonight, but Papa made me.'

'Weather doesn't really matter in the city,' Ellie Vuich said. 'But did you know that when Natasha Meller was married last November, the bridegroom was almost two hours late because the roads were all snowed up? Wasn't it awful for Natasha? I would have cried right in front of the altar.'

'Natasha probably just sat down and waited.' Sophie laughed. 'I would have made a scene!'

'Who is her husband?' Sashette asked.

'A landowner. His estate and that of Natasha's parents touch,' Marie Vuich explained. 'Now Natasha can spend her life in the country and be close to her parents. Just what she always wanted.'

'She is the first of our class to get married,' Masha said pensively. 'And Sophie will be the second.'

'Stephanie and Nadia are both travelling abroad. Maybe they will marry foreigners,' Katish suggested.

'Stephanie might, but Nadia writes that seeing new

places is so interesting she has no time for romance,' Sophie answered.

When the girls began to say good-bye, Sophie held Masha back. 'I told the footman to hold your carriage. I want to talk to you,' she whispered.

'What is it? You look upset,' Masha asked as soon as she and Sophie were left alone.

'I am not really upset, just annoyed.' Sophie plumped herself down on a footstool. 'You see, I was planning to have such a wonderful time, ordering my trousseau and shopping. Instead, I am to be packed off for a month's visit to my aunt Daria. I tried to argue with papa, but he wouldn't listen.'

Masha looked interested. 'Your aunt Daria? Isn't she your Godmother?'

'Yes, yes,' Sophie interrupted impatiently. 'She's Papa's elder sister. I've told you about her before. She wanted to adopt me when Mamma died, and when Papa refused she became so angry she said she'd never see him again. And she hasn't, in all these years. But when I became engaged to Mark, Papa told me I had to write to her about it. She answered immediately, very kindly I must say, and invited me to visit her. Papa says this means the end of the feud and that I simply must go. Rodnoye is quite far, somewhere near Pskov, and when I think of travelling in January, with all that snow, into the deep country…brr…' Sophie shuddered.

'Pskov…' Masha repeated. 'Why, Anna Wulff lives near Pskov! Do you remember Anna? She was a White when we were Browns.'

'Of course I remember Anna. Have you kept in touch with her? I had no idea!'

'We don't write often,' Masha admitted. 'But I got a letter from her only last week. She never says much about herself, just that she lives a quiet country life with her mother and sisters. Her step-father died a few years ago. In her last few letters, though, she has mentioned a young man, a neighbour, who often visits them. He is a poet. She doesn't give his name, but she said, right at the end, "I am becoming more interested in him than I should".'

'Now that really *is* interesting!' Sophie hugged her knees in delight. 'Aunt Daria undoubtedly knows Anna's family. Everyone knows everyone else in the country. We will find out all about that young man. We may even meet him!'

'*We?*'

'Yes, certainly,' Sophie's tone was carefully nonchalant. 'You are coming with me, you know.'

'I am coming with you?'

Sophie rocked with laughter. 'Masha, dearest! Don't look so startled. Aunt Daria is expecting you. She told me in her letter to bring a friend to Rodnoye as she is afraid I might be lonely in the country. *Do* say you will come. Miss Alice will chaperone us. Alexandra Feodorovna will let you go, I am sure.'

'She probably will, but I still see no reason why I should go,' Masha protested, but in her heart she knew that Sophie would win as usual.

The feeling proved to be right. A week later, Masha found herself sitting with Sophie and Miss Alice in a carriage on runners instead of wheels and drawn by four horses.

Both girls were wrapped in furs. Miss Alice hugged around her a wide brown cloak brought from England.

It was barely six in the morning. Men armed with brooms were sweeping snow off the pavements. Newspaper boys ran past, screaming out the latest news. Wagons loaded with milk-cans clattered by.

Shuttered shops, bakery doors opening and closing, letting out clouds of steam and the smell of freshly-baked bread, an elderly sexton opening the doors of a church, the city gates, and at last the open road.

Everybody started to settle down for the long trip. Sophie produced the latest issue of *The Northern Bee*, in spite of Miss Alice's admonitions that young ladies should not read newspapers; Masha hemmed a handkerchief. From Miss Alice's bag came knitting, a bottle of medicine against colds, an extra shawl, a copy of *The Ladies Pocket Magazine*, and finally a small leather-bound book. The carriage on runners moved much less jokingly than one on wheels.

'Here is a fascinating and instructive book,' Miss Alice announced. 'It is called, *The Voyage into the Land of Virtues*. I am going to read aloud, and you, Sophie, can translate from English to Mademoiselle Fredericks, excellent practice for you.'

'Oh, no,' Sophie groaned. 'Let's practice our French instead. What about a nice French novel?'

'Sophie!' Miss Alice sat upright. 'What would your papa say if he heard you! To read those wicked French books. The very idea!'

But after a couple of days of travelling, the girls found that even the dullest story sounded exciting. Miss Alice was afraid to travel after dark, so the trip took much longer than it might have.

'Is it going to last forever?' Masha wondered drowsily, breathing on the frosted glass to look through, but seeing only snow banks piled high alongside the road.

The nights spent in inns were uncomfortable and the carriage seemed to grow smaller and smaller. Every time the impatient Sophie made a sharp movement, her elbow hit the big tea caddy standing on the seat beside her, as Miss Alice did not trust the tea served in the inns. Sitting in her corner, Masha was uncomfortably aware of her feet resting on a box containing small porcelain jars of spices, a gift for Sophie's aunt. 'I am so afraid of breaking them, I sit like a stone statue,' she complained.

'Well, I wanted to have a special carriage for the luggage and take a maid along, but Papa said it was all nonsense,' Sophie grumbled.

The last day of the trip was clear and windy. The tall lime trees waved their branches as the horses pulled the carriage along the wide snowy avenue towards Rodnoye.

Masha had expected a big manor, and was surprised to see a low rambling house, with a mezzanine rising in the centre and a low, open porch. It reminded her of her own childhood home. 'It must be pretty here in summer,' she thought, looking at the shapes of the flower-beds under the snow and the shrubs and trees massed around the house. Behind, rose the roofs of barns and stables.

A young servant-girl, running across the yard, a shawl around her shoulders, saw the carriage and darted back into the house. A minute later, the front door burst wide open and people surged onto the porch. Before Masha knew what was happening, they were surrounded by a crowd of servants, helped out of the carriage and up the porch steps.

The front hall was a big empty room with high-backed wooden benches along the walls. At the sight of Sophie, a white-haired footman, sitting in a corner and knitting a stocking, jumped up exclaiming, 'The image of mistress! Might be her daughter!' and rushed to kiss Sophie's hand.

Maids bustled around the girls and Miss Alice, taking off their wraps. Other servants were carrying in boxes and trunks.

There was a click of heels behind the door. A short, round-faced woman with a mop of fluffy white hair and very pink cheeks rushed into the room. 'At last!' she cried, throwing her arms wide open as if she was trying to embrace all the three visitors at once. 'We were expecting you two days ago. We…' She stopped and glanced uneasily over her shoulder as a loud voice called, 'Well, Emma! What is taking you so long? Are they here or aren't they?'

The woman's blue eyes blinked and her strong German accent became more pronounced. 'It is your aunt,' she whispered to Sophie. 'She had an attack of gout last night and can't walk. She is getting impatient. Follow me, please.'

'Emma, do you hear me?' the voice came again. There was a threatening note in it, and Masha hurried after Sophie, Miss Alice bringing up the rear.

The big drawing-room was flooded with the mellow light of the winter sun. A glass cabinet was full of china and ivory figurines; an embroidery frame stood by the window. Heavy, damask-covered furniture seemed to have grown out of the green rug.

Daria Ivanovna Gradov was seated in a high-backed armchair, her dress of purple silk spread around her, one foot stretched out on a footstool. An enormous white lace bonnet crowned her grey hair, its long streamers falling on her shoulders and framing a massive face with an aquiline nose. Sharp black eyes were fixed on the door. 'Sophie, dearest girl!' she exclaimed.

Sophie quickly crossed the room and bent to kiss her aunt's hand, but the old lady offered her cheek instead. Seeing the two faces close together, Masha thought that the footman was right. Aunt Daria was old and Sophie young, but there was a strong resemblance, especially in the stubborn chin and upsweeping eyebrows.

'Not bad, not bad,' Daria Ivanovna murmured, holding Sophie's hands and studying her. 'No wonder you got snared so quickly. A very suitable match, I understand. And this is your friend? Welcome, Mademoiselle Fredericks. Oh, I see you brought your heathen too, Sophie.'

Surprised by this last remark, Masha gave a glance around and saw that Aunt Daria's eyes were fixed on Miss Alice. She felt thankful the governess could not understand Russian.

'And now I am sure you are all hungry,' Sophie's aunt

declared. 'Tidy yourselves and we will have luncheon.' She clapped her hands and two maids appeared to escort the girls and Miss Alice to their rooms.

The clumsy, calico-clad girls, clattering around in their heavy home-made shoes, reminded Masha of her home, but at the same time filled her with misgivings. 'Don't you think we had better unpack ourselves?' she whispered to Sophie, watching the maids drop a perfume bottle, that luckily did not break, and giggle as they handled Sophie's diaphanous underwear.

Sophie was indifferent. 'Let them do it. They can't do much harm and it amuses them. Better think on how we are going to sleep in this elephant,' she pointed at the enormous bed under a heavy canopy, and loaded with pillows.

Before Masha could answer, another maid burst into the room, covering her mouth with her hand, her shoulders shaking with laughter. Behind her came Miss Alice, a frown on her face, a big sponge in her hand.

'Will you please explain to this poor ignorant creature,' Miss Alice told Sophie, 'that all civilised people use sponges. She keeps staring at me in a most aggravating way.'

'Poor Miss Alice will find it difficult here,' Masha said after the governess had gone to her own room.

'I am afraid,' Sophie answered, 'that we may find it somewhat difficult ourselves.'

The difficulties began as soon as luncheon was served. Used to the plain fare of Smolni and the dainty cooking of French chefs, the girls felt as if they had been invited to a giants' feast. Thick soup and an enormous leg of veal, were followed by chickens smothered in gravy. A rum soufflé did not end the meal. Dishes of preserved fruits appeared and had to be at least tasted.

All through luncheon, Masha felt Daria Ivanovna's sharp eyes on her face. She realised that her hostess was trying to find out what kind of a friend her niece had, but it was very uncomfortable. Sophie, at ease as usual, chattered gaily about St. Petersburg and Smolni. 'And by the way, Aunt Daria,' she said, 'An old schoolmate of ours lives in this part of the country. Her name is Anna Wulff. Do you happen to know her?'

Daria Ivanovna looked up from her plate, 'Anna Wulff? Yes, of course I know her. Her mother's estate is only about five miles from here.'

'Really!' Sophie cried, 'But that is splendid! Anna doesn't know we are here. We could drive over tomorrow and surprise her.'

Daria Ivanovna frowned. 'Well, my dears,' she laid down her napkin and addressed both Sophie and Masha at once, 'I am sorry to disappoint you, but as long as Anna doesn't know you are visiting me, I would prefer you not to go. Not that I have anything against Anna herself. She seems a nice enough girl, though I really prefer Alma, her step-sister; more character. The youngest, Zizi, is just a brat of sixteen, a cheeky brat too. However, that is not the point. What I don't like is the way these girls are brought up. That most undesirable young man, Alexander Sergeivitch Pushkin, I daresay you've heard about him, is constantly in their house, courting all the three sisters at once. They are allowed to walk in the park with him unchaperoned, they read his poems! Just imagine, young girls reading *The Gipsies*. I can't understand what their mother is thinking about!'

'But Aunt Daria, couldn't we visit Anna just once?' Sophie pleaded.

'No,' her aunt answered emphatically. 'I know what would happen. The whole family would return your visit, then you will be asked again... No, no, Sophie, I have made up my mind. Have some more potatoes?'

'Has Pushkin been sent to his country estate by the emperor?' Masha asked timidly, remembering the conversation in Empress Elizaveta's apartments.

'That is right,' Daria Ivanovna attacked her food again. 'And when he got here he was so arrogant with his parents, they packed and left for St. Petersburg! Don't know how they could afford it; they are half-ruined already. The house is in a terrible state. Not that Pushkin cares! Has an old nurse who would do anything to make him comfortable, simply dotes on him. No fool like an old fool, Lord forgive me for saying it.'

The girls looked at each other. There seemed no hope of meeting Anna again.

Luncheon over, Emma helped Daria Ivanovna back to her chair, advanced the footstool and put a snuff-box and a big silk handkerchief on a small table within the old lady's reach.

'If you want to see the house, Emma will show it to you while I rest,' Aunt Daria told her guests. She put the handkerchief over her face and crossed her hands on her lap.

Emma (everybody seemed to have forgotten her last name) explained to the girls that she used to be a German governess to Daria Ivanovna's daughter. The girl died while still a child, and Emma remained as Daria Ivanovna's companion. 'She is not always easy to be with, but I have a great respect for her,' she said, marching in front of the girls, opening the doors and parting the curtains.

Sophie yawned and dragged her feet, but Masha loved the half-darkened rooms, full of old tapestries, dim mirrors and bronze figures all speckled with green mould. Shadowy paintings stared from the walls, grandfather clocks stood lifeless, their hands pointing at different hours. There was a strange smell of rose petals, mould and mice. The old parquet floors creaked, steps echoed in the high ceiling of the deserted ballroom.

Miss Alice said softly, 'It reminds me of the old country house in England where I was born.'

'An English country house!' Sophie exclaimed. 'But surely they must be very different.'

Miss Alice shook her head. 'No, my dear. All houses look alike when they are taken over by the past.'

'How did you like it?' Daria Ivanovna asked when the explorers came back.

'Very much,' Masha answered sincerely, while Sophie muttered something.

'Ha!' Daria Ivanovna snorted, 'It is all moth-eaten.'

'But I still like it,' Masha insisted, wondering at her own boldness, 'Just as it is. It feels like *home*.'

'Ha!' Daria Ivanovna said again and took a pinch of tobacco from her snuff-box. 'Strange you should say that.' She eyed Masha with interest.

'I don't think even gun-fire could wake me up,' Sophie muttered sleepily that evening when she and Masha were installed in the big canopied bed.

Instead of answering, Masha suddenly sat up. 'Sophie! Do you hear that strange rustling noise? Just outside our door.'

Sophie instantly became wide awake. 'Yes, I can hear it. What could it be? Wait, I am going to look.' She jumped out of bed and ran to the door.

In another minute, she was back. 'It is one of the maids,' she informed Masha, crawling under the bed clothes. 'She is sleeping on our doormat. Remember Aunt Daria said she gave orders for a maid to be at hand in case we might want something at night.'

'I didn't realise she meant it literally,' Masha said, perplexed. 'I don't like the idea of that girl sleeping on the floor.'

Sophie shrugged her shoulders. 'I don't like it either, but we can't change Aunt Daria's orders. She would be furious. Of course it could never happen in our house. You know how Papa is always telling me not to forget that servants are human beings like the rest of us.'

'And Mark?' said Masha, carefully. 'What is his opinion?'

'Mark is even worse,' Sophie said, 'He wants to abolish serfdom. He tells me that many of his friends think the same way and they are all trying to work out a plan to make all peasants free.'

So, in an indirect way, Mark had told Sophie about the Freedom Society. A weight lifted from Masha's breast. She would have liked to find out how much more Sophie knew, but Sophie buried her face in the pillows. 'Let's sleep,' she suggested. 'Aunt Daria says that tomorrow right after breakfast, she is going to show me a few things she wants me to have as a part of my trousseau. I want to wake up early.'

The 'few things' took up most of the long table, brought for that purpose into the drawing-room. Sophie stared with fascinated wonder at the large casket where gold brooches, earrings and bracelets lay in their nests of faded blue velvet. 'All this for me?' she gasped, 'Oh, Aunt Daria!'

Daria Ivanovna, comfortably installed in her chair, waved her hand. 'Just trinkets, love. Nothing to talk about. Better open that long case and have a look.'

Sophie obeyed. This time she did not even exclaim. She stood with shining eyes, staring at the long pearl necklace hanging from her fingers.

'Wear it as often as you can,' her aunt instructed. 'Real pearls like to be close to the skin, otherwise they may die. Now, see that red velvet box? Those are loose pearls. You can use them on your ballgowns. But not on your wedding dress, mind! Pearls mean tears.'

Masha also came to the table and admired the massive silver settings for twenty-four persons and the beautiful vases of old china.

'Mademoiselle Fredericks,' Daria Ivanovna called and Masha went over to her.

'First, I would like to call you by your Christian name, if you don't mind, and I give you permission to call me Aunt Daria,' the old lady said. 'Second, here is a small gift from me. I want you to have it because you are Sophie's friend.' She took Masha's hand and slipped on her finger a slender gold ring with a single large sapphire.

Masha blushed with surprise and pleasure. She tried to thank Daria Ivanovna as warmly as possible, but her mind was busy imagining how different it would have been, had Sergei put the ring on her finger.

'You love him very much?' Daria Ivanovna asked unexpectedly.

Taken unawares, Masha murmured, 'Yes,' and blushed even more.

The older woman sighed. 'I hope you will be happy, my dear. But you are not Sophie, you will want more from love than she does. All I can say is: may life be merciful to both of you.'

Sophie interrupted the conversation. She rushed up, glowing with excitement, wrapped in a peacock shawl. 'Aunt Daria, this is so beautiful! You don't see this colour any more. I wish I could wear it for my wedding.'

'Goodness, that reminds me!' Daria Ivanovna thumped the table with the flat of her hand. 'I have forgotten the most important thing. Polia!'

A thin child of about twelve, sitting cross-legged on the floor by the door, jumped up, received an order to bring a blue silk bundle from Daria Ivanovna's room, and scuttled away.

She was back in a minute, a blue silk shawl over her arm. At the sight of the shawl, Daria Ivanovna's face became dusky red. Seizing the girl by the arm, she pulled her nearer and with the other hand gave her a heavy box on the ear. 'I said *blue silk bundle*,' she emphasised the words with another blow. 'Hurry now!'

The girl disappeared like a scared rabbit. Daria Ivanovna groaned, leaned back and fanned herself with her handkerchief. 'Ogh, she made me so hot! Just what makes people so stupid, I ask you?'

Masha fidgeted in her seat, hoping that the question was not addressed to her. She pitied the child from the moment she saw her, sitting motionless hour after hour, her frightened blue eyes on her mistress' face. Should Daria Ivanovna drop a handkerchief, or motion towards a book on the table, the girl would jump up, pick up the handkerchief, or present the book, then once again take her position on the floor.

'How can the poor child be intelligent if she is treated like a trained monkey,' Masha wondered, watching the slight figure in a skimpy brown dress hand the bundle to her mistress and hastily step back, afraid of a fresh blow.

But Daria Ivanovna was completely calm again. She carefully unfolded a square of blue silk on her lap. Creamy folds of something light and foamy streamed to the floor.

'Old Venetian lace!' Masha exclaimed, 'The grand duchess has some. Oh, how beautiful!'

'Where? Let me see too,' Sophie dropped a jewelled fan and ran to her aunt.

'It is your wedding veil,' Aunt Daria announced, holding up the lace. 'You will be the fourth bride in the family to wear it. Here, try it on.'

'It is so beautiful, I am afraid to touch it,' Sophie murmured. She adjusted the veil with hairpins, draped the folds around her shoulders and went to the tall console mirror.

'Oh, Sophie!' Masha said and could go no further. In her simple white wool dress, her bronze curls gleaming under the fine web of the lace, Sophie gazed into the mirror with an eager look, as if trying to steal a glimpse into the future.

Suddenly, without any reason, Masha felt frightened for

Sophie. The feeling lasted only for a second, but it was so strong, tears rose in her eyes. 'It is because Sophie is getting married and I am going to lose her,' she tried to explain it to herself.

'My daughter would have been about your age now,' Daria Ivanovna said huskily. Taking a pinch of snuff, she stuffed it into her nostrils, sneezed violently, then said in her usual brisk tone, 'That is enough admiring yourself. Take that thing off. It brings bad luck to parade in bridal finery before the wedding.'

11

In the woods

As the days passed, Masha found it harder and harder to recall St. Petersburg with its crowded streets. Smolni, Anichkov Palace, even the grand duchess seemed far away from the snow-bound world in which she now lived.

At the same time, almost forgotten memories came back. One night she dreamed that she was in her old country home, opening the creaking doors and stepping over the high thresholds. In her dream she knew that Sophie was somewhere in the house, but she could not find her and when she tried to look out of the window, all she could see were dense woods. She cried, 'Sophie, where are you?' and felt a slight touch on her shoulder.

'Wake up,' Sophie's voice said, 'You are dreaming aloud.'

Masha opened her eyes and saw the frost-patterns on the windowpanes shining red and gold in the rising sun. Sophie was stretched beside her, yawning.

'Sorry, I woke you up,' Masha muttered sleepily.

'You didn't really,' Sophie propped herself on her elbows. 'I've been awake for some time, making plans for today. Did you hear the sleigh bells, just now?'

'I think I did, through my sleep. Why?'

'It was Aunt Daria driving off to Pskov for that luncheon the bishop is giving.'

'Yes, I know. She said it would be too boring for us. I suppose she was right. Don't you think so?'

'Of course, of course,' Sophie sounded impatient. 'That is not what I meant. Do you realise that without Aunt Daria we can do *anything we want* today?'

'Not quite; there is Miss Alice.'

'Bother Miss Alice,' Sophie frowned. 'Well, I don't think she can say anything against our going out for a drive. Remember how you enjoyed it last week when we drove all over the grounds in that one-horse sleigh?'

'I suppose we could do it again, if Miss Alice approves,' Masha agreed, getting out of bed.

Miss Alice's approval lacked enthusiasm. She sat at the breakfast table nursing an aching tooth, her face swathed in a warm scarf. 'Not that I think it is suitable for two young girls to be alone among all these savages,' she told Sophie. 'However, since your aunt permitted it the first time, there is nothing for me to say.'

'If your governess would like something for her tooth,' Emma offered, 'perhaps some herb tea…'

Sophie started to translate, but Miss Alice did not let her finish. 'No, my dear, I have no faith in all those home-made remedies. And do you know what the maid said when I asked for some hot water for my tooth this morning? She suggested summoning a man from the village who would stop the pain by casting a spell. Yes, yes, I understood her perfectly. Her mimics were clear enough. And this is the nineteenth century!'

'What is she saying?' Emma asked anxiously, rolling her blue eyes in Miss Alice's direction. Sophie explained and Emma threw up her podgy hands. 'Oh, dear! I understand so well how she feels! I used to think the same myself when I first came here. But Daria Ivanovna uses that man; we all do, and he is really helpful.'

'Do you think your aunt really believes in such things?' Masha asked later, when she and Sophie were dressing for their outing. 'What an odd mixture. I saw Voltaire among her books; she reads all the St. Petersburg newspapers, even if they are several days late, and then…a man who casts spells.'

'I can't think about it now,' Sophie grumbled, pulling at the ribbons of her bonnet. 'Everything is going against my plans. Breakfast was late, then all that fuss about Miss Alice's tooth, then the sleigh runners have to be greased. Then just as I thought we were ready, Emma insists we have something more to eat. It is almost one o'clock now and the weather is changing. Look at all those clouds.'

But Masha refused to get ruffled. 'Does it really matter? We are not going far.'

'Hmm,' Sophie picked up her gloves. 'Let's be off.'

A stable-boy tucked the fur-lined blanket around the girls' feet and handed the reins to Sophie. The small sleigh glided smoothly along, drawn by an old grey horse.

'I wanted a friskier animal, but they wouldn't give me one,' Sophie commented as they drove out of the gates. 'Oh!' She pulled sharply at the reins as a group of people suddenly appeared almost under the horse's hoofs.

Two young lads were supporting the third, who reeled and stumbled, red-faced and dishevelled, singing a boisterous song. Behind the trio walked two women, a young and a very old one, both crying and wailing at the top of their voices. Several men followed, one of them with an accordion over his shoulder.

'Who are they?' Masha asked, watching the little procession move towards the servants' quarters.

'I think the man who was singing must be a recruit,' said Sophie. 'One of the maids told me there are several recruits being taken from the village. The rest of them were probably his family and friends.'

'Poor people,' Masha sympathised. 'Military service is very long, isn't it?'

Sophie answered, 'Twenty-five years. A lifetime.'

For some time neither of the girls spoke. At last Masha said, glancing around, 'Sophie, aren't we rather far from home? I am sure we've never been here before.'

'What?' Sophie peered from under her bonnet. 'I've really not been paying attention for these last fifteen minutes,' she confessed. 'But I am sure we are on the right way. This is Sorot,' she pointed with her whip at the wide curve of the river under its sheet of ice. 'All we have to do now is to follow it to the next bend, turn left and then just keep straight ahead.'

'Straight ahead to where?' Masha wanted to know.

'To Anna Wulff's home.'

'To Anna! But your aunt forbade us to visit her. Sophie, you mustn't.'

'Calm yourself!' Sophie gathered the reins in one hand and put the other on Masha's sleeve. 'Surely Aunt Daria won't object to our driving *past* Anna's house.'

'Then I don't see what good it will do to us. There is probably a park, or at least a garden between the house and the road. We will only see the roof.'

'Well…with all this snow it is hard to say where the road ends and private property begins. After all, the stable-boy gave me only general directions. I may drive through the park by mistake. If we happen to meet Anna, or if we are seen from the windows, it wouldn't be my fault, would it?'

'That is what you used to say when you got us into mischief in Smolni,' Masha groaned, but Sophie only answered impatiently.

'Gracious! What a fuss you are making. Suppose we *did* visit Anna. It would be too late for Aunt Daria to say much.'

'Let's get there first,' Masha suggested, looking at the dense white sky. 'It is starting to snow… Shouldn't we turn back?'

'What? Turn back because of a few miserable flakes?' Sophie glanced with contempt at the small white stars clinging to her cloak and touched the horse with her whip.

The river made a bend again and the road forked. Looking very sure of herself, Sophie took the left turn. The snow stopped, then started again, heavier this time.

Time passed. Uneasily Masha watched the horse's broad grey back become white. The sky seemed to be getting lower and lower. Drifts of snow accumulated under the trees. 'Sophie,' she said firmly, 'We *must* go back. It looks like a real snowstorm.'

To her surprise, Sophie did not argue 'You are right,' she agreed. 'We can try to see Anna some other time. Hold tight now; there isn't much room to turn.'

But the old horse did not want to turn. He continued to pull forward in spite of Sophie's manœuvres with the reins. 'What is the matter with that animal?' Sophie exclaimed impatiently, 'Doesn't it want to get back to the stables? At last!' she announced in triumph as the sleigh made a wide semi-circle, leaning precariously on one side.

'Do you know the way?' Masha asked.

'Naturally. We will be home in no time,' Sophie answered with such conviction, Masha felt reassured. Thrusting her hands deeper inside her muff, she leaned against Sophie's shoulder and closed her eyes.

A sharp jolt made her sit up and clutch at Sophie's arm. The sleigh had stopped. Through the net of snow, she could see the dark wall of woods bordering a clearing. 'Where are we?' she asked.

'I don't know,' Sophie's voice sounded alarmed. 'I don't think we have passed this place before. I don't remember any woods, just a few groves, and look,' she pointed at several tree-stumps, barely visible under the snow, 'we are not even on the road any more.'

Masha's heart made a frightened leap, but she tried to keep calm for Sophie's sake. 'Maybe we should try and get back to the place where we turned around,' she suggested. 'The horse could have been right after all, and we were really going in the wrong direction.'

Sophie shook her head. 'I will never be able to find that place any more. It is no use pretending. We are lost.' She gulped at the last words.

Masha felt sorry for her friend. 'Sophie dear, please don't cry, I'm sure we'll be all right. Here, let me drive while you rest.' She gave her muff to Sophie and took the reins.

The sleigh moved, grazing the stumps. Branches loaded with snow grazed the girls' bonnets. In some places, the horse went knee-deep in snow.

'Careful!' Sophie cried warningly.

The sleigh plunged down, making the girls clutch at each other. For a second, the horse seemed to be somewhere above their heads. There was a loud creaking of branches and Masha realised they were climbing out of a ditch. The horse breathed heavily, pulled, almost wrenching Masha's arm out of its socket, and both girls called out at once, 'The road!'

But it soon became clear that this was not the road they wanted. Narrow and almost buried in snow, it seemed to lead straight into the woods. 'Still, it is better than wandering among the tree-stumps,' Sophie declared, taking the reins again. 'It is bound to lead us somewhere.'

Masha felt less optimistic. 'It may go on for miles,' she said, 'but we have no choice.'

'Even if it does, we may meet someone who would show us the way,' Sophie insisted cheerfully, urging the horse to go faster. Her cheerfulness did not last long. The horse soon resumed his slow pace and the road went on and on.

'What time do you think it is?' Masha spoke in a whisper without knowing why.

Sophie whispered back, 'I don't know, but it is getting darker and colder too. The wind is rising.'

Masha looked over her shoulder. The deep furrows made by the sleigh-runners were almost instantly obliterated by the falling snow. Drifts rose here and there, whirled and merged together.

'We must move faster,' Sophie muttered, 'Ho! ho!' she cried in her best imitation of the coachman, and brandished the whip. But the horse was tired and did not care; only a hollow echo answered from the woods making the girls shiver.

A strong gust of wind came, followed by an even stronger one. The dancing snowflakes blotted out the horse's head. Soon the storm was raging full force buffeting the sleigh and tearing the reins out of Sophie's hands. It was completely dark now. The shadowy pines bordering the road seemed alive, waving arms instead of branches.

The girls pressed against each other, trying to protect their faces from the wind.

Suddenly the sleigh veered and went down a slope. The horse was moving now as if he knew exactly where to go. Sophie cried, 'A light! A light!'

Masha stared at the two lighted windows that looked as if they were hanging in the space, and held her breath, afraid they might vanish again.

The sleigh stopped in front of a tall gate, dimly outlined in the darkness. A man bundled in a sheepskin coat ran towards the girls, bending against the wind and holding on to his fur cap.

'Where are we?' Sophie called.

'Mikhailovskoye,' the man called back, 'The village is over there,' he pointed somewhere into the distance. 'This is…' the wind carried his voice away. Masha only made out, 'Pushkins' estate.'

'Pushkin!' Sophie exclaimed, but Masha was too weary to feel any excitement.

The man took the horse's bridle and led it into the yard, shouting something in the direction of the house.

Immediately, two more windows lighted up and a pale

rectangle of a door shone out against the dark mass of a house.

The man helped the girls out of the sleigh. They staggered up the icy porch steps into the house. The door closed behind them, shutting out the night and cold.

12

Pushkin

After the darkness outside, even the light of a candle standing on a big wooden chest in the anteroom seemed blinding. Masha took a careful step forward, blinked and finally distinguished an elderly woman with a round wrinkled face, a big black mole under her left eye, and thick grey plaits woven around her head partly hidden by a dark scarf. Masha smiled and every wrinkle smiled back at her. Behind the woman several servants craned their necks to get a better view of the unexpected visitors.

A door opened and a young man peered out. What could be seen of him was wrapped in a worn-out green dressing-gown. The sight of his curly fair hair and olive skin made Masha realise that this must be the poet himself for she knew he was said to be descended from an Arab brought to Russia by Peter the Great. He started when he saw the girls, clutched his robe at the throat, muttered, 'Excuse me,' and vanished.

Sophie introduced herself and the old woman threw up her hands. 'Daria Ivanovna's niece! Out in this weather!' She turned to the gaping servants. 'Quick all of you! Help the young ladies take off their wraps. Make sure the guest-room is well heated and have tea ready.'

The master of the house arrived just as the tea was brought in. He was fully dressed, a blue scarf tied in a bow around his neck. After the introductions, he put his arm around the shoulders of the woman, busy with the tea-cups.

'This is Irma Radionovna who used to be my nurse,' he

said, and Masha noticed the deep warmth in his voice. 'Now she is my housekeeper, friend, listener… What else are you?' he asked her laughingly.

Irma Radionovna shook him off. 'Oh, you and your jokes!' she said, pretending to be cross and tucking her hair into place. 'Better sit down and entertain the young ladies. We don't often have company.' There was wistfulness in the last words.

The drawing-room was almost too hot. Masha felt weariness creep over her body and a slight headache press on her temples. She slowly sipped her tea and looked around, wishing that her eyelids were not so heavy. Here was none of the faded elegance of Radnoye, only frank shabbiness. The green silk covering the walls was becoming detached in several places. The sofa sagged; the arms of the chairs were threadbare. Even the silver on the table looked worn out, the monogram almost obliterated. But there was a warm atmosphere that was not only due to the big green-tiled stove in one corner. 'It is the old nurse who makes it a real home,' Masha thought, watching the short stout figure move with dignity around the table, offering home-cured ham and crusty home-baked bread.

Masha became so absorbed in her thoughts, she started when Sophie touched her arm.

'Masha,' Sophie said, 'our host is speaking to you.'

'I am sorry,' Masha apologised, 'You were saying?'

'Merely, that I have just learned you are a lady-in-waiting, Mademoiselle,' Pushkin answered. 'You are indeed privileged to be so close to their majesties and their high-nesses. But isn't it rather…awesome?'

Masha ignored the note of irony in Pushkin's voice. 'Not when you come to know them,' she answered simply.

Sophie filled the awkward pause by telling Pushkin about their unsuccessful attempt to visit Anna Wulff.

'You were going to Trigorskoye!' he exclaimed. 'What an

immense circle you have made. Did you say you started after one? It is six now.' He glanced over his shoulder at the big clock of redwood standing between two windows. 'This means you have been on the road for five hours!'

'I did not realise it was so late,' Sophie said, looking worried. 'My aunt is probably back from Pskov. She will be frantic. We must return as soon as we can, if you would only give us someone for a guide…'

But both Pushkin and his old nurse did not let Sophie finish. It would be a folly they said for the girls to take a drive again on such a cold night. A man who knew the roads well had already been dispatched on horseback to let Daria Ivanovna know Sophie and Masha were safe. Beds were ready for them in the guest-room and the stove red-hot.

Masha breathed easier. The mere idea of facing the darkness and snow made her shiver. She was thankfully reaching for her second cup of tea, when Sophie's foot touched hers.

'We are very disappointed not to have seen Anna Wulff. She is an old schoolmate of ours and we are very fond of her,' Sophie said, her eyes on Pushkin's face.

'One of the three graces,' he said gaily. 'But you would not have found her at home anyhow. The whole family went to Pskov for the same bishop's luncheon your aunt was attending.'

'Her sisters, then, are they as nice as she is?' Sophie went on innocently.

'Each one is capable of making a man lose his head and heart,' Pushkin answered lightly. 'I am afraid I rather abuse of their good nature and their mother's hospitality. Whenever I am out riding, my horse turns towards Trigorskoye by itself. Sometimes I walk. It is so close. A daily visit has become a habit with me.'

'Such nice, kind young ladies,' Irma Radionovna put in.

'God bless them.'

'Do you have many other neighbours?' Masha asked Pushkin.

His rather thick lips parted in a roguish smile. 'Not many, but every one is a character. Try to put them into a novel or a poem, and people scream, "Caricature! Exaggeration!" but I assure you there is no need to exaggerate. Here, for instance…'

For the next hour, the girls were treated to a series of portraits that made them almost sick with laughter. Pushkin's voice and mimicry were perfect. It was a fireworks display of wit, sometimes merciless, but always funny. Masha recognised some of the people who visited Daria Ivanovna. Later, reading *Eugene Onegin*, she recognised even more of the characters they 'saw' that night.

Irma Radionovna sat by the stove, knitting needles flashing in her hands. From time to time, she glanced at her nurseling over her glasses, smiled, and went back to her work.

The old clock hissed, moaned and struck eight. Irma Radionovna folded her knitting and said that the girls must be tired after their adventures.

Two long sofas meeting at an angle and made up with sheets and blankets were waiting for the girls in the guest room. A maid brought some hot water and made clumsy efforts to help them undress. As soon as she was gone, Sophie raised her head from the pillow.

'How did you like him?'

'I really don't know,' Masha answered thoughtfully. 'Of course he is a great poet, and he is clever and amusing, but I wonder if there is anything sacred enough for him not to make fun of? And I don't think he is happy. If he were, he would be different.'

'You may be right,' Sophie agreed. 'But one thing I am sure about, he is not in love with Anna.'

Masha did not comment, but only said, 'Shall I put out the candle?'

'You don't want to talk?' Sophie asked, disappointed.

'No, I am very tired. Good night.'

Yet sleep would not come to her. Lying in the dark, Masha thought of the love that breathed wistfully through Anna's letters, and just for a little she allowed herself to think of Sergei. 'I wonder if Anna knows that Pushkin doesn't care for her. Or is she still waiting for the next time, hoping that he will take her hand in his and not let it go?... As I did... As I do; for once it seemed so near...No, no, I will not remember!' Masha pulled the blanket up to her chin and closed her eyes tight, but her cheeks were already wet. 'I will not think about it,' she told herself resolutely, but still the tears trickled slowly, silently, from beneath her eyelids. Poor Anna. Poor Masha.

When she woke next morning, it was broad daylight and Sophie was already up, brushing her hair. 'It is a perfect day,' she announced, 'and we are going home right after breakfast. Aunt Daria has sent a coachman and a big sleigh for us. A stable-boy has already taken our sleigh home.'

The girls hurried through their breakfast because Sophie, with her uneasy conscience, did not wish to keep Aunt Daria waiting. Irma Radionovna poured out coffee and seemed disappointed that the girls were leaving so soon. Pushkin looked sullen and muttered something about it not being fun to wake up every morning and find that one was still in a cage.

Masha did not know what to answer and kept her eyes on her plate. Her silence seemed to irritate Pushkin. When they rose from the table, he bowed to her, saying, 'I regret I cannot look forward to meeting you again in St. Petersburg, Mademoiselle. It is considered that the country air is...er... better for my health.'

'I keep telling him that everything is for the best in life,'

Irma Radionovna put in, 'But he is so restless, he won't listen.'

'We must really start getting ready. Come on, Masha,' Sophie urged, putting an end to the conversation, to Masha's relief.

When the girls came down again, warmly wrapped against the cold journey home, they found their host on the terrace waiting to see them off.

'Why everything is different in the daylight,' Sophie cried. 'I was sure the house was standing in the woods. But it isn't. One can see Sorot from here. Is it an orchard on the left? Of course it is lonely in winter, but I wouldn't a bit mind living here in summer. What do you think, Masha?'

'I wouldn't mind living in the country all year round,' Masha answered sincerely, 'but I think that autumn here should be even lovelier than summer. Imagine all these trees red-gold and reflecting in the river!'

For the first time, Pushkin looked at Masha with sympathy. 'You are right,' he said. 'Autumn is the most beautiful season in these parts. That is the time to ride horseback for hours, get intoxicated with air and colours. Then back home, grab a pen, even if one's fingers are stiff with the first frost, and write, write till midnight.' His face softened and his eyes lost their cynical gleam.

'That is how I will try to remember him,' Masha decided following Sophie to the sleigh. Pushkin helped them in and stepped aside.

The horses took off. The sleigh glided along the long avenue of pines. Masha looked back for the last time. Pushkin was standing still, shading his eyes against the sun, his figure tall and dark against the sparkling snow.

13

Anna Wulff

Daria Ivanovna looked very grim when the girls were ushered into her presence. Masha had the distinct impression that she was not in the least taken in by Sophie's glib explanation of how they came to be lost in the snowstorm. However they got off with a severe lecture tempered by the fact that they were both obviously coming down with severe head-colds, the direct consequence, Aunt Daria pointed out, of their thoughtlessness and folly. However they recovered quickly and Sophie began to talk about going home. But Daria Ivanovna declared that they could not possibly go until she had given a large ball in their honour.

'All my neighbours are offended because I have not taken you two on a round of visits,' she said. 'My gout and the weather are not considered good enough excuses. So we may as well invite them all at once to have a look at you.'

'Anna Wulff too, Aunt Daria?' Sophie said meekly.

'Anna and her sisters too, or you might run away and get lost again,' Daria Ivanovna answered shaking her finger at Sophie. 'And I fear we must invite Pushkin as well,' she went on, frowning over the list of names. 'After all you stayed in his house and we must return the hospitality. But for heaven's sake, don't ask him to read any of his poems, Sophie. Don't even mention them. I forbid you! When I think that a young man from such a good family writes verses for money…but there is a black sheep in every flock, I suppose.'

Preparations for the ball took two full days. Servants

bustled all over the house, moving the furniture, polishing floors, putting fresh candles into the chandeliers and sconces. Daria Ivanovna sent a note to her neighbour, a retired colonel who owned hothouses, asking for flowers. The colonel wrote back that he was very sorry but all his flowers were either preparing to bloom or had bloomed already.

'All nonsense!' Daria Ivanovna cried, crumpling the letter and throwing it on the floor. 'The old rascal! He is simply annoyed because I refused to sell him my bay mare. Take his name off the invitation list, Sophie. Immediately!'

'This makes four persons you have taken off, Aunt Daria,' Sophie remarked, giggling.

'What do you mean four? Show me that paper.' Daria Ivanovna put on her glasses and pored over the list. 'Hmm... Well, you may put that woman back; the one at the bottom. It is true she did not bow first when I saw her in church last week, but I shall overlook it this time.'

Everything was ready, even to the piano player. He arrived from Pskov on the eve of the ball and was ushered through the back door. A thin, sick-looking man, with a long face emerging from his high collar, he spent the whole afternoon tuning the old piano. Masha saw him eat hungrily at a small table in the pantry, where meals were served to those who could not be treated as servants, and yet were not considered 'the real guests'.

The girls had a long discussion about the dresses they were going to wear. 'The main thing is for us not to look overdressed,' Sophie insisted, 'or people will think we are trying to impress them with our city finery.' They finally decided on simple tarlatan gowns with scalloped flounces, since Sophie had brought one in yellow, and Masha one in white, which made them look almost like sisters. Before taking off their paper curlers, both girls knelt down in front of a low table and let the maid press their tresses with a warm iron.

'It really works!' Masha marvelled, rolling rippling curls around her finger. 'How did you think of it, Sophie?'

'A maid in Smolni told me,' Sophie mumbled through pins in her mouth.

When the girls came downstairs, they found Egor, the old footman, dressed in a black livery all rusty at the seams, his white stockings yellow with age, going from room to room 'sweetening the air'. Masha watched with interest as the old man took a shovelful of red-hot coals and dropped some aromatic crystals on it. A spicy smell became mixed with the acrid smell of tallow. Masha suspected that not all the candles were made of wax.

'Here you are at last!' Daria Ivanovna's voice boomed from the drawing-room. 'I was just going to send for you. Our guests will be here soon.'

'It is only six,' Emma reminded her timidly, 'and the invitation said seven.'

Daria Ivanovna waved her away. 'They will arrive at least one hour earlier,' she declared. 'I know them.'

She was right. The first guest was already entering. It was the colonel of the hothouses, who chose to ignore being in disgrace and came without being invited. His bald head shining, a broad smile on his ruddy face, he presented Sophie's aunt with a very small nosegay of roses.

'All that my poor rosebushes would give me,' he announced, 'but I see that you have two blooming roses already.' He made a military salute in the direction of the girls and they curtsied, trying not to laugh.

The colonel was obviously preparing even more elaborate compliments, when suddenly his jaw dropped and his eyes became fixed on Miss Alice coming down the stairway. Clad in a beruffled green dress, a green taffeta butterfly mounted on a wire trembling in her hair, she gave the colonel a stiff bow and sat down on a straight-backed chair by the wall.

'Miss Alice is going to lure all our partners away from us!' Sophie whispered to Masha.

Soon the guests were arriving in droves. Egor grew hoarse announcing them. Cloaks and wraps accumulated in the hall.

Masha's first thought after seeing their girl guests was, 'Goodness, and we were afraid of appearing overdressed!' Each girl looked as if she had put on every ribbon, every flower and every scrap of lace she possessed. The girls themselves seemed silly and affected, speaking in thin high voices and laughing without any reason, but after she and Sophie had taken a group to their bedroom for last minute repairs, she realised that these were only 'party manners'.

The guests became so interested in Sophie's array of bottles and boxes, they forgot their company airs and eagerly offered their own home-made recipes for face-washes and lotions against sunburn. When they found out that Masha was a lady-in-waiting, they clustered around her asking questions. Was it true that Grand Duchess Alexandra owned ten thousand dresses? Did they have balls every night in the palace? Could Masha show them how to make a court curtsey?

Sophie good-naturedly produced her hats and gowns. The girls examined every gown, tried on the hats and exchanged opinions. 'Look at these ribbons, all moire glacé. You don't find these even in Pskov.' 'This is a pretty colour but it would fade in the sun.' 'My mother would never allow me to wear *that* gown.'

They became so interested it took Masha and Sophie some time to get them back to the ballroom.

Soon dancing was in full swing. There was no graceful gliding across the floor as in St. Petersburg. The parquet shook, the chandeliers swayed, dripping wax, men's coat tails and ladies' sashes flew, faces glistened, fans waved, blowing out the candles.

Between dances, Sophie ran up to Masha and whispered that Anna Wulff has just arrived. 'Her mother and her sisters are with her,' Sophie said, 'Come quickly. They are greeting Aunt Daria.'

'Anna here!' Masha forgot about the next dance and ran, threading her way among the dancing couples. There was a group of women standing near the door of the ball room. A very young girl, almost a child, with a round mischievous face was curtseying to Daria Ivanovna. 'Probably Anna's youngest sister, Zizi,' Masha guessed and at the same time felt someone's arms around her shoulders.

'Masha!' Anna's voice exclaimed. 'I was just going to say how changed you are, but you are not really. You are still my little Masha, only not in brown uniform. Oh, how happy I am to see you!' Anna kissed Masha tenderly. 'And Sophie! Old enough to be engaged! Let me introduce both of you to my family.'

At the first glance Masha did not like Praskovia Alexandrovna, Anna's mother. Still young-looking, with a lively, intelligent face, she gave an impression of haughtiness because of her slightly-protruding lower lip. But Masha's antipathy vanished as she met the kind brown eyes. 'Anna mentioned you in every letter when she was in Smolni,' Praskovia Alexandrovna told Masha. 'We used to call you "Anna's little daughter".'

Alma, Anna's step-sister, was a thin, very serious-looking girl, a striking contrast to the sprightly Zizi.

'And this,' Anna said turning to a young woman in a daringly low-cut evening dress, who stood talking to Daria Ivanovna, 'is my cousin – an Anna too, Anna Petrovna Kern to be exact, but I am sure she will want you to call her Annette.'

'Certainly,' the young woman said, 'I will be delighted. Anna has told me so much about her life in Smolni, I feel as if I knew all her friends personally.'

'How lovely she is,' Masha thought, looking at the deep blue eyes under the fine brows, the small straight nose, the arched mouth. But at the last feature Masha stopped. There were wilful lines in the corners of the lips and something slightly calculated in the smile.

'I have only just arrived from St. Petersburg,' Annette said, 'I am afraid I will be leaving in a few days. You too, I understand?'

'Yes, shortly,' Masha answered, but was aware that Annette was not really listening. She was looking over Masha's shoulder, a slight blush mounting in her cheeks. Masha glanced back. Pushkin was just entering the ballroom.

Daria Ivanovna greeted the poet cordially but with a shade of severity, as if she expected him to do something dreadful any moment. Masha thought that Sophie's aunt was needlessly worried. There was no trace of the mocking, arrogant, self-assured Pushkin that evening. He had barely entered when his eyes found Annette Kern and an eager, longing look made his face almost boyish.

Annette stood quietly, her blonde head bent a little, watching Pushkin bow to Daria Ivanovna and Praskovia Alexandrovna. But as soon as he made a step in her, direction, she turned to the nearest man and, with 'Isn't this a lovely waltz?', fluttered away in his arms.

'She is teasing him,' Masha thought while Pushkin was greeting Anna and Alma. He said a few polite words to Masha and Sophie, and stopped in mock admiration in front of Zizi who immediately claimed him as a partner.

The next moment, Alma too was invited for a dance. Anna Wulff seized Masha's hand. 'I don't want to dance. Could we go somewhere and talk just for a few minutes like old times?'

'We could go to our room,' Masha said doubtfully, 'but I

don't know…'

'You go, Masha,' Sophie said generously. 'I will stay and help Aunt Daria receive.'

'Come,' Masha pulled Anna's hand. The two girls slipped out of the ballroom and sped down the corridor.

'I don't know where to begin,' Masha said, perching herself on the arm of Anna's chair. 'So many things have happened since we left Smolni.'

'To you,' Anna corrected. 'And you are barely out. To me these last six years seem so exactly alike…' she interrupted herself. 'No, not quite maybe. Two years ago a gale destroyed the crop of fruit and last year Zizi was sick with measles. The biggest event was a fire in the attic. But don't ask me just when it all happened. I am losing track of time.'

'Oh, Anna,' Masha murmured.

'Don't be sorry,' Anna touched Masha's cheek. 'It is not so bad really. We receive newspapers and magazines. The news may be a little stale but to us it is quite fresh. Neighbours come visiting. We play parlour games, sing, play the piano. If we happen to dream about something special, we look it up in Martin Zadeka. That's a book, in case you don't know. Every possible dream is listed alphabetically. You can buy it from any peddler.'

Anna became silent. Leaning back in the chair, she was fingering the russet ribbons on her dress. 'I am not telling the truth,' she said at last in a low voice, her eyes looking into space. 'Last year *was* different… *He* came.'

'Pushkin?' Masha breathed.

The older girl nodded. 'Yes. I was out in the garden, reading when he came for the first time. I looked up and saw him walking up the path. My mother had known him before of course, his family are our neighbours, but I was away in Smolni and knew him only by name. And now…' she sighed and ended almost in a whisper, 'I can't bear the thought that one day he will go away again.'

'She loves him so much and he doesn't care,' Masha thought, watching Anna's face.

'He treats my sisters and myself like a brother or a cousin,' Anna said, as if in answer to Masha's thoughts. 'But when it comes to Annette…it is quite different. He met her a long time ago in St. Petersburg.'

'Surely she is married?' Masha interrupted. 'I heard her addressed as "Madame".'

'Yes, she is married. Her husband is a general, twice her age. She does not love him and tries to be away from him as much as possible, visiting relatives, coming here. The admiration of Pushkin and other men is like a breath of fresh air to her. They make her realise she is young and beautiful and she enjoys it.'

'I don't like her,' Masha said vehemently.

'Oh, no!' Anna sat up in the chair and looked at Masha. 'You mustn't. I know what you are thinking, but you are mistaken. I am not jealous of Annette, that is I am not jealous of the longing, the passion, he has for her. These are not the feelings I want from him.' She smiled a strange whimsical smile. 'You have been in Pushkin's house, haven't you? You have seen his old nurse? It is Irma Radionovna of whom I am jealous! To be always at his side, take care of his smallest needs, make it possible for him to write without being bothered by petty worries, comfort him in hard moments. . . that would be enough for me. That is all I ask.'

'But it still may happen,' Masha groped for the right words, 'He may realise that…'

Anna did not answer. With a quick movement, she brushed a tear away from her lashes, then said dreamily, 'One day, last summer, we were all walking in the woods, I fell behind and my hair got caught in some prickly branches. I called for help and Pushkin came. He untangled my hair and…and I felt him lay his face against it, just for a second. I don't believe he realised I noticed. We were all alone.

Maybe I should have said something. Only I did not dare to. We just walked on and joined the others. Masha!' she turned and peered into Masha's face. 'You are crying. Why? Have you... Are you in love with someone?'

Her face on Anna's shoulder, Masha whispered. 'Yes. Only I want him to love me with all his being, with his every heartbeat, as...I love him.'

'Doesn't he?' Anna asked.

Masha murmured, 'I don't think so.'

The door opened and a maid put her head in. 'If you please, Miss,' she told Masha, 'Barinia is wondering where you might be.'

Masha rose to her feet, keeping her face away from the maid. 'Tell Barinia I am coming.'

Anna rose too. For a moment, the girls held to each other tight, cheek against cheek.

A minute later, they were coming down the stairway, their faces freshly powdered, their hair smoothed. Anna was invited for a dance almost as soon as they entered the ballroom. Left alone, Masha went in search of Daria Ivanovna. She found her playing cards in the library.

'Why did you run away like that?' Daria Ivanovna asked briskly. 'I feared you were not feeling well.'

Masha felt guilty. 'I was upstairs with Anna Wulff, talking.'

Daria Ivanovna's keen eyes swept over Masha. 'Confidences?' she asked, and without waiting for an answer added in a milder tone, 'Go and dance.'

Waltzing with a thin, long-legged young man, who had to bend down to reach her, Masha caught sight of Pushkin. He was dancing with Sophie, but his eyes were following Annette's emerald earrings, sparkling and disappearing again among the whirling couples.

The ball ended after midnight, a very late hour for the country. Sleighs and coaches began to drive up to the porch.

The drivers shouted at the horses, the hall buzzed with good-byes.

'Sophie and I are coming to see you the day after tomorrow. Your mother has invited us to lunch,' Masha told Anna, 'So it is not good-bye yet.'

In the ballroom the chandeliers were already extinguished. In the dim light of a solitary candle only the musician could be seen, crouched over the piano. Handel's solemn music rose and fell, chasing away the light dance-tunes still lingering in the air. He struck the last chord and closed the piano. The floorboards creaked slightly when he went out, then it became very quiet, until a mouse began to gnaw in the woodwork. The long years of silence were taking over again.

At the end of the week, the girls left for St. Petersburg. At first Sophie rejoiced at the prospect of seeing Mark and her father, but when she saw the packed trunks, she flung herself, weeping, on her aunt's neck. 'I hate to leave you all alone in this old house,' she sobbed.

'Daria Ivanovna is not alone,' Emma protested, shocked. 'I am always at her disposal and all her wishes are attended to immediately.'

'Be quiet, Emma.' Daria Ivanovna looked at her companion sternly over Sophie's head. 'Never mind, dear child,' she said soothingly, 'I will see you again soon. You forget that I am coming to your wedding in April.'

Masha walked all over Rodnoye for the last time, saying good-bye to every room. In the last room she visited, the shrouded ballroom with its drawn curtains, she was disconcerted to find that her silent farewell to the old house had been observed by Daria Ivanovna. She had thought her hostess occupied in overseeing the bestowal of the luggage, but there she was, standing in the doorway, her shrewd old eyes taking in Masha's loving pat of the old damask, her lingering glance at the shelves and alcoves.

It was impossible to explain, but Daria Ivanovna seemed to need no explanation. 'Come here, my dear,' she said, and as Masha stood before her, she took both her hands and looked seriously into her face.

'I am glad that you are Sophie's friend,' she said. 'Don't ever let anything come between you.'

There was even less room in the carriage going home. Jars of home-made preserves and boxes of dried fruit, Daria Ivanovna's presents, filled every corner. The jewels and Sophie's wedding veil were to be brought separately, later, by Daria Ivanovna herself, but Miss Alice kept counting the bags and boxes to make sure everything else had been safely packed in.

Masha and Sophie were both silent, wrapped in their separate thoughts. The day had begun cloudy and mild but dusk crept on before anybody expected it and it became colder. 'Sophie, tell the coachman to start looking for an inn,' Miss Alice ordered. 'What is he stopping for?'

'There is a party of convicts crossing the road,' Sophie replied, pressing her face to the window, 'Look.'

Masha leant forward. A long line of ragged figures plodded along, averting their faces from the wind. Armed guards walked alongside.

'Where are they taking them?' Miss Alice asked.

'To Siberia, I suppose,' Masha said, 'I know that they must have committed crimes, but I can't help being sorry for them. Did you see that woman in the last row, Sophie? Could you imagine yourself walking with those people?'

'Walking with convicts!' Sophie exclaimed, 'No, I could not imagine that. What made you think of it?'

'I don't know,' Masha answered truthfully.

'Ah, here is the inn at last,' Miss Alice remarked with satisfaction.

Lighted windows appeared in the dusk. The horses ran faster.

14

Sophie's wedding

Sashette was engaged. Masha heard the news from Ally Ayler almost as soon as she reached Anichkov Palace. 'It is a wonderful match for Mademoiselle Rossett,' Ally commented. 'Everyone knows she has no dowry, while her fiancé is quite well off and has a brilliant career in front of him. Many a mamma tried to snare him for her daughter, yet he has chosen Mademoiselle Rossett. They must be greatly in love.'

Sashette's own view was different. 'Please don't wish me happiness,' were her first words when Masha came to see her in the Winter Palace. 'I don't expect to be happy. Smirnov asked me to marry him not because he is in love with me, but because I am attractive enough and intelligent enough to make a good governor's wife, and he is almost sure of his nomination. I accepted him because I want to escape the Ladies-in-Waiting Corridor and the necessity of counting every penny. My brother is already in St. Petersburg being coached for the Naval Academy.'

'What can I say?' Masha thought, looking at Sashette's tightly-drawn black brows. 'When is the wedding?' she dared to ask.

Sashette's face darkened even more. 'Not till the end of this year. Smirnov's mother wishes us "to get to know each other better". All nonsense of course. She simply hopes her son may change his mind about marrying me. I am too poor for her.'

'I am sure your fiancé will not even consider changing

his mind,' Masha said hastily.

'*He* won't,' Sashette agreed, 'but his mother is a scheming woman and he is very much under her influence. I won't feel safe until we are married. November seems far away.'

Masha did not stay long; she felt too ill at ease. As she was leaving, Sashette said suddenly, 'Don't ever do what I am doing,' and turning away, went to the window. 'Goodbye,' she said, without turning round.

Masha breathed freely again only after she was back in Anichkov Palace, but Sashette's troubled eyes and bitter words returned often to haunt her as she slipped back into the familiar, happy round of duties, reading to the grand duchess, attending balls with her, romping in the nursery with the children. Days and weeks seemed to fly by. Lent came, theatres were closed, there were no more balls or receptions. Then it was Palm Sunday. Branches of pussy-willow were distributed in churches, their fluffy grey bails announcing spring.

Easter was in the middle of April. Anichkov Palace smelled deliciously of the white lilac and hyacinths standing in vases and baskets in every room. In the nursery, little Alexander and his sisters were playing with coloured eggs. In her room, Masha admired her own collection. Alexandra had given her a small jade egg to be worn on a chain around her neck. The big one, made of red velvet and opening like a box, came from Sophie; inside were small scissors and a silver thimble. A blue and gold enamel egg, a gift from Empress Elizaveta, held a miniature copy of the New Testament.

Even Nastia had presented Masha with a big wax egg that had a panorama of a monastery inside. Pressing her eye to the small oval and holding the egg against the light, Masha thought that the white-walled monastery looked like the one near St. Petersburg where Sophie's lingerie was being embroidered by the nuns. She had accompanied Sophie to help her chose the designs and afterwards they had eaten tea and honey in the superior's small white cell with geraniums on the windowsill.

The lingerie was all ready now, for Sophie's wedding was to take place the first Sunday after Easter. Masha blinked and put the egg down. She was happy for Sophie but it was hard to get used to the idea that from now on she would be sharing her friend with Mark. She hoped she would not cry at the wedding.

But when the day came, Masha found she was too busy to cry. The ceremony was to begin at four. Sophie started to get dressed at two. The two bridesmaids, Masha and Katish, helped to pin on the priceless veil. A maid, armed with a needle, stood at attention, ready for any small adjustment on Sophie's ivory wedding gown with a long train.

Daria Ivanovna, installed in a deep armchair, was giving orders. 'Bring the veil up a little higher on your side, Masha. Keep still, Sophie! Has anybody remembered to put a gold coin into her shoe for luck?'

The door opened a crack and General Brozin's voice could be heard. 'Is she ready?' He sounded anxious. 'It is getting late.'

'Oh, Papa, it is much too early!' Sophie laughed. 'Do you want us to get to church before anyone else?'

'Your father doesn't really mean the time, Sophie. He just wants to make sure you are not hysterical or changing your mind at the last moment,' Daria Ivanovna said briskly, and called to her brother, 'Everything is quite in order. Close the door, please.'

'Changing my mind? I was never so sure and happy in my life! I feel as if I had wings!' Sophie pirouetted joyously.

The door opened again and Mark's seven-year-old nephew burst into the room, dressed in white silk suit, fair hair sticking out like a halo.

'Don't step on her dress!' several voices cried, and Daria Ivanovna asked impatiently, 'Where is that Miss Alice of yours, Sophie? I asked her to keep an eye on him.'

'She is in the library,' the white silk cherub explained, calmly taking out of his pocket a half-eaten slice of bread and jam. 'I pinned her dress to a chair, so she can't move,' he added between bites.

'Of all the little imps—' Daria Ivanovna began, but at that moment Sophie announced in a tragic tone that one of her long white gloves had a stain on it.

There was a general commotion. Lemon-juice was rubbed on the stain and failed. A maid was dispatched to the nearest shop, brought back the wrong size and rushed off again.

The 'imp' was dragged to the washbowl and cleaned up in spite of his protests. He promptly burst into a roar and calmed down only after Sophie had persuaded him that he was the most important person in the ceremony. 'There is always a boy walking in front of the bride and carrying an ikon,' she told him. 'And you know something? The bride usually gives her good-luck coin to the ikon boy after the wedding.'

The last argument won the day, though Daria Ivanovna muttered something about a sound spanking being just as persuasive.

At last Sophie was ready and stood quietly, with clasped hands, her blue-green eyes dark and wide.

Sitting in the carriage with Katish, Masha wondered why the horses were moving so slowly, until she heard Katish's awed whisper, 'Heavens! We can hardly pass. It looks as if the whole of St. Petersburg is coming to Sophie's wedding.'

'All St. Petersburg, except Sergei,' Masha thought, staring out of the window at the throng of carriages. As if in answer to her thoughts, Katish asked, 'What about Sophie's cousins? Aren't they going to be present?'

Masha forced her voice to sound indifferent. 'The younger is on manœuvres with his regiment. The older is still abroad.'

She congratulated herself for having successfully phrased her answer in such a way as to avoid pronouncing Sergei's name and hoped that Katish wouldn't ask more.

Katish did not. She simply said, 'Really? I thought Sophie mentioned that they would do their best to come. Oh, look, we're there!'

The girls were not too early. Sophie arrived a few minutes later, accompanied by her father and Daria Ivanovna. She walked with light steps, her head held high, her face serious and eager at the same time. Masha and Katish took their places behind her. Magnificent singing rang out in the old church.

Her throat tight, the palms of her hands moist, Masha stood rigid, listening to the centuries-old words binding two lives together. Sophie seemed calm, but Mark's hand shook slightly when the rings were exchanged. Katish was breathing heavily and making quick dabs at her eyes with her handkerchief, but for Masha the feeling ran too deep for tears. Too deep and too confused, with joy and sorrow inextricably intertwined.

It was all over at last. Radiant, Sophie stood surrounded by relatives and friends, blushing every time someone addressed her as Madame.

Masha was threading her way towards Sophie too, when she suddenly saw Michael leaning against a pillar. 'Oh, you were able to get away from the manœuvres then?' she exclaimed, 'Wasn't Sophie a beautiful bride?'

'Sophie?' he asked wonderingly, then seemed to shake himself, smiled and said, 'Sorry. I am afraid I was daydreaming.'

'It must have been a very absorbing dream,' Masha retorted, offended for her friend.

Michael did not seem to notice. 'Yes, very,' he said simply.

Masha had no time to talk further. Katish was at her side, saying that the carriage was waiting.

Even General Brozin's big house could hardly hold all the guests. Footmen did their best to pass through the crowded rooms without spilling the champagne. In church all the faces seemed a blur to Masha, but now she saw many familiar ones. Madame Adlerberg, Maman, was present, Marie Divova and Sashette, the two Vuich sisters, dressed alike as usual. Lena Mandrika had come from Moscow especially to be at the wedding. 'We arrived only this morning,' she explained to Masha, hugging her. 'I was so afraid we were going to be late. I barely had time to buy a new hat. The one I brought with me was crushed by a trunk.'

'You look beautiful, and so fashionable!' Masha said admiring Lena's lace gown. 'I suppose…' She stopped.

Lena said calmly, 'I know what you were going to ask. No, I have not decided yet whether I am going to be a nun or not. I am still finding out.'

The conversation with Lena had to be cut short. Masha was called to help Katish distribute the wedding souvenirs: white satin bags, Sophie's initials embroidered on them, filled with bonbons.

Masha had just disposed of her last bag when a voice close to her said, 'Well, you might have kept one for an old friend.'

It was Sergei.

For a moment the room spun in a joyous, multi coloured whirl. She knew she had to say something, but no words came. It didn't seem to matter though, for Sergei's next remark was wholly inconsequential.

'That is a remarkably well-chosen ornament,' he said, looking at the small crown of forget-me-nots on Masha's head. 'They are the colour of your eyes.'

Masha's confusion increased. She sought desperately for some light social remark, but under Sergei's intense gaze she seemed bereft of speech.

'You have missed the ceremony,' she managed at last. Sergei began to laugh. 'Guilty,' he said, 'But it is really Sophie's fault. Why did she have to be married in April? In Germany it is the rainiest of all months. Travelling was simply impossible. I was afraid the horses would drown in the puddles.'

'Masha! Masha!' Ellie Vuich came running. 'Where are you? Sophie is getting ready to leave.'

Masha ran upstairs. Sophie was changing into her travelling clothes, while maids were rushing around, getting into each other's way. 'Help me on with this collar,' she begged Masha, 'These women only aggravate me, and it is getting late.'

'Just stand still,' Masha started to adjust the collar. 'What is the hurry?' she asked, 'I thought you were going to travel in easy stages, staying with all those relatives of Mark's for a day or two on your way to Paris.'

'We are certainly going in a round-about way,' Sophie agreed. 'No, there is no hurry, really, only…' she suddenly hugged Masha, 'Mark and I are so anxious to be together and alone at last,' she whispered into her ear.

'Oh, Sophie!' Masha said helplessly, returning the hug, 'If you only knew how hard it is to let you go.'

'You will see me in June,' Sophie said consolingly. 'Mark and I are expecting you to spend at least two months at Otrada. He is sure you will love the estate. It has been in his family for generations.' She lowered her voice, smiling at her friend. 'Sergei is coming…and Michael too,' she added.

Masha smiled back, her eyes shining, but all she said was, 'Of course I will come. How could I resist the promise of an old house?'

'You and your old houses!' said Sophie, laughing. 'Aunt Daria can't get over your appreciation of Rodnoye. She says I have no proper feeling for such things and holds you up as an example. But remember: even though I am married, nothing can change our friendship, ever.'

The April evening was chilly, but Masha, Katish and the crowd of guests stood on the entrance steps, waving until the carriage with Sophie and Mark disappeared behind the street corner. Another carriage, loaded with luggage, and bearing a valet for Mark and a maid for Sophie, followed.

Coming into the drawing-room, Masha noticed a small figure behind a curtain. It was Sophie's young ikon bearer. He stood beaming at a gold coin on his palm. Lifting his blue eyes at Masha, he asked, 'Will you give me your coin too when you are married?'

'Certainly,' Masha promised, laughing, 'But you may have to wait a long time.'

The small boy shook his head, 'No, I won't. You will be married next, Uncle Mark said so.'

'To whom?' Masha asked quickly.

'To Uncle Sergei, and Uncle Sergei did not say anything. He only looked funny. Ugh, don't kiss me, I am not a baby!' He wriggled out of Masha's arms and fled.

Masha stood looking after him, the colour coming and going in her face.

15

Otrada

The weeks following Sophie's wedding were very quiet ones for Masha. The grand duchess was expecting a fourth child in August and there were very few dinners or receptions at Anichkov.

'As dull as the Winter Palace,' Sashette commented. 'I mean our empress's domain. It is always gay in Maria Feodorovna's apartments. Thank goodness I've been chosen to accompany her to Germany again this summer. Sometimes I think I am going to die of sheer boredom!'

At the end of June the court left for Tzarskoye Selo, but as usual the grand duchess had acceded to Sophie's pleas and Masha was excused from summer duty so that she might visit Sophie's new home. Alexandra stipulated only that she should have a suitable chaperone for the journey—it would not be proper for her to make so long a trip by herself—but luckily one of the older ladies-in waiting, Mademoiselle Dubois, was going to Tula to visit some friends and it was arranged that Masha should travel with her.

The voyage turned out to be quite an ordeal. Half-French, Mademoiselle Dubois did not believe in fresh air. The carriage rolled along the country roads with tightly-closed windows to avoid draught. Suffocating in her corner, Masha counted the hours that separated them from the next halt. Unfortunately Mademoiselle Dubois was also 'artistic'. As soon as she saw a beautiful landscape, she made the carriage stop and installed her easel on the roadside. The sun rose high; the horses emptied their feed-bags; Mademoiselle Dubois was still painting, her head on a long bony neck thrown back to admire her work, her elaborate coiffure bespattered with paint. 'We will never arrive at Tula this way, never!' Masha thought in despair, sitting on the dusty grass and looking at her parasol which was beginning to fade in streaks.

But they reached it eventually, late one afternoon. As the carriage was rolling down the main street the sky which had been cerulean all the exasperating journey darkened and rain began to fall in sheets. Masha pressed her face to the window, wondering if anyone would be there to meet her after all the delays. To her intense relief and pleasure, she saw Mark's face smiling at her from the doorway of an inn.

Mademoiselle Dubois went on to her friends and Masha urged Mark to start at once for Otrada, but he insisted on their having something to eat first. They had plenty of time and perhaps the rain would stop. It would only take them about two hours to reach Otrada.

But instead of stopping, the rain became heavier. Dusk gathered and it was still raining. At last, Mark ordered the coachman to put up the hood of the landau and they left Tula to the sound of the rain drumming on the road and the carriage-top, only to stop after the first two miles because of a broken front wheel. The coachman repaired it after a long struggle, but it was past midnight when the landau at last drew up before a tall house with white pillars, all dark except for a few lighted windows. 'Don't disturb, Sophie. The maids will show me to my room,' Masha told Mark as they entered the hall. But there was a familiar light step on the stairway and in another minute Sophie's arms were around her.

Soon Masha was comfortably installed in bed, with Sophie curled up in an easy chair nearby. The clock on the landing struck two before the murmuring voices ceased and

Masha lay alone in the welcoming darkness, secure in the knowledge that Sophie had kept her word and that she had not lost her friend after all.

It was almost eleven when she left her bedroom next morning. Walking along the corridor, she saw Miss Alice coming towards her.

'Sophie has invited me to spend the summer here,' the old governess explained. 'There are many young people in the party. Then in the autumn I must look for a new position.' She spoke calmly but there was anxiety in the faded eyes.

'I do hope she is going to find a nice family,' Masha thought, as she approached the morning-room from which came Sophie's voice, '…and so when the housekeeper told me we didn't have enough eggs and tried to assure me that hens lay only once a day, I knew she was lying.'

'Really? And what did you tell her?' Mark's voice was full of interest.

'I told her that hens lay at least three times a day and that if we haven't enough eggs, it means that someone is stealing them,' Sophie answered triumphantly.

'You did? Sophie, sweetest! You are priceless!' Mark was choking with laughter, 'What did she say?'

'She said, "That must be St. Petersburg hens, barinia. We don't have such hens in the country.' Why are you laughing? *Do* hens really lay only once a day?'

'I see that Sophie is wrestling with housekeeping,' Masha said entering.

Mark, sitting in an armchair, was wiping tears of laughter from his eyes. 'She's managing by trial and error. But never mind. She will learn.'

'It is not easy,' Sophie sighed. 'Especially with such a crowd of guests in the house. All Mark's cousins and nephews and nieces are spending summer with us. It is a family tradition to gather at Otrada. They all have to be fed and I am out of ideas for menus. But at least we have a new cook. The last one was always drunk.'

'I had a wonderful breakfast served to me this morning,' Masha said, 'Everything tasted better than in the city, and cream was so thick it floated in the cup.'

Mark looked pleased. 'We have good cows,' he said. 'Our butter and cream are famous all over the countryside. We sell a great deal in Tula. When I inherited this estate after my father's death, it was heavily mortgaged and in such disorder, everyone advised me to sell it. I am glad I didn't, but it has taken time to put it back into shape.'

'Mark is fearfully proud of Otrada,' Sophie said, looking at her husband with admiration. 'He is up at dawn every day, making sure everything is done just right. And do you know something, Masha? He never sells old horses. They are sent to pasture till the end of their days.'

Mark looked a little embarrassed. 'I am not being sentimental about horses,' he explained to Masha. 'I simply believe that everyone deserves a pension. Ah, there's Michael walking in the garden. Shall I call him?'

'Yes, do,' Sophie answered. 'He can show the grounds to Masha while I struggle with the menu for today.'

'Wait,' Masha said quickly, 'I will surprise him. No, don't send anyone. I'll find the way.'

There was still a morning freshness in the air as she walked out onto the wide terrace. Roses climbed up the white pillars. Bees flew in and out of jasmine bushes. A swallow passed low, almost touching the ground, and flew towards the many nests hanging over the upper floor windows. In front of the terrace was a grass-plot bordered with irises, a sundial in the middle.

Michael was coming up the sanded avenue between two rows of trimmed acacia trees. He was sun-tanned, in light summer uniform. At the sight of Masha he stopped, then took a few slow steps forward.

'Well, you don't seem to be very eager to meet me,' Masha said, laughing.

To her surprise, he coloured and mumbled something inaudible, but quickly pulled himself together, bowed, and offered her his arm in a somewhat formal manner.

'Mark and Sophie order you to show me the grounds,' Masha continued, a little perplexed at his confusion, but to her relief he smiled and said easily, 'That can only mean the flowers and the river. I would never dare show you round the dairies and the stables! Mark likes to do that all himself.'

Their path lay through a garden of roses in full bloom, then down a gentle green slope towards the silvery haze rising from the calm surface of a river. It was beginning to get hot. Masha was glad she had put on a light dimity dress with short sleeves.

A few more steps and they came to a low wooden jetty. Nearby was a boat-house. On the opposite shore, a yellow ribbon of a road wove its way among rolling meadows and vanished in the distance. A little further up the river, the thatched roofs of a village could be seen, and beyond them a tall belltower.

'The river is called the Upa,' Michael explained. 'The village belongs to Mark. There is no bridge; we use a boat to cross. I would take you on the water now, but all the boats are out. Otrada is full of guests and they are all fishing, or rowing, or riding. You will see them all at lunch.'

To Masha 'all' meant only one person. She longed to ask Michael about Sergei, but something held her silent, she did not know quite what. She was desperately trying to formulate an inquiry that would be sufficiently offhand when a voice hailed them from the garden and Sergei himself came striding down towards the jetty. He was in riding-clothes and was shading his eyes with his hand.

Masha turned her face to the light breeze coming from the Upa, hoping it would cool her flaming cheeks; the next moment Sergei had taken possession of her hand.

'We have been expecting you for days,' he said reproachfully. 'We had begun to believe you weren't coming.'

Masha answered something, she did not know herself what, too preoccupied with keeping the joyous lilt out of her voice. But it kept creeping in anyway.

'Sophie has been ordering your favourite dishes for every meal,' he continued gaily, 'wringing her hands in despair when they were wasted on the rest of us. What has taken you so long?'

'It takes time to paint a landscape,' Masha laughed, and began to tell Sergei about her trip. They walked side by side, talking. When they passed through the flower garden, Masha wondered why she never noticed before how intoxicating roses could smell. Suddenly, she realised that Michael was not with them.

'But...' she began stopping, 'Your brother...'

'Don't imagine you can compare with the joys of fishing' Sergei answered. 'Michael has just taken it up and it occupies all his waiting hours. I haven't the patience, but Michael never gives up.'

Before Masha knew it, they were in front of the house. Several guests who were assembled on the terrace waved, and Sophie ran down the steps to greet them. 'Come and meet everybody,' she cried.

For the next few minutes, Masha dutifully curtsied, bowed and tried to remember names and faces. Among the guests was General Volkonski, son of Princess Volkonska who had served as Masha's chaperone on her first evening at Anichkov Palace. Tall and serious looking, he seemed much older than his wife Marie, a slender dark-haired girl, with a vivid face and enormous black eyes.

'We call Marie "the maiden of the Ganges",' Sophie said gaily, 'and what do you think Masha! Marie knows Pushkin, quite intimately too.'

'Do you really?' Masha asked Marie, when the two girls were wandering in the park that afternoon.

Marie smiled. 'I really do. He travelled all over Crimea with my family. It was three years ago. I was only fifteen then. My father is General Rayevski. I suppose you have heard about him.'

'The whole of Russia knows his name,' Masha answered with awe.

'I will never forget that summer,' Marie Volkonska said dreamily. 'I remember once, we stopped by the sea and I ran races with the waves until my shoes were all wet. Pushkin teased me about it for a long time.'

'He wrote about it too!' Masha exclaimed. '*How I envied the waves who were kissing her feet.*'

Marie nodded and blushed, 'I think he was a tiny bit in love with me,' she confessed.

Masha did not answer. She was thinking about Anna Wulff, denied even that 'tiny bit' of love.

After dinner, everyone gathered in the big drawing-room. The tall windows were open, but it was so calm not a curtain stirred.

A young man, short and sturdy, constantly shaking off a lock of hair falling on his forehead, sauntered to the piano. After a few chords, he turned to Mark. 'Really, Mark, this is a most excellent piano!' he said enthusiastically. 'I never expected to find such a fine instrument in the country.'

At the sound of his voice, Masha jumped up. 'It is you?' she exclaimed. 'Remember the flood in St. Petersburg last year? You were pleading with someone to save the piano. Your name is Glinka.'

'Masha, what do you mean?' Sophie asked in astonishment.

The young man seemed surprised at first, then recollection dawned on his face. 'You are right, Mademoiselle,' he told Masha. 'I was living in a small apartment with a friend at that time. It was on the first floor, and I was asking the men who were moving the furniture upstairs to take the piano first.'

'Michael Glinka is our future great composer,' Mark said. 'Just now he is engaged in a great battle against Italian music. He thinks that we should have our own Russian opera and use Russian folk-melodies in it. Quite a few people are shocked by his ideas.'

'Let them be shocked,' the young musician answered stoutly, 'Enough of those over-romantic Italian arias. We have our own music and we shouldn't be ashamed of it. Just wait until I study Russian folk-singing a little more. In the meantime, here is Gluck for you.' He touched the piano keys and the music flowed.

It was past midnight when the gathering broke up. The house was quiet for a few hours, and then the sun was up again and gay voices echoed on the terrace, in the park and by the river.

Riding parties raced along the tree-shaded avenues into the fields and meadows; the river reflected laughing faces and gay parasols; the serious fishermen could be heard begging everyone to keep away from certain spots. A bevy of Mark's young cousins and nieces, aged from fourteen to sixteen, followed by their youthful admirers, made every effort to escape Miss Alice's supervision. Their light dresses fluttering in the breeze, they ran through the park and towards the depths of the birch grove, jumping ditches and scrambling over fences to escape their chaperone. But Miss Alice in a stout tweed skirt and sensible shoes jumped and scrambled too. No sweet murmurs accompanied by fond glances were exchanged except in her presence.

Sophie took part in all the gay doings, but sometimes was seized by pangs of conscience about her duties as a mistress of the estate. On those occasions she rose early and visited the dairies. Keeping a watchful eye on the horns rising above the stalls, she gave a vague glance at the milk pails, urged the dairymaids to wash their hands and distributed cakes of pink soap.

'A great improvement in dairy life,' Mark declared. 'Now we can expect the cows to begin giving pink milk.'

'He is always teasing me,' Sophie complained to Masha, 'and you can see that it is not easy to run a house in the country!'

Masha felt a little guilty about not sharing Sophie's household responsibilities. But it was impossible to resist when Sergei offered to take her out on the river, or suggested a walk. Every day he gave her a riding lesson. Soon Masha was able to ride in the park, then on the roads. When the weather was too hot for riding or walking across the sun-drenched fields, they climbed the small hill at the end of the park, following the narrow path between the tall ferns until they reached an old stone bench half-hidden in the greenery. It seemed their own special secret place. Sergei would read aloud, or they would look at the pictures in one of the many illustrated magazines from the house, their temples almost touching as they bent over the pages. A few times, they saw Michael in the distance, going to the river with his rod. He never seemed to see them and they never called him. Other guests left them alone. It was summer in the country; everyone was wandering round, enjoying the liberty.

The evenings were spent in the big drawing-room. Glinka played, sometimes accompanying Marie Volkonska who had a beautiful contralto voice. Forfeits and other games were accompanied by shrieks of laughter. The nights were so beautiful, it seemed a sin to go to bed.

But no matter how late Masha went to sleep, she always woke up in the small hours of the morning. Sitting up in bed and looking out at the sleeping garden, she would wait with fierce, suffocating impatience for the dawn to come. When at last the sky became touched with red, she would fall on her pillows and cry desperately, without knowing why.

At the end of July more guests arrived. Among them was a young army officer, Paul Pestel, with a heavy-featured somewhat wooden face and a commanding manner. When he talked, there was always a note of authority in his voice with just a shade of contempt.

With Pestel's arrival the gay life in Otrada changed. Instead of boating or riding, most of the men spent long hours talking in the library.

Sitting on the terrace, near the open library windows, Masha caught snatches of heated discussions, with the words 'freedom' and 'equal rights' always coming up. The young voices were eager and full of faith, ringing with courage. Then Pestel would begin to speak, long heavy sentences falling like stones in the sudden hush, until someone would recall a funny anecdote and everybody would forget politics and start laughing.

Michael was one of the few men not involved in these mysterious discussions and Masha instinctively turned to him for company. She was a little afraid at first that he might be offended because she had neglected him lately, but he did not show any resentment. When she murmured something about having been busy with her riding lessons, he answered, 'I've been busy too, trying to learn from Mark how to manage an estate. He is really wonderful you know, not a cruel master at all, but an exacting one, and that is how it should be. Otrada is flourishing and Mark is liked by peasants and by his own people.'

'You are still thinking about your country house then?' Masha asked.

He answered slowly, tracing a design on the sanded path with a twig, 'Yes, I have kept that part of my dream.'

Masha always felt at ease with Michael. Settling herself more comfortably on the garden bench, she took off her straw hat and fanned her face. 'You may think it strange,' she told Michael, 'but even though I find Otrada a real paradise, I like Rodnoye, Daria Ivanovna's house, better.' She half-closed her eyes, 'I can imagine it now. The shrubbery is probably all tangled and the flowers are all growing wild. I don't think Daria Ivanovna is interested in the garden and most of her men servants are old. Yes, I can see it… The trees are unpruned and that is why there is greenish light in the rooms…' She broke off. 'I know I am talking nonsense. You can't possibly understand.'

His eyes on Masha's face, as if trying to memorise every feature, Michael answered in a low voice, 'You are not talking nonsense and I do understand.'

They both started. There were voices behind them and General Volkonski, Sergei, Pestel and several others passed by, going towards the house. 'They did not see us,' Michael said, 'those bushes are too high.'

'They are probably going to have one of their meetings again.' Masha lowered her voice. 'It is Freedom Society, isn't it? I hear them talking about…such things.'

'Don't mention it to my brother,' Michael cautioned. 'He may not like your knowing about the society.'

But Masha did talk to Sergei on that subject, in the evening, when they were sitting in their favourite hidden spot. He looked annoyed. 'I never realised we could be overheard,' he said. 'Well, anyway, we were discussing the questions that should concern every civilised person. 'Don't you agree,' he gestured towards the village on the other side of the river, 'that it is time to give human rights to those people and change their lives?'

Masha looked at the distant huts and at the woman going to the well with two buckets, then glanced back at Sergei. 'What do you know about them?' she asked.

Sergei frowned. 'What a strange question! Surely, the most important thing is to give them freedom first. We can always look into their other needs later.'

'Why doesn't Mark set them free then?' Masha was sorry the minute she said the words. Sergei bit his lip and looked irritated. 'Mark offered them freedom as soon as he was twenty-one and able to dispose of his estate,' he answered. 'The fools chose to remain slaves.'

'What?' Masha exclaimed.

'They wanted land as well as liberty,' Sergei explained. 'Mark told them that they could rent it from him, but they refused.'

Masha was at a loss to know what to say. It was certainly difficult to imagine peasants without land and she was not sure they could afford to pay rent. On the other hand, it did not seem fair to make the landowners give their property away. She poked at the bushes with her parasol and wished she had never started the conversation.

'Mark can't be expected to chop his land to pieces and distribute it to the peasants,' Sergei said. 'That is why we need clear-headed men like Pestel to work out a plan that would satisfy everybody.'

'A plan that would satisfy everybody...' Masha repeated, her eyes still on the distant village. 'There are several million peasants in Russia. It would be an immense task...'

Sergei did not answer. He sat frowning and fingering the white silk scarf on his neck until it was all tied in knots. Then, abruptly, he suggested they return to the house. Masha wished she had followed Michael's advice, and yet when she reviewed the conversation she was not sorry. Somehow it seemed to have bridged a gap that had existed between them and brought them closer to each other.

16

High Summer

Pestel left a few days later and the conferences behind the closed doors stopped. The smell of ripe apples from the orchard chased away the stale odour of pipe-smoke still lingering in the library.

Sophie, heartily tired of her visits to the dairy, devoted her energies to organising a giant picnic a few miles away on the edge of the woods. The company started off early in the morning, some on horseback, some in open carriages. A wagon loaded with food, rugs and extra wraps, had been sent in advance.

Everyone was delighted with the spot Mark had selected — a mossy clearing guarded by centenary oaks and pines. Rugs were spread and a big fire lighted. A thin column of smoke rose in the air. The coachmen grouped themselves around their own fire. The unharnessed horses grazed nearby.

It seemed to Masha that she had never enjoyed herself more than on this care-free day. There was not a cloud in the sky.

Grown-ups and children, all ate ravenously, though Sophie complained that the delicious dishes she had provided were neglected in favour of half-burned potatoes baked in the ashes.

'There is poetry in those potatoes that one can't find in the cold veal, dearest,' her husband explained.

'And insects in the tea add to the poetry,' Sergei joined in, fishing a struggling grasshopper out of his cup with a blade of grass.

After the meal, the picnickers rested or wandered in the woods. The children played games on the clearing under the watchful eye of Miss Alice.

Masha leaned her head against a tree trunk and watched a butterfly fly low over the grass, feeling too lazy even to shake off the green cricket sitting on her sleeve. She smiled and closed her eyes.

'Wake up!' someone said. Masha started and brushed her hand across her face. Sergei was standing beside her. 'Sorry,' he said. 'I shouldn't have disturbed you, but I want to show you something worth seeing, Glinka in a trance. Come quickly.'

Still half-awake, Masha followed Sergei across the clearing into the woods. 'There,' Sergei whispered.

Masha saw Glinka standing in the middle of a narrow path, an ecstatic expression on his face, his right hand moving in the air as if directing an invisible orchestra. Masha's ear caught distant singing. In another minute it became more distinct and soon three peasant girls in loose sleeveless dresses of bright blue, worn over white blouses, came from behind the trees, singing. They saw Glinka, blushed and began to giggle. But as they went on and disappeared behind the bend of the path, the song broke out again.

Glinka turned around and stared at Masha and Sergei as if he couldn't recognise them, then seemed to shake himself and came nearer. 'Did you hear?' he asked, 'Each voice distinct and what a harmony. That is the Russian folk-song that we are trying so hard to twist into a drawing-room piece. And when I think that with all our natural riches we still don't have a Russian opera…'

'Write one,' Sergei suggested.

'I might,' the musician answered seriously. 'I have even thought of a subject.' He turned to Masha. 'Have you read

Pushkin's *Russlan and Liudmila*? Wouldn't it make a beautiful opera?'

'I really don't know,' Masha answered doubtfully. 'It is a fairytale. I can't very well imagine it on the stage.'

'It will make a beautiful opera,' the young musician repeated stubbornly, 'and the public will love it.'

Marie Volkonska had joined them, a big bunch of wild flowers in her hand. 'How I hope Pushkin will be allowed to return to the capital,' she said. 'Life in the country must be very dull for him.'

'He did seem bitter about it,' Masha admitted.

Marie became pensive. 'You have seen that young woman, Madame Kern. Is she really so beautiful?' she asked Masha.

'Yes, she is beautiful,' Masha said, surprised. 'But how do you know of her?'

'A friend in St. Petersburg sent me a copy of a poem he wrote about her. '*A moment I recall enchanted*, it begins,' Marie explained. 'I showed it to our great composer here and he has put it to music. I may sing it this evening.'

'Isn't someone calling us?' Sergei asked suddenly.

'Ho-o-o! We are leaving!' Mark's shout came. 'The horses are being harnessed.'

'Coming!' Glinka called back and the little group hurried on. They came to the clearing just as several figures with leaves in their hair and stains from wild berries on their clothes, began to pour out of the woods. Michael arrived at the last moment, running and holding a basket filled with mushrooms.

'Michael, you could have been left behind and perished in these woods,' Sophie scolded.

'Wait until you have tasted these mushrooms in cream sauce. It was worth it,' Michael defended himself, climbing onto the saddle.

It was late in the afternoon when the merry party arrived

home. For a while everybody rested, but as soon as the terrace became white in the moonlight, couples came to stroll in the garden and a group of music-lovers gathered around the piano in the drawing-room.

Masha felt strangely tense and irritable. The candles in the chandeliers seemed to burn too brightly, the music and the voices sounded too loud. 'I am tired after the picnic,' she thought, slipping through the glass door onto the terrace.

It was very warm. Black clouds floated past the moon and distant lightning flashed on the horizon.

Masha stood for a few minutes, leaning on the stone balustrade. The air was heavy with the scent of flowers and freshly-watered earth.

A shadow appeared in the door and Sergei's voice asked, 'May I join you?'

Without waiting for an answer, he came out and leant on the balustrade beside her.

A chord of music came through the open windows and Marie Volkonska began to sing an aria.

Sergei said, 'It is from Beethoven's *Fidelio*. I heard it in Vienna last year. Beethoven himself was present. He had to be turned around to see the public applaud. I will never forget the grief in his eyes as he stood there, all alone in the world, unable to hear the music he had created.'

'It is tragic,' Masha murmured, 'but why do you say "alone"? Didn't Beethoven marry that girl, Theresa... Braunsweig, I think her name was. I read in the papers that he was engaged to her.'

'I understand the marriage is off. She is from a wealthy family. He is poor in spite of his great works. Or, more likely, he did not want the woman he loved to share his burden. Quite right too. Don't you think so?'

The clouds had veiled the moon completely. The terrace was dark except for the reflection of the lighted windows on the flagstones. Darkness gave courage to Masha. 'No,' she said firmly. 'It is not right. I don't know why men think that all a woman ever wants to share is wealth or fame.'

Sergei did not answer. Masha was silent too. Behind them in the drawing-room, the music started again. Marie was singing the Pushkin lyric of which she had spoken: *A moment I recall enchanted.*

Masha and Sergei listened, hardly breathing, as Marie's voice rose in the air, putting love and longing into every note.

'I don't know who is the greater genius!' Sergei exclaimed when the singing ended, 'The poet or the musician.'

'But those lines should not have been written for Annette Kern!' Masha cried, her throat suddenly tight with tears. 'For her it is just another trophy won by her beauty. I know someone else who loves Pushkin, loves him deeply, humbly. Why…'

'Why?' Sergei's voice was very low. 'Because a man does not always recognise the right woman, and even when he does, he hesitates because he is afraid she might make him forget his life's aim. He battles with himself, he goes away from her, only…to come back again.'

A silhouette appeared in the lighted window and Sophie's voice called, 'Masha, are you there?'

Masha opened her lips, but Sergei reached for her hands and held them tight. 'No,' he whispered, 'Don't answer. I want you to listen to me. I want to tell you something.'

'Yes,' Masha murmured, her heart beating so hard she could hardly pronounce the short word. The touch of Sergei's hands sent a thrill through her whole body. It seemed to her that every sound around her had become hushed, except that ardent whisper near her ear.

'For several years now,' Sergei said, 'I considered myself committed, dedicated only to one idea—to deliver my country from the taint of slavery, to give the humblest subjects the same rights that we, the privileged ones, enjoy now. Love did not mean anything to me. I considered it a weakness. Then one day I met you at Sophie's. You can't know how touching you were in your ignorance of life, how fresh, how pathetically eager to enter the world that was opening before you. In spite of myself I began to think how lucky would be the man who would show you that world, and...love was born. But I fought it and I thought I'd won. Then I saw you growing up: no longer a naïve child, but a young girl strangely untouched by the society intrigues, unspoilt by her life at court, faithful to her friends. And love came back. It was harder to fight, this time. The day of the flood I almost told you how I felt about you. Later, when I met you in the street, when we stood on that plank, so close to each other, I forgot all my resolutions, all the promises I had made to myself. I was going to take you in my arms and shout to the whole world that I loved you. But someone came by and I was reminded that I was not free to love.'

'How well I remember,' Masha thought, 'That day when the happiness was snatched away.'

'I came to Otrada,' Sergei spoke slowly, almost haltingly, 'because...I couldn't bear to be away from you. I kept telling myself that it would be only for a short while, that we were simply friends. But the summer days began, the long walks, the exchange of thoughts, of opinions. I realised that the girl was becoming a woman, warm, thoughtful, understanding. I could not pretend any more. I knew that I loved you more than ever, that I could not live without you.

'Masha,' he said, bending over her, his voice deep and tender, 'I love you. But there is something you must understand. I shall never be able to talk to you about...about my friends' plans and ideas. I am under oath not to reveal anything. Do you still feel you could trust me enough to become my wife, to stand by me, to give me courage and faith to fight for the freedom of the millions of slaves? Do you love me enough for that?'

For a second Masha stood still, almost overwhelmed by the immense wave of awed happiness that was mounting from the bottom of her heart. 'Yes, yes,' she murmured, swaying closer to Sergei. 'I trust you, love you. I want to help you make your dreams come true.'

'I hoped and prayed you would say that,' Sergei said fervently. He gathered Masha in his arms and held her close. 'Look into my eyes,' he whispered, 'You will see your image there, and the same image is in my heart. We are united already, and soon we will be united before God. You are mine, mine…'

His lips found Masha's and she returned the kiss.

17

The legend of the cross

Masha returned to St. Petersburg in the last days of August. She listened to the coachman's 'Make way! Make way!', looked at the stream of carriages with liveried footmen hanging behind, at the granite embankment of the Neva, and felt as if she had been away for several years.

The trip home, in company with Marie Volkonska and her husband, had been very pleasant. Masha was sorry that Marie was not staying in St. Petersburg, but General Volkonski had to rejoin his regiment in the south of Russia.

'I do hope we shall see each other again,' Masha said to Marie. The young woman smiled, her dark eyes soft and mysterious. 'Something very wonderful is going to happen to me in December,' she said, 'I am going to have a baby. If everything goes well, I am planning to be present at your wedding in February.'

Masha blushed. 'We would like to be married in February, but of course nothing is official until I have asked Her Highness' permission and approval.'

As Masha spoke the last words, she remembered Sergei's face when he pressed her in his arms saying good-bye. 'Why do you have to ask permission to get married?' he said impatiently. 'I could understand your asking your parents, but…'

'But Grand Duchess Alexandra and the grand duke are like parents to me,' Masha had answered and smoothed the frown with a kiss.

Marie gave Masha a keen glance and laughed. 'I don't

think you will have to tell Her Highness much,' she remarked.

Marie was right. Masha had barely pronounced Sergei's name, when the grand duchess kissed her and wished her happiness. 'I feel exactly as if I were losing a daughter!' she said warmly. 'We have all become so attached to you, my dear. Only yesterday, the Empress Elizaveta was asking for you.' Alexandra's face suddenly became grave, 'I might as well tell you now, Masha. Her Majesty is not at all well. She had a bad fit of coughing a few days ago and fainted afterwards. It may be very serious.'

All Masha's joy fled. 'I am so sorry!' she exclaimed. 'But the doctors must do something, find some medicine…'

The grand duchess shook her head. 'The doctors have tried everything. Now they have decided that the empress should spend a few months in Taganrogue. The emperor is going first to see that everything is prepared for her arrival.

At the name of Taganrogue, something stirred in Masha's memory. She remembered herself in Smolni, a small girl in Browns' uniform, listening to the geography teacher say as he pointed out a place on the map, 'This is Taganrogue, a small town on the shore of Azov sea. The climate is noted for its strong north-easterly winds.'

'But… but if Her Majesty has lung trouble, won't the climate be too raw for her?' she began.

Alexandra interrupted her wearily, 'Masha, please! Everyone seems to ask this same question. The doctors have recommended it and I am sure the doctors know best. You may accompany me to the Winter Palace tomorrow and maybe see Her Majesty for a few minutes.'

Sashette was on duty, when they arrived. From the way Sashette's eyes flashed and from the two red spots on her cheeks, Masha realised that the empress's lady-in-waiting was in bad temper.

'Wait with Mademoiselle Rossett, please, Masha,'

Alexandra said. 'I will ask Her Majesty if you may come in a little later.'

As soon as the grand duchess disappeared behind the tall inlaid doors leading to the empress's boudoir, Sashette pounced on Masha. 'Just think!' she announced in a tragic tone, 'I am one of the victims chosen to go to Taganrogue. We are going to stay several months in that hole! It is a living death! I am desperate.'

'Can't you say you are to be married soon?' Masha suggested, mentally resolving not to mention her engagement to Sashette until later. 'Surely that is a good enough excuse.'

'I am not going to be married soon,' Sashette snapped. 'Smirnov's mother has sent him to his country estate to settle some dispute about taxes or boundaries, I don't know exactly what. He's to be away for about two months, and when he gets back I shall be in Taganrogue. As soon as the emperor heard that no definite date for my wedding has been set, I was doomed. "You will be going to accompany Her Majesty to Taganrogue," he told me, "You have a good reading voice and two ladies-in-waiting will be enough." I should think two is enough! I understand the whole suite is going to be packed into a few rooms. And of course my companion is to be Mademoiselle Valuyeva with her open mouth and eternal bad colds. I cried so much last night, my eyes are all puffy.'

She glanced at the mirror as she spoke, and tidied a stray ringlet. In fact she was looking unusually handsome.

'Your new hairstyle is beautiful,' Masha risked, hoping to distract Sashette from her woes.

'Do you really think so?' For a moment Sashette brightened. 'But what is the use! Who is going to see me in Taganrogue? I am tired being a lady-in-waiting! Ally Ayler was married last month, you are engaged…'

Caught unprepared, Masha could only stammer, 'How

did you know?'

Sashette laughed, 'Because there is a golden halo around your head. Seriously, I expected it. No, I did not really know, but I watched you and Sophie's cousins at her wedding and wondered which one you were going to choose.'

'Which one?' Masha was so astonished, she wondered if she heard right. 'But…it was always Sergei…I never thought…'

Without saying a word, Sashette watched Masha's face, a strange smile on her lips. 'Of course it was always Sergei,' she said at last in a soothing tone. 'I must have imagined that the other one… Oh, never mind, I wish you much, much happiness.'

'She looks so very much older than I,' Masha thought, 'and we are almost the same age.' She had just begun to thank Sashette, when there was the sound of a silver bell. 'It is Her Majesty,' Sashette exclaimed and went to the boudoir.

'You are to come in,' she told Masha, coming back.

Elizaveta's thin face with the blue veins standing out on the temples was almost transparent; her slim hands looked deathly white against the dark blue silk of her gown. Masha, listening to the gracious congratulations and good wishes, felt pity grip her heart and hold it tight.

After a few minutes, the grand duchess made a discreet sign to Masha and began to take leave.

'If you don't mind, Alex, I would like to keep Masha for a little while longer,' the empress said suddenly. 'She can help me to sort my books. I am trying to decide which ones to take to Taganrogue.'

There were only a few rows of books left on the rosewood bookshelves near the fireplace. Masha read the titles aloud and waited for the empress's order. Most of the books were replaced on the shelves. Only a few were laid aside in a small pile. A bible, Pushkin's poems, a volume of

Schiller's poetry, a few books of memoirs.

A letter frayed at the edges flew out of one of the books. Not knowing what to do, Masha picked it up and paused, the letter in her hand. She looked at the empress.

'Burn it, my dear,' Elizaveta said, 'Yes, poke the fire.'

The thin sheet of paper curled, became red and fell apart. The sick woman leaned back and closed her eyes, but by the firelight Masha saw a tear slide down the pallid cheek. She hurriedly turned back to the shelves. 'I think that is all, Your Majesty,' she announced, 'Oh, no, there is one more book, wedged behind the others.'

It was a flat square volume: an atlas.

'Give it to me, please.' The empress opened her eyes, took the book from Masha and spread it open on her lap. 'It is such a long time since I have seen this,' she said, smiling. 'Once, when the emperor and I were both very young, we used to study these maps and dream. He would tell me how he would give up the throne and we would both settle in Germany, on the shores of the Rhine, in a vine-covered cottage.' She followed the river with her finger and turned the page. 'Sometimes, we even planned to go to America and live there. Yes, I can see the mark in ink he made. Here it is, between Boston and New York. We both really believed in those dreams then.'

'And they never came true,' Masha whispered.

'No,' the empress answered gravely, 'they never came true, and it was right that they should never come true. What were we actually planning to do? Shirk the burden God placed upon us. Each of us has a cross and we must carry it to the very end.'

Kneeling in front of the fireplace, Masha was far away from the palace and the etiquette. 'And if the cross is too heavy?' she asked.

'If it is too heavy…' Elizaveta repeated and became silent. Several minutes passed. Then a log fell apart in the fireplace, sending up a shower of sparks. The empress lifted her head. 'You see, my dear,' she said, and her voice sounded stronger, 'No cross is ever too heavy. There was a tale I read once in an old book and I never forgot it. It was about a man who always complained that his cross was too heavy for him. One night, he dreamed that he was standing in a big white hall that was full of crosses. There were small light crosses made of twigs, heavier ones of wood, stone or marble, even a giant cross of pure gold. The man was wondering where all those crosses came from, when he heard the voice of God, "In this hall are the crosses of all people in the world. Take whichever you wish in exchange for the one you find too heavy." 'The man started to try the crosses,' the empress went on. 'He began with the light ones, but their sharp edges cut his shoulders. He tried those of wood and marble, but they crushed him. He wanted to try the cross of gold, but he could not even move it. Only after many hours did he find what he wanted. It was a heavy cross made of solid oak, but somehow it fitted his shoulders and he could carry it without too much discomfort. "This is the cross I want," he said, and God's voice answered, "Take it and carry it, for see it is your own cross, the one that you found too heavy".'

The thin voice ceased. Obscurely Masha felt the story was not meant for her. Elizaveta was pleading with someone else not to throw away the God-given cross. Without speaking she lifted the empress's frail hand and touched it with her lips.

The older woman bent down and kissed the girl on the forehead. 'Good-bye, my dear,' she said. 'May God keep you from all harm.'

18

The news from Taganrogue

In the middle of October, Masha received a letter from Sashette.

'We have been in Taganrogue for over a month now,' Sashette wrote, 'but I shall never get used to it. The palace is near the sea and the constant sound of the surf gets on my nerves. I really don't know why I say "palace". It is an ordinary green-roofed villa, all on one floor. The rooms are too small and the ceilings are too low. There are mice. Valuyeva, who is the silliest person in the world, jumps on the nearest chair and screams whenever she sees one. The town itself is just a hole. There isn't a single good shop. I am counting on you to buy some things for me. Send them with the next messenger, please. I need some rose-water, garters, blue if possible, some *Peau de Nymphe* powder, a pair of pink-striped stockings…'

Masha scanned the list of items necessary for Sashette's happiness and went to the next paragraph.

'I did hope at first that Her Majesty would get tired of this wilderness and we might go abroad or at least to Crimea, but she is delighted with everything. It is true that the emperor has had all her favourite furniture sent here and arranged everything himself, even driving the nails for the pictures with his own hands. I suppose you could call it cosy, but oh, how I long for my uncomfortable room in Ladies-in-waiting Corridor! I shall soon forget how to dance. Walks are our sole amusement. Her Majesty goes out on foot every day. I must admit that the local air seems to be doing her good. She looks years younger, talks and laughs as she has never done before. She even dresses differently, in bright colours and wears jewellery every day. The emperor is with her most of the time. They sit for hours on a bench above the sea. Do you know what people here call them? The newlyweds!

'I suppose Sophie is back from the country. Do you see her often? I hear that Stephanie is back and planning to give several balls this season…'

Masha folded the letter and went to the window, looking dreamily out at the falling leaves. "The newlyweds",' she thought, 'The emperor and empress together, away from the court, almost as they had once dreamed.'

She smiled. February was getting nearer and her own dreams were coming closer every day. She saw Sergei often, mostly at Sophie's and he was constantly sending her flowers, small unexpected presents, a new book she wanted to read.

But at the thought of Sophie, Masha's face clouded. Something was wrong there but she did not know what. Mark was looking for a house in St. Petersburg, but in the meantime, General Brozin was more than happy to have the young couple living with him in the big old house on English Quay. Everything seemed as usual. Sophie's rooms smelled of her perfume, her French novels and fashion magazines were piled on every chair, silks and laces were thrown on the rug. Yet something was wrong. Somehow the old Sophie was missing.

Masha felt more and more anxious about a certain look in her friend's eyes, sudden uncharacteristic silences.

'Where is Mark?' she would ask sometimes, 'I hardly see him any more.'

'He is out,' Sophie would answer and change the conversation.

One afternoon in early November, Masha invited Sophie

to go shopping with her, hoping that it might distract her friend to give advice on a suitable trousseau. 'Buy anything you want,' the grand duchess had said, 'and have the bills sent to Anichkov Palace.' When Masha tried to thank her, she stopped her with, 'No, it is only a small return for the many daughterly services and loyal devotion.' The girls were already seated in the court carriage, when Masha had an idea. 'Let's shop in Gostinni Dvor,' she suggested. 'I have been there only once, when I was quite small.'

'Very well,' Sophie agreed with a return of her animation. 'But we mustn't buy gloves there. You need a French shop for that. Let's look at dress fabrics, and maybe at the shawls. I heard someone say that there is a good choice of shawls in Gostinni Dvor.'

The choice proved to be even greater than they had expected. It was drizzling outside, so Gostinni Dvor was less crowded and noisy than usual. The girls spent a good hour selecting shawls, then passed on to dress materials and ended in the haberdashery.

'You were certainly right about coming here,' Sophie said gaily as she and Masha came out of Gostinni Dvor, a boy loaded with packages at their heels. 'I don't remember having seen such lovely trou-trou shawls anywhere else. And that forget-me-not blue silk is just right for you. Do you think we bought enough lace for the trimming? Oh, look! It is not raining any more! Let's go to that hat shop I told you about!'

'Why not? It is still early and we have plenty of time.'

Masha was so glad to see Sophie gay again, she was ready to go anywhere. 'Wait a moment until I find some money for the boy.'

She was fumbling in her reticule when a curious nasal voice suddenly sounded close by, rising above the street noises. 'God have mercy on us,' it chanted, coming nearer. People began to turn round.

Masha paled. 'It is Annoushka,' she whispered frantically, clutching at Sophie's arm. 'The madwoman! The one who predicted I would live in a palace! I am afraid of her! Let's get into the carriage. Quick!'

Sophie had no time to answer. The gaunt figure in its shabby black dress was already in front of them. It seemed to Masha that Annoushka had hardly changed at all since she first saw her so long ago, on the day before she entered Smolni. Annoushka's round expressionless face still looked unnaturally blank and white, like a paper doll's. Only her eyes looked older, sunk in orbits under greying eyebrows in the ageless countenance.

'Ah, here you are again!' Annoushka cried, coming close to Masha. 'Buying the pretties? Too early! They will be out of fashion by the time your wedding day arrives.' She turned away from Masha and addressed Sophie, 'And you, my beautiful, smile, laugh, be gay! You'll not laugh much longer. Tears are in store for you and I don't see the end of them. Now don't forget what I said, both of you!'

'Come,' Masha gasped, dragging Sophie after her. The two girls almost ran the few steps that separated them from the carriage. The court footman, who had watched the scene with amazement, was holding the door open. Masha fell onto a seat, Sophie followed. The footman took the packages from the boy and put them on the front seat. The coachman began to gather the reins.

As the carriage moved, Masha caught sight of Annoushka standing on the edge of the pavement, shouting something. Behind her a crowd had already gathered.

Sophie spoke first. 'What do you think she meant?' Her voice had panic in it.

But Masha put her hands over her ears. 'Don't talk about her!' she cried. 'It was only madwoman's talk. Let's go for a long drive and forget all about it.' Opening the window, she ordered, 'Just drive slowly…anywhere.'

Sophie drew a deep breath and said with a forced laugh, 'I am going to admire our purchases.' Leaning over, she took a package from the seat and began to unwrap it.

For the next half-hour the girls discussed each shawl, ribbon and piece of lace as if their lives depended on it. Strangely, it helped. Masha began to feel calmer and even a little drowsy. 'Like after an illness,' she thought, settling herself more comfortably against the cushions and listening with half an ear to something Sophie was saying about a length of velvet. Behind the carriage windows shops and houses glided by and disappeared. Masha realised they were somewhere near the Blue Bridge, a part of the city she did not know.

A big sign on a solid-looking grey building caught her attention. She read, 'Russian-American Company' and wondered idly if it had something to do with Alaska. At the same time, she became aware that Sophie had stopped talking and was staring out of the window. Following her gaze, Masha saw Mark coming out of the building. Behind him came Sergei and several other men, among them General Volkonski and Pestel.

'Let's call them!' Masha exclaimed, but Sophie hissed, 'No! Be quiet,' and drew the curtain down the carriage window. Masha had barely time to notice a slim young man, with a boyish, olive-skinned face, who was obviously the host. He shook hands with the others and stepped back into the house. It took Masha a few minutes to remember where she had seen him before. Then it came back to her. The narrow street, the dripping roofs, the young man calling to Sergei and reminding him of a meeting. 'Do you know him?' she asked Sophie, 'I mean the host.'

Sophie said curtly, 'I have met him once. His name is Riliyev. He works for the Russian-American Company. That is his apartment on the ground floor, the one with the grille-work on the windows.'

'I still don't understand why you did not want to be seen,' Masha said somewhat impatiently. She glanced through the back window, but Sergei and the others were already out of sight Turning back to Sophie, she saw with dismay that her friend was crying.

Masha pushed aside the tumbled purchases and moved closer to Sophie. 'What is the matter? Won't you tell me?' she asked gently.

'It is nothing, really,' Sophie wiped her eyes and straightened her bonnet. 'It's just that…that Mark spends most of the evenings nowadays with his friends, that Riliyev, Pestel and the others. They talk about matters I am not supposed to understand. I…feel lonely, and I wish he wouldn't.'

Masha felt at a loss. Sophie had apparently only a vague idea of the Freedom Society. But would it help to tell her more? Sophie was not interested in the society, she only resented it because it was taking Mark away from her.

'Are you not taking it too seriously?' she asked.

'Maybe,' Sophie agreed. 'Do you remember last summer in Otrada, how Pestel and most of the men used to sit in the library and talk? I happened to tell Marie Volkonska that it annoyed me, and she said, "We ladies have our own amusements. Why not let our husbands have theirs?" That is why I did not want Mark to see me now. I don't want him to think I spy on him.'

'No, of course not. But don't you think that Marie was sensible in what she said? I'm very sure they'll all get tired of talking eventually. We must just be patient with them.'

Sophie's face cleared. 'You sound as though you were married already! But you're right. I will try not to fret too much.'

The incident soon faded from both girls' minds. There were pleasanter things to think about. Sergei had bought a house on the English Quay, not far from General Brozin's.

He and Masha spent many delicious hours in Sophie's small drawing-room, poring over the plans and comparing samples of upholstery and hangings. It seemed to Masha that she had never even imagined being so intensely happy.

'Everything will be ready by May,' Sergei said, folding up the plans. 'Our own house, just as we want it, my darling. There it will be, waiting for us when we return from our honeymoon. We will probably have a month or so in St. Petersburg and then I may be sent abroad for a short while but you will accompany me. Then maybe we will go to Otrada. Sophie and Mark are expecting us.'

'But,' Masha said timidly, 'Are we not going to have a summer home too? Not something grand,' she added quickly, afraid that Sergei might think she wanted too much. 'Just an old house in the country…'

Sergei looked amused. 'Darling,' he said, taking her hand and kissing it. 'That is for when we are much older, when we have a family. We are young and free now, and neither of us has inherited an estate like Otrada, thank goodness! I haven't Mark's talent for being a gentleman farmer. No, we are going to travel! I will show you Italy, the south of France, Scotland, the world! Just imagine the two of us walking in the streets of Rome or standing on the shores of Lago Maggiore.' He turned her toward him and looked into her eyes. 'Don't you remember the very first time we met?' he said softly. 'I said that someone would show you the world?'

'Oh, yes, yes!' Masha cried, carried away. She did not know why she felt a slight stab of pain in her heart. Who would want an old house in the country with all the world to wander in?

That evening she wrote to Sashette telling her about the house and their future plans.

Sashette answered promptly. 'I am glad you are enjoying yourself,' she wrote. 'I can't say the same. The emperor is away in Crimea. Just a short trip, but Her Majesty is fretting and is sad again. I am so bored, I have even started to play solitaire in the evenings, like an old maid.'

Masha felt sorry for Sashette and even a little guilty for her own happiness. It was with relief that she read the postscript, 'His Majesty is back from Crimea and thank goodness the gloom has lifted before I went out of my mind.'

But the next messenger from Taganrogue brought bad news to Anichkov Palace. Emperor Alexander had caught a chill on his return voyage from Crimea and was in bed with fever. Soon another message came, the emperor's health was better. He was up but not going outside yet. Almost without interval a fresh report arrived. Alexander had suffered a relapse, was laid up again and his condition was serious.

A feeling of anxiety settled over the palace. Faces were grave. Balls and receptions were cancelled.

'I tremble every time a messenger arrives from Taganrogue,' the grand duchess told Masha. 'Everything was going so well, and now this sudden illness... The doctors call it "Crimean fever", but they don't seem to know much about it.' She frowned and wrapped her shawl tighter around her shoulders. All the ladies-in-waiting knew that this gesture meant Alexandra was worried.

Only the children seemed unaffected by the atmosphere of anxiety and Masha was thankful for their effect on their troubled parents. In the nursery, the grand duke and duchess resolutely put aside any forebodings they may have entertained and for a brief while appeared to have a little surcease from care.

It was on the dull and rainy evening of November 2 that Masha, making her way to the grand duchess's rooms, met Grand Duke Nicholas coming out of Alexandra's apartments. He said curtly, 'We have bad news, Masha,' and walked on without another word. With a sinking heart, Masha tapped at the door.

Alexandra was sitting in her small drawing-room, her face in her hands. She looked up as Masha came in and the girl saw that she was very pale. 'The emperor is dying,' she said quietly. 'Go and rest, my dear. We will all need our strength soon.'

Masha went to her room, but her thoughts were chaotic and jumbled. If the emperor was dying, who would inherit the crown? Alexander and Elizaveta had no children, so that there was no direct heir. The throne must then go to one of Alexander's three brothers, presumably to Konstantin, the eldest. But Konstantin cared nothing for Russia. He was married to a beautiful Polish countess and lived an elegant idle life in Warsaw. It was rumoured that he had long ago declared his unwillingness to reign. The Grand Duke Nicholas came next, then the youngest brother, Michael, who also lived in St. Petersburg. He was nice but insignificant, was devoted to the military service and spent most of his time with his regiment. Would it not have to be the Grand Duke Nicholas? Masha wondered, fearfully, seeing in her mind's eye the proud sad face of her beloved Alexandra. Who would it be?

The same question was whispered all through Anichkov Palace the next day and discussed all over St. Petersburg.

No more news came from Taganrogue. It was announced that on November 2 there would be a solemn mass with special prayers for the emperor.

Standing in the Winter Palace church, among other ladies-in-waiting, Masha studied the severe profile of the Grand Duke Nicholas. Beyond him stood his mother, the Dowager Empress Maria Feodorovna. Her stout figure looked hunched and her usually elaborately-dressed coiffure was sagging. The grand duchess Alexandra stood with bowed head, the children in front of her. The two little girls fidgeted but their brother did not move, mindful of his tutor's eye on him.

Masha realised she was not paying attention to the service and forced herself to listen.

'…and grant health to Thy servant, Alexander,' the priest was praying. His voice faltered and stopped. Masha looked up. The grand duke was gone.

A lady-in-waiting standing next to Masha whispered, 'His Highness was summoned outside. A messenger has just arrived from Taganrogue.'

A wave of hushed comments rose and died down. The singing stopped, the altar doors closed.

There was a sudden movement near the door and the grand duke reappeared. He walked slowly along the red-carpeted aisle, turned and faced the congregation. 'By the will of our Lord,' he began, 'His Imperial Majesty, the Emperor Alexander passed away on the morning of November 19th'.

Masha saw people around her cross themselves and bow their heads. Somebody at the back of the church started to sob. The dowager empress swayed and sank down on the floor. Several courtiers rushed to help her up. Little Ollie began to cry and hid her head in her mother's skirts. Masha swiftly made her way to Alexandra's side and gently lifted Ollie. Looking over the child's head, Masha saw that a small table with a crucifix and a copy of the New Testament on it, had been placed before the altar. Nicholas, his face wooden, was directing a long line of men, who each in turn laid his hand on the holy book and kissed the crucifix, pledging allegiance to the new Emperor Konstantin.

Yet Konstantin was far away in Warsaw, not even aware that he was called upon to reign.

'A strange situation,' an old courtier said behind Masha.

19

The new emperor

St. Petersburg was in mourning. Priests were officiating in black robes. Mounted heralds in mediaeval clothes, black capes flapping in the wind, were riding over the city, proclaiming the death of Emperor Alexander. Street lamps were veiled in black. In churches, people knelt shoulder to shoulder, lighted candles in their hands.

But no tolling of bells or singing of prayers could drown out the steadily mounting murmur of dissatisfaction. People gathering on street corners, in taverns, in elegant drawing-rooms, were whispering to each other that the Grand Duke Nicholas should not have proclaimed his brother Konstantin Emperor without his consent. Konstantin was still in Warsaw and showed no intention of coming to the capital. Soon it became known that Emperor Alexander had left a will in which he named Nicholas heir to the throne.

But the Grand Duke Nicholas continued to say firmly, 'Even an emperor has no right to bequeath the crown. My brother Konstantin is the rightful heir, not I.'

'I refuse every claim to the throne,' Konstantin wrote from Warsaw. Nicholas immediately wrote back, insisting that his brother come to St. Petersburg. The troops had already sworn allegiance. Konstantin was the official sovereign.

Public indignation rose even higher. 'Konstantin and Nicholas are playing ball with the Russian crown, tossing it to each other,' people said.

Even those who were close to the Grand Duke Nicholas could not understand his actions. Some said that the late emperor had forced Konstantin, the rightful heir, to promise he would refuse to reign and Nicholas was trying to repair the injustice. Others argued that Nicholas was afraid he might be accused of usurping the throne without having the birthright to it.

The palace was full of rumours. The grand duchess remained in her rooms. Bewildered and sad, Masha fled to Sophie's for reassurance, but Sergei was not there and Sophie, preoccupied and oddly strained, only complained that Mark was away from home more than ever.

Even the servants kept whispering and exchanging glances. One evening, Masha could not restrain herself any more. 'What is the matter with you all?' she asked Nastia sharply. 'What is it you are always whispering about?'

Nastia looked frightened. 'it's…it's nothing, Miss,' she mumbled.

'Something is wrong,' Masha insisted. 'Tell me.'

Nastia looked at Masha's face, then silently nodded and going to the door closed it tighter.

'It is about His Majesty,' she whispered, coming close to Masha. 'They say…they say…'

'What do they say?' Masha said impatiently. 'Go on, Nastia.'

'It's what the soldiers say, Miss. The ones who were at Taganrogue'. Nastia glanced around and lowered her voice still more. 'At dawn, they say, on the morning the emperor died, the sentry on duty saw the emperor walk out of the door, cross the yard and go out of the gates. He swears it was the emperor, and he was surprised because he knew His Majesty was sick and in bed, but he did not think much about it until…until…' Nastia shuddered and became silent.

'Until what?' Masha asked sharply, and Nastia whispered, 'Until the emperor's death was announced.' She licked her dry lips and looked furtively at her mistress.

Masha stood still. Dying men do not walk. The tale seemed incredible, and yet in a disquieting way it fitted in with an odd episode that had happened in the grand duchess' boudoir only two days ago.

Alexandra had been reading and Masha was sitting sewing in a low armchair, when the grand duke suddenly entered. He did not notice Masha, half-hidden by a tall ivory screen. Going straight to his wife, he asked abruptly, 'Where is your diary? I must have it.'

The grand duchess answered in a surprised tone, 'My diary? It is right here. But why?'

'Because there are pages that must be destroyed. This one for instance.' There was a sound of torn paper and Nicholas' impatient voice, 'Do you remember noting down that extraordinary thing Alexander said about how he would stand in the crowd and cheer at my coronation? I am sure it is here but I can't find the place. Maybe it would be better to burn the whole diary.'

Alexandra said, 'Oh no! Wait! We can go over it, page by page. If you think... She made a sign to Masha who rose thankfully and slipped away. It had seemed strange at the time, but now, too, the words of the Empress Elizaveta came back to her: 'He would tell me how he would give up the throne... We used to study these maps and dream...' Had the cross proved too heavy?

Next morning, the palace was teeming with news. A messenger had arrived from Warsaw, bringing Konstantin's ultimate refusal to inherit the throne. Nicholas was to be proclaimed Emperor of Russia and the small court of Anichkov was moving to the Winter Palace that very day.

For the last time, Masha looked around her pretty room. 'It doesn't really matter. I would be leaving it soon anyway,' she told herself, but all the same she felt sad.

The Winter Palace seemed very big and unfriendly,

compared to the cosiness of Anichkov. Masha was relieved to find that her new room was not in Ladies-in-waiting corridor, but near Alexandra's apartments. She left Nastia unpacking and went along to see the children in their new nursery. She found them looking forlorn and peevish. Ollie was crying because her favourite doll had been accidentally left behind in Anichkov, Mary had spilled milk on her dress, and the young Alexander stubbornly refused to let Mimi wash his face. Before anyone could stop him, he darted out of the nursery and raced through the palace, Masha in hot pursuit.

At the head of the wide stairway, Masha almost caught the fugitive, but he was too quick for her and sped on in the direction of the library. Masha knew that the grand duke had made the library his temporary bedroom to be near the council hall. She ran faster, then stopped as the library door opened and Nicholas came out, followed by Count Miloradovich, the governor of St. Petersburg. Masha caught sight of a narrow camp bed standing by the window, an oval table with a big silver inkstand on it, a half-opened suitcase on the floor.

The grand duke was saying to Miloradovich, 'I cannot arrest people who have not yet done anything criminal. It would only make martyrs of them. Besides, Count, you assured me yourself, and not so long ago, that they were simply lovers of literature who met to discuss books and read poetry. Of course, I agree with you that the matter should be thoroughly investigated. It may be...' His eyes fell on his son and he exclaimed, 'What are you doing here?'

Not in the least abashed, Alexander hung on his father's arm. 'Papa, when are we going back to Anichkov? I don't like it here.'

Nicholas bent over the child. 'We are not going back to Anichkov, my boy. You will have to get used to your new home. After all, your mamma and I are finding it very new too. Now run away, I am busy.' He patted the boy's head and handed him over to Masha, with a reproving glance from his pale blue eyes.

Order finally restored in the nursery, Masha slowly returned to her room, thinking of what she had overheard. Could it be the Freedom Society that must be thoroughly investigated? She felt apprehensive and uneasy, and almost cried out when she opened the door of her room to find a slim girl in black sitting by the window.

'Sashette!' Masha exclaimed, 'Is that really you?'

'Certainly, it is me, don't scream,' Sashette answered sharply, getting up and coming forward. Her face was thin and haggard as if after a sickness.

'You don't look well,' Masha said anxiously.

'I am deadly tired,' Sashette lowered herself into an armchair and stretched her arms with a weary gesture. 'But don't be sorry for me,' she went on as Masha opened her lips, 'It is really lucky that I look so dreadful, otherwise I would still be in Taganrogue. We were all exhausted after all those sleepless nights and church services. It ended in my fainting almost at the empress' feet. She decided I was too ill to stay and sent me back.'

'Her Majesty hasn't returned then?' Masha asked, 'I suppose she is going to accompany His Majesty's body? But won't it be too tiring for her? They are going to stop in almost every town to let people say good-bye to the emperor. They say that the trip may take two months.'

Sashette gave Masha a long look from under her black lashes. 'You will be very much surprised at what I am going to tell you,' she said slowly. 'The empress is not going to accompany the body, nor is she coming back. She is staying in Taganrogue until spring. Doesn't it sound strange? She loved the emperor so much. But after all if what people say is true... You know what I mean.'

'No,' Masha said cautiously, and waited.

'Oh, yes, you do,' Sashette made a sign to Masha to move her chair nearer and looked full into her face. 'Listen to me,' she said urgently, 'I promise that once out of this room, I will never mention the subject again, not even to my future husband, but now I must talk. I shall go out of my mind if I keep it all to myself. Have you heard the story about a sentry who saw the emperor at the hour he was supposed to be dying? Yes, or no?'

'Yes,' Masha whispered, 'but it can't be true. There were doctors at His Majesty's bedside. A priest had been called to hear his confession. The grand duchess showed me the reports.'

'You don't understand,' Sashette interrupted impatiently, 'It is all correct. The emperor *did* catch the Crimean fever. He *was* very sick, the priest *was* called. But he was not dying, he was getting better.'

'Everybody saw him die.'

'Who is everybody?' Sashette raised her eyebrows. 'There were not many of us in that so-called palace. We should all have been gathered around the emperor's deathbed. But who actually was there at the moment of his death? I was not. The Empress Elizaveta and the doctors were present, that is true. But if you ask the others, you will find that none of them really saw the emperor die. We saw a body and were told that it was his, but the face was so dark, he was barely recognisable. They said it was due to the fever. I don't believe it. It was not the emperor's body. It was someone else.'

Masha was still not convinced. 'It is simply not possible. How could a body be substituted? It is too difficult.'

'For an ordinary person, yes,' Sashette agreed, 'But not for a sovereign. Presumably a few trusted friends had to know in order to carry out the plan. And I think that the empress knew too. The emperor spent several hours locked in her room before he left for Crimea. When she came out, she was completely changed. All that happiness I wrote to you about was no more.'

'No one has the right to throw away the God-given cross,' the empress' tired voice sounded in Masha's ears.

'But why? *Why* should he want to do it?' she cried.

Sashette shrugged her shoulders. 'Guilt of his father's death, disappointments, fatigue... Maybe he simply had no more strength to reign. But I have not told you the most terrible thing yet. It is said that a few days after the emperor's "death", a tramp was arrested not far from Taganrogue. He was in his late forties, or early fifties, with blue eyes, blond hair with some grey in it, had rounded shoulders.'

'Yes?' Mas prompted. She thought of the emperor's bowed shoulders, standing in the moonlit garden at Peterhoff. How long ago?

Sashette took a deep breath. 'The man was riding a beautiful white horse, a pure-breed Arab, but he had no passport and refused to reveal his surname. "I am Feodor Kuzmich and I have no home," that was all he would say about himself. He was accused of stealing the horse and besides you know how severe are the laws about tramps. The man was whipped and sent to Siberia. Just think, *whipped!*'

Dusk started to gather, but Masha did not ring for a lamp. She tried to picture the peasant who called himself Feodor Kuzmich, but her mind refused to imagine the Emperor of Russia trudging along the roads with tramps and criminals.

At last Sashette rose to leave. 'We must forget what we have talked about today,' she said. 'And in particular don't say anything about it to Sophie. She chatters too much. Has she told you about the Freedom Society that her husband belongs to?'

For a moment Masha simply stared at Sashette, feeling

hot and cold at once.

'No?' Sashette pursued. 'Perhaps Mark has been discreet after all.'

'What do you know about the Freedom Society?' Masha managed to say.

'So you have heard of it!' Sashette said. 'I hope for your sake that Sergei is not a member. It was one of the few diversions of the autumn. An army officer named Sherwood arrived in Taganrogue bringing a list of names of the principal members of the Freedom Society and a detailed report on their aims and activities. I know all about it because His Majesty discussed it with the empress. It seems that this Sherwood had been a member himself, then became disillusioned and decided…well, let's say it, to betray the others. The emperor said something about despising traitors, no matter how well intentioned. He also said that he had known all about the Freedom Society and was not going to take any action against them. He mentioned the names of a lot of men—Mark Panov among them—and said they were serious young men with noble ideals. But there will be a new emperor now and Grand Duke Nicholas is very different. He does not admit any libertine ideas. Sherwood's disclosures will pass into his hands now. You can imagine what it may mean. Poor Sophie.'

Masha was glad of the concealing dark. 'No, Sophie has never said anything,' she faltered.

'Well, it may come to nothing,' said Sashette, 'and I am sure your Sergei wouldn't be so foolish. At least I am back in civilisation—and back in Ladies-in-waiting Corridor too.'

The two girls kissed each other. As Sashette walked away down the corridor it seemed to Masha that her black dress merged with shadows that were not altogether those of evening.

20

December fourteenth

When Nastia drew aside the curtains next morning, Masha was reminded of the day of the flood. The same sort of ominous sky, with black clouds rolling from every direction, shed the same grey light that made everything look bleak and sad.

Standing in front of her dressing-table, Masha adjusted the folds of her black velvet dress and mourning veil. A solemn mass on the occasion of Nicholas's accession to the throne was to begin at eleven. The immense halls of the Winter Palace were already filled with courtiers and military personnel, all in full uniforms, with medals and ribbons. Ladies in elegant mourning gowns seemed to be dressed for a ball rather than for a church service.

Yet there was a sense of uneasiness in the air. Men talked to each other rapidly and glanced at the windows, ladies, their elaborately-dressed heads close together, whispered and murmured, and from their tense faces one could see that they were not exchanging drawing-room gossip.

As she moved through the salons towards the royal party, Masha learned from snatches of conversation that there was restlessness in the troops. Grand Duke Konstantin was popular among the soldiers and they refused to believe that he had renounced the crown of his own free will.

It was almost time to enter the church, when there was a sudden murmur of excited voices and Masha saw Emperor Nicholas leave the gathering, his back very straight, his step heavy and purposeful.

Everyone was talking now. Newcomers had brought appalling tidings. A rebellion had broken out in the Moscow regiment. Several officers and soldiers had refused to swear allegiance to Nicholas. The rebels left the barracks and were now marching towards Senate Square.

'Mark!' Masha said aloud. 'It is his regiment.' Nobody seemed to hear her. Panic was already reflected in shrill exclamations and startled faces. Alexandra stood very still with clasped hands. The Dowager Empress Maria Feodorovna kept repeating in German, '*Mein Gott. Mein Gott!* It can't be possible.'

A young courtier standing near Masha was saying with an obvious effort to appear unconcerned, 'A trifling incident. Nothing to worry about. A couple of those rascals hanged on the nearest lamp-post...and the revolt will be over.'

Sashette came, threading her way to Masha. Her dark eyes looked enormous in her pinched pale face. 'The insurrection is growing,' she said in a low voice. 'I have just talked to one of the officers of the guard. He said that other regiments are joining in and the civilians too. They are all assembling in Senate Square. He also said,' Sashette put her hand on Masha's arm. 'I am sorry, but...he said that...he noticed your fiancé among the civilians. I thought it better that you know.'

'Sergei? With the rebels?' Masha felt as if the parquet floor under her feet had suddenly moved. For a moment everything around her looked out of focus. She struggled for breath and at last found her voice. To her own surprise, it sounded steady. 'Then I must go to Senate Square and find him,' she said.

Sashette stared at her. 'To Senate Square? What for? You must be out of your mind!'

'I must go,' Masha repeated stubbornly. 'If something

happened to Sergei, this would be our last chance to see each other. I am going. It is only a short way.'

Without paying any heed to Sashette's frantic, 'Wait! You can't go alone!' she brushed past her and out of the door. She reached her room almost running and snatched up a long grey cloak with a hood and lined with fur. It was only a matter of seconds to throw it over her shoulders. She was ready.

The quiet in the streets was reassuring. Instead of armed soldiers advancing on the palace, a thin throng of pedestrians struggled against the wind, obviously preoccupied with their own affairs. A few empty cabs rattled by.

The peace did not last. A group of ragged urchins appeared from behind the corner and tore down the street with whoops and cheers. Masha stopped abruptly. A detachment of soldiers ran past her, headed by a young lieutenant, who was carrying a feathered three-cornered hat on the end of his sword. They shouted 'Long live Konstantin!' and went on running in the direction of Senate Square.

Masha waited until her heart stopped jumping in her breast, gathered her cloak around her and went after them. A rhythmic beating of drums and shouts of 'We want constitution!' became more and more distinct. Senate Square, when she reached it, appeared immense to her frightened eyes. She looked round for shelter and saw a big pile of granite blocks piled on the Neva embankment. They seemed to offer some protection. Slipping on the icy ground, she went over and stood close to the cold stones.

'I mustn't lose my head,' she admonished herself. 'It is no use rushing around. If I just stand here quietly and watch, I am bound to see Sergei or maybe Mark. There are not many people, and I can see well from here.' Huddled in her cloak, she waited, scanning the gathering throng. From her position she could see most of the square.

Uniformed figures were hastily forming in ranks at the foot of the monument to Peter the Great. Masha recognised the uniforms of the Moscow regiment, but even to her inexperienced eye it was evident that this was only part of the regiment.

The motionless ranks of soldiers seemed even quieter in comparison with the agitated crowd that was rapidly approaching from every direction. Masons in working-clothes spattered with plaster, climbed the granite blocks beside Masha. Men and boys sat astride the wooden fence surrounding the half-finished building of St Isaac's Cathedral. Women muffled in shawls fought for a better place to watch. An itinerant merchant set down his load of wicker baskets and climbed a lamp-post to get a good view.

Masha was becoming desperate. It would be impossible to find Sergei among all those people. For a second, she thought she saw Mark's face, but she was not certain. She stood rubbing her cold hands, wondering what to do next, and listening with one ear to the conversations around her.

'They say Konstantin is in prison.'

'Yes, yes, he is, and in chains.'

'In chains! Good heavens! The rightful emperor.'

'Never mind, the soldiers over there will set him free. They will show Nicholas how to take the crown away from his older brother. Look at them! They are ready to fight. And the tails! Just look at the tails! They are armed too.'

It took Masha a few minutes to realise that by 'tails' people meant civilians whose coats ended in tails. Several of them were holding pistols or rifles and stood among the rebels. A strange figure in peasant clothes was darting here and there, waving his hands and talking to the soldiers. Masha thought he resembled the man Riliyev.

At the same moment she caught sight of Mark. This time she was sure and cried desperately, 'Mark!' but he did not hear her, turned, and vanished out of sight. She was just going to call again, when a movement passed across the crowd and Count Miloradovich, the governor, on horseback, came cantering into the square. In full uniform, the blue ribbon of the Order of St Andrew across his chest, he approached the rebels as calmly as if they were lined up for a parade. Holding back his rearing horse, he studied the faces in front of him, and started to speak. His voice carried effortlessly across the square.

'That is enough nonsense! Go back to your barracks. His Highness, the Grand Duke Konstantin is not in prison. He is in Warsaw, free and in good health. He refused the crown of his own free will. You all know how devoted I am to him. This golden sword is his gift.' Miloradovich took the sword from its sheath and flashed it in the air. 'How could you think I would turn against him? Have I ever deceived you? Ask those of your comrades who fought by my side in the days of Marechal Suvorov. They will tell you that you can trust my word.'

A murmur of approval passed across the ranks, but a young lieutenant, Prince Obolenski, stepped out and caught the count's horse by the bridle. 'Please leave the men alone, Excellency,' he shouted.

A pistol-shot cracked. Watching in horror, Masha saw Miloradovich lift his right hand, sway and slide sideways from the saddle. The frightened horse reared and backed.

But it was not Obolenski who had fired. A tall man in a sheepskin jacket stepped back into the ranks, a pistol still smoking in his hand. Masha recognised him immediately. It was that same Kahovski who had once waited for the Emperor Alexander in Peterhoff's park.

Shouts of 'Hurrah for Konstantin!' and 'We want Constitution!' rang out, accompanied by a rapid stutter of the rebels' guns.

They were merely firing in the air, but Masha did not know it and was too terrified to care. Clinging to the granite blocks, she closed her eyes and felt that her knees were giving under her.

'May I be of assistance?' somebody asked. Masha forced herself to turn and saw an elderly gentleman with a silver-topped cane. He stood watching her with growing amazement on his round pink face. 'But…if I am not mistaken…' He peered closer at Masha through his gold-rimmed glasses. 'This is Fraulein Fredericks! Do you remember me?'

'Herr Erhardt!' Masha was almost sobbing with relief. 'Of course I remember you. You taught German in Smolni. I am so glad to see you.'

'The pleasure is all mine,' Herr Erhardt bowed. 'And now, may I escort you from this dangerous place! If I recollect rightly, you are in Her Majesty's service. It will be the Winter Palace then?'

'Yes, I am lady-in-waiting to…' she was about to say, 'the grand duchess Alexandra,' then corrected herself, 'to the Empress Alexandra Feodorovna. But I can't go back. I must find my fiancé, Sergei Davidov. I must talk to him. He is with them, I am sure of it.' She pointed at the rebels.

Herr Erhardt looked sharply at her but seemed unperturbed. 'Davidov? I know him slightly. His brother, Michael, was one of my students in the Cadets' School. I am sure I can find your fiancé for you, Fraulein Fredericks, but I would prefer you to wait in safer quarters. Allow me.' He took Masha's elbow and led her around the edge of the crowd to the Senate building.

It was deserted. 'All the clerks and other personnel were told to go home when the disorders began,' Herr Erhardt explained, 'We shall not be disturbed.' He ushered Masha up the stairs and into a small office on the ;second floor. 'My nephew works in here,' he said, offering her a chair. 'Please rest while I find one of the watchmen and send him to look for Herr Davidov.'

'Thank you,' Masha murmured, sitting down, 'You are

very kind.'

Herr Erhardt's absence was short. 'The man is on his way,' he announced, rubbing his hands with satisfaction. I have described Herr Davidov and he will ask, but it may take time.'

It did take time. Half an hour passed. No one came. Feeling too nervous to remain seated any longer, Masha rose and joined Herr Erhardt who was standing by the window.

She looked out and gave a startled exclamation. In that short while, Senate Square had completely changed. In place of scattered flocks of spectators, the whole place was swarming like a disturbed ants'-nest. People stood on the roofs, clung to rain-pipes, rolled up empty barrels to stand on, mounted on each other's shoulders.

The rebels still occupied the same position at the foot of the monument. 'There are more of them now,' Masha remarked, pressing her face against the glass. 'The Grenadiers have joined too.'

Herr Erhardt's answer was non-committal. 'Yes,' he said, 'and now look over there.' He pointed at the shining armour of the Chevaliers of the Guard lined up by the wooden fence boarding St Isaac's Cathedral. Further on stood the Semeonovski regiment, the part of the Moscow regiment that had remained faithful to Nicholas, and several others whose uniforms were not familiar to Masha. Every exit from Senate Square was blocked by government troops.

'Michael is with *them*,' Masha thought. 'Just as he feared: brother against brother.'

A burst of cheering made her forget Michael. She watched with amazement as a detachment from the Navy passed through the government troops and joined the ranks of rebels.

Masha turned to Herr Erhardt, 'I don't understand it. Why were those men allowed to pass?'

'Because the government is using excellent strategy,' Herr Erhardt took off his glasses, wiped them, and addressed Masha as if he were lecturing in Smolni. 'The emperor knows what he is doing. He wants to make sure who is with him and who is against. Now the situation is clear. Also, it is much easier to have all the rebels here in a mouse-trap instead of fighting them all over the city. See! That is exactly what I mean,' he finished triumphantly as the cavalry appeared and took its place near the Admiralty Boulevard. The rebels were taken in a steel ring.

'But why is there no fighting?' Masha insisted. 'Why are the rebel troops just firing in the air?'

'Why?' There was sadness in the old man's voice. 'I've been teaching in many select schools of St. Petersburg. I know most of these rebel leaders. They are fine young men who want freedom and prosperity for everybody, but they simply do not realise it cannot be done overnight, nor do they understand that liberty given to millions of people without preparation may be dangerous. They are willing to fight for their ideals, but they have no idea how to fight. By this time they could have attacked the Winter Palace, or Peter and Paul fortress, maybe have the city in their hands. Did they do it? No, and they never will. The officers brought their soldiers, but did they bring cannons?' He turned away from the window, and said, shaking his head, 'Static revolution.'

Masha was giving only scant attention to what the old gentleman was saying. Tears of impatience were slowly mounting in her eyes. They had waited for almost an hour. Perhaps the watchman could not find Sergei.

Somewhere in the building a clock struck one and at the same time familiar steps sounded in the corridor outside the office. Masha wanted to cry, 'Sergei!' but instead only a sob came. She reached the door just as he was entering and almost fell into his arms. Herr Erhardt muttered something and discreetly shuffled away.

Masha did not even notice he had gone. She was touching Sergei's face with her hands, murmuring, 'Thank God you are safe.'

'Masha, darling!' Sergei kissed her avidly. 'I knew you would come! I felt it! This is the day of glory and you will see us win! Our dreams are about to come true, dearest. Freedom is almost at the door!' He gave her a playful shake. 'Come, smile! Why this serious face? Aren't you happy for me?'

'Wait, Sergei!' Masha disengaged herself and placing her hands on Sergei's shoulders looked up at him. 'I want to understand something first,' she said. 'Grand Duke Konstantin is safe in Warsaw. You know it. Why were the troops told he is in prison? Why do you want him on the throne? Do you really believe he will grant constitution to Russia?'

'Konstantin on the throne!' Sergei laughed, a young, exuberant, reckless laugh. 'Imagine the narrow-minded, self-indulgent Konstantin signing the constitution charter!'

Taken aback, Masha murmured, 'But the troops...'

Sergei laughed again, 'The troops, the troops! They are merely shouting what we told them to shout. We chose our moment well. The government has been weakened by these days of interregnum. But we couldn't have stirred up a rebellion without a cause, a popular cause. Konstantin served that purpose. Men like him because he was never above telling a joke, or sharing food from the common pot during the campaigns. He is only a pawn. We need to have power in our hands. The troops don't even know what the word 'constitution' means, but they shout it anyway. Oh, our plans are working out perfectly.'

'By "we" and "our" you mean the Freedom Society?' Masha asked.

'Naturally!' Sergei's eyes were shining; his voice had a

triumphant ring in it. 'We can talk about it now. No more dark secrets! From now on there will be only light. A new dawn is rising over Russia…'

Masha repeated, 'A new dawn…'

Sergei frowned, 'You sound so doubtful. Don't you believe me?' Throwing off his long cloak, he put his arm around Masha's waist and drew her to the window. 'Look!' he commanded, pointing down at the ranks of rebels and at the jostling crowd. 'Here they all are, ready to fight and to win. Look at them!'

Masha answered steadily, 'I *am* looking, but I also see the government troops blocking every exit, just as Herr Erhardt said they would. 'Even…' she broke off and shrank away from the window. 'Sergei! The cavalry, they are going to attack!'

Sounds of flying hoofs filled the room. The cavalry with bared swords rushed at the rebel ranks. But the horses slipped on the icy ground and several riders were thrown. The rebels fired in the air and lowered their rifles.

Masha hid her face in Sergei's breast, but he forced her to look again. The cavalry was retreating to its original position. Many of the rebels were helping their opponents back onto their horses.

'You see! You see!' Sergei kept repeating, as though drunk with joy. 'The regular troops can't do anything against us! It is too difficult to attack at a close range on such a slippery ground. Besides, the men themselves are not eager to fight, when it means brother against brother. Just give us time and as soon as it becomes dark, all the regular troops will come over on our side. And if they don't, people from the poor quarters from all over town will join us! Peasants from the nearby villages will arrive. They will be carrying axes and stones instead of rifles, but we will welcome them.' He straightened up, smiling, as if he could already see the crowds coming, 'We are not a group of dreamers talking in the library of Otrada any more; we are a legion!'

Leaning against the window-frame, Masha was silent. Sergei stopped speaking and looked at her. 'You have said nothing, my darling,' he said reproachfully. 'Don't you see that this is the hour of triumph? The triumph of freedom!'

Masha forced herself to speak. 'No,' she said, 'That is where you are wrong. You are still just a group of men talking and dreaming. . . alone. The mob will not share your dreams, at least not in the way you want it. You are teaching them to kill and that is what they will do, and you may be the first victims. Fraternity, equality...they will use these to make *you* their slaves. Sergei, you must realise it. You are stirring up forces that will do nothing but destroy.'

Sergei's face darkened. 'What are you trying to suggest?' he asked slowly, almost threateningly, 'That we surrender?'

Masha cried, 'Oh, no! But you could talk to the government. Surely the emperor realises the situation is serious. You could come to terms, obtain his promise to start reforms.'

'Never!' Sergei looked beside himself with anger. 'We will fight until the last of us gives up his life. Don't you understand?'

Suddenly, the anger got hold of Masha too. 'It is you who don't understand,' she retorted. 'You are talking about a honourable death on the battlefield, and I am thinking about those axes and stones the mob will turn on you, on all of us.'

A fresh roar from the crowd, 'We want constitution! Hurrah for Konstantin!' drowned out Sergei's answer.

Volleys of rifle shots followed. A bullet struck the windowsill and became embedded in it.

Sergei rushed to the window. 'It is a cavalry attack again!' he exclaimed, 'But they are retreating.' He turned away from the window and saw Masha, trembling all over, tears hanging on her eyelashes.

'Masha, dearest!' Sergei was beside her, taking both her hands in his. 'Are you hurt?'

Masha tried to smile. 'No, only frightened. That bullet…'

'Of course you were frightened,' Sergei was tender again, 'This is no place for a woman, I want you to leave.' Awkwardly, he tried to pull Masha's hood over her head. 'Sophie's house is not too far,' he said, 'I will have you escorted there. You can stay with her for a few days and when…when everything is settled, we will get married.'

'You want me to go to Sophie?' Masha was so amazed, she wondered if she had heard aright. 'I can't! I must go back to the palace.'

Sergei answered dryly, 'You are not going back to the palace ever again. Your duty at court is over. You are not committed in any way. At least I don't suppose you took vows like a convent.'

The irony stung. Masha felt her tears dry up. 'I am committed by gratitude if nothing else,' she said firmly. 'And did it ever occur to you that affection and devotion can be more binding than any vows?'

'Gratitude…devotion…what beautiful words,' Sergei's tone was more ironical than before.

'Feelings not words,' Masha corrected him.

He said bitterly, 'Of course, *feelings*. With you, it couldn't be anything else. Very well, there is only one thing I want to know Masha. That evening in Otrada, when I held you close to my heart for the first time, I thought you were with me, with us. Now . . . I don't know any more.'

Masha took a deep breath, 'I didn't know there were sides. I believed that each of you would try to find the best way to liberate the serfs, provide them with land and teach them how best to cultivate it and persuade other landowners to do the same, show the government what could be done. I heard Mark talk about it. I was eager to share your plans, help you all I could. I never knew that you were preparing…bloodshed.'

She drew her cape closer around her. 'I am going back to the palace not because I am taking sides, but because that is where I am needed most. Her Majesty may be in danger and I must be with her.'

'No!' Sergei stood between Masha and the door, 'I will not let you go. There is nothing you can do for Alexandra Feodorovna or for any of them. They are doomed.'

'Doomed?' It seemed to Masha that the word struck her, bounced against the walls and echoed all over the empty building. 'Doomed?' she whispered.

His eyes on his clenched hands, Sergei said heavily, 'I mean it. If we are to have a republic in Russia, and most of us want that form of government, we cannot let the Romanov family live, at least not the male members. Not all our members agree on this, but it is the only way. There will be no peace as long as there is a pretender to the throne.'

Masha stared at him in total disbelief. 'The child?' she exclaimed, 'Young Alexander? You mean you would kill a child?' And lifting her hand as if to protect herself against something terrible, she cried, 'No, don't say anything. I can read the answer on your face.'

The corners of Sergei's mouth tightened. 'Every revolution entails executions. It is the order of things.'

'Executions?' Masha retorted, 'You mean *murder*!'

Sergei answered angrily, 'Yes, if you call destroying a tyrant like Nicholas, murder.'

She said reproachfully, 'Tyrant? At least give him time to become one. He has not been twenty-four hours on the throne.' She took a step forward, 'May I pass please?'

'Not yet,' Sergei stepped back and put his hand on the doorknob. 'You are making your choice now, Masha. If you leave for the palace there will be nothing more between us. We may as well forget each other.'

Masha lifted her eyes to his. Her voice was perfectly steady. 'I have no choice. You have made it for me. When you said "they are doomed", you doomed me too, because I shall die with them.'

They stood silent, facing each other. Sergei spoke first. 'You think that is your last word, don't you? he asked. 'Well, it is not.' Seizing Masha by the shoulders, he pulled her close. His hands bruised her arms; his mouth crushed hers. 'Now,' he whispered passionately, '*Now* dare to say that you want to leave me for ever.'

'Let me go!' Struggling desperately, Masha freed herself and stood pressed against the wall, one hand out to prevent Sergei from coming nearer.

He stood breathing heavily, his eyes glittering and angry. 'You shrink from me as if I were a stranger,' he said. 'Have you no love left?'

She cried back, from the depth of the despair that was filling her heart, 'I don't know. How could I? You are right, we are strangers to each other. Today is the first time we have really met.'

Sergei said softly, 'I see. It is all over then,' and she wondered whether it was her imagination that his face suddenly looked thinner and older.

Somewhere underneath them, a door banged, light steps ran up the stairway and two young voices shouted together, 'Sergei! Sergei Davidov! Where are you?'

Sergei said rapidly, 'My friends are looking for me. I must go. Masha, for the last time, have you made your decision?'

She bowed her head. 'Yes. Good-bye, Sergei.'

'Good-bye, Masha.' Very formal and cold, he took her hand, kissed it lightly and let it drop. 'Are you sure Herr Erhardt will escort you?'

She nodded and whispered, 'May God keep you safe.'

Sergei said, 'I am surprised it matters to you.'

The next moment he was gone. She heard him call out, 'I am here.' Voices answered; footsteps echoed through the corridors.

Masha stood rigid, listening. When the last sound of the footsteps died away, and the silence came, she flung herself on the floor, sobbing in agony and biting her hands to retain the anguished, 'Sergei, come back!'

At last she pulled herself up, tears streaming down her face, and stumbled to the window.

There was no sight of Sergei, only the crowd, thicker than ever, swarming everywhere.

21

In Senate Square

Herr Erhardt returned a few minutes later. He did not ask about Sergei. After a keen glance at Masha, he suggested that she step into another office where she could be more comfortable.

But Masha was not even listening. In a frenzied hurry, shaking all over, she kept repeating, 'Please take me back to the Winter Palace, Herr Erhardt. Please. I have been absent too long already.'

The old gentleman looked somewhat perplexed. 'Fraulein Fredericks, it is dangerous outside. The artillery may open fire any minute.'

'Artillery?' Masha could not believe her ears, 'Would the emperor use cannons on men who have nothing but rifles and pistols? Oh, no, he will never do that.'

Herr Erhardt answered gravely, 'My child, he has his empire to save.'

Masha's pale face became even paler. 'I must return anyway,' she murmured. 'Don't worry about me, Herr Erhardt. The palace is so close, I can go alone.'

'Fraulein Fredericks! I could never let you do such a thing!' Herr Erhardt protested, shocked. 'I only tried to warn you, but if you really must return, I am at your service.' He put on his top hat and took his cane. 'Now, if you are ready, we can start,' he said, holding the door open for Masha.

At the foot of the stairway, he cautioned her, 'Hold on to my arm, please. The crowd is very dense and agitated. We could easily become separated

Masha found Herr Erhardt was right, as soon as they stepped out of the building. Senate Square was filled to overflowing. Still, the first few steps were not too difficult. Herr Erhardt pushed on steadily, doing his best to protect Masha from the milling mob. People grumbled, but let them pass.

A burst of shouting came so unexpectedly, Masha started and let go Herr Erhardt's arm. There was a rumble of wheels and everybody began to run. Pushed from all sides, Masha gasped for breath and tried to grasp Herr Erhardt's sleeve. It was no use. He was already too far from her. A large man, smelling of fish, stepped on the hem of her cloak, making her stagger and almost lose her footing. She regained her balance somehow, just in time to see Herr Erhardt's agitated face bobbing in the distance, his glasses askew. She cried, 'Here! I am here!' but he was already gone.

The crowd began to press forward again. 'There must be something they all want to see,' Masha thought dazedly as she was forced on, her feet hardly touching the ground.

A sharp command, 'Stop! Don't come any closer,' made her realise that the rebels' picket-line was near. The crowd stepped back and Masha saw an old-fashioned coach with large plate-glass windows and very high gilded wheels. An elderly man in clerical robes, his white hair touching his shoulders, was climbing out. Masha knew him. It was Archbishop Seraphim, who that very morning had been supposed to officiate at the solemn mass in the Winter Palace.

Holding a big golden cross in his hand, the archbishop resolutely marched towards the rebel troops. Immediately, every rifle was lowered and every head bared.

Wedged in the crowd, Masha found herself almost in the front rank. In spite of her discomfort, she noticed that one of the rebels, a young man in working overalls under his shabby quilted jacket, a rifle over his shoulder, kept staring at her from under his battered grey cap.

His face looked familiar to Masha, but she had no time to give it much attention. The archbishop was speaking. His elderly voice was weak and Masha could only catch separate words, 'Lay down your arms…I swear to you…His Majesty …every right to the throne…Listen…'

The rebels' faces remained stony, but there were angry murmurs in the mob. 'Don't try to deceive us!' someone cried, and was followed by several voices shouting, 'Shame on you!' Men near Masha clenched their fists and lurched forward. The archbishop's voice was drowned out and he hastily retreated to the coach which moved away, followed by a shower of stones. At the same time, Masha noticed a rift in the crowd and moved towards it, hoping to get out of the square. But there was no time. A volley of rifle shots made the mob run back, engulfing her again. She was swept along, crying helplessly, 'Let me go! Please…I can't…'

As the mob halted she realised that she had been carried close to the fence by the cathedral where the regular troops were standing. A rider on a white horse, in green uniform, was silhouetted clearly against the grey planks. It was the Emperor Nicholas himself. His face was white under the black three-cornered hat. His hands tugged nervously at the horse's bridle. Yet, even as she watched she saw him leave the protection offered by the corner of the fence and emerge into the square. Bricks and stones flew through the air; the generals of his suite rushed after him, gesturing and pleading with him to think of his safety. He brushed them aside and tried to speak to the mob. Some people took off their hats and seemed to listen, others shouted insults.

The chimes on the Admiralty building struck three. The wind had become colder and a light snow started to fall. Masha felt as if she were in the grip of some terrifying nightmare. Pressed close around her, as far as she could see, was the dark mass of the mob, and beyond them the closed ranks of the regular troops. Somewhere in the fast-gathering dusk Sergei was standing too—among the rebels. He had said that the government troops would go over to the rebels as soon as the night came. It was dark enough now, but the troops did not move. Michael would be in Senate Square too. Whatever happened, *he* would never go over, not even for his brother's sake.

The thought of Michael always so calm and trustworthy gave courage to Masha. Giving a quick glance around, she selected a spot where the crowd seemed thinner and tried to push her way through. She succeeded in making a few steps and was trying to push further, when a broad-shouldered young sailor caught her by the waist. 'What's your hurry, my beauty? Better come with me,' he mumbled, his drunken breath close to Masha's face.

Gathering all her strength, Masha thrust the man away, and turned blindly back into the thick of the crowd, her heart pounding, her legs shaking.

She could not get away, but at least she had escaped the man and he could not distinguish her in the crowd where she now stood.

Breathing heavily, Masha tried to pray, but could only whisper through chattering teeth, 'God, help me. Please, help me.'

She noticed that a change had come over the crowd. Round the edge were gathering ragged tramps, drunks from nearby taverns, strange men with faces hidden in their collars: the dregs of the city hoping for plunder.

A quiver of fright ran through her. She rubbed her freezing hands and pulled the hood further down her face. She realised that it would be madness to try and escape now. Her safety lay in staying with the crowd.

Staring into the darkness, she thought how different everything looked. Even the familiar buildings looked strange and somehow menacing. She could not imagine this was the St. Petersburg she knew, of Smolni Institute, Anichkov Palace, the shabby house with the sign *Furnished rooms of Widow Iziumova*, where she had stayed on her very first day in the city.

Now why had she thought of the furnished rooms of Widow Iziumova? The answer came quickly and unexpectedly: the young rebel in the battered grey cap was Mitia! Masha forgot the dark Senate Square. She was remembering herself, a small girl in a quaint home-made dress, talking to a boy only a little older than herself. The boy had a pair of enormous boots under his arm and his face was smudged with shoe-blacking. She had met him again, years later, a young apprentice who had helped her and Sophie when they were lost at the Easter Bazaar. He must have recognised her. Maybe he could have found Sergei for her. But it was no use finding Sergei. He said that everything was finished…that she had made her choice…

A sudden tremor passed through the crowd. At first she could not understand what everyone was saying. Then, all too clearly, she heard, 'The cannons! The cannons!'

Four cannons had been rolled up and directed at the Senate. The generals were gathered around the emperor. The mob pushed and swayed. Masha could see General Toll bend over from his saddle and say something to the emperor, pointing at the rebels and then in the direction of the Winter Palace. She saw General Benkendorf gallop off. He returned about ten minutes later, calling out that the ammunition for the cannons was on its way.

Soon, the command, 'Load!' rang across the Senate Square.

Around Masha, the crowd buzzed. Everyone was wondering why the rebels continued to stand still instead of attacking the regular troops. Stones rattled against the fence. The rebels began to shout, 'We want constitution!' and drums began to beat. But the sound was not loud enough to drown out the command, 'Fire!'

The emperor's hoarse 'Dismiss' came almost simultaneously.

Three more times the command to fire came and three times it was dismissed. The cannons loomed in the darkness, ready to destroy. The fourth time, the salvo boomed, but the cannon-balls flew high, well above the heads of the crowd.

Instinctively, Masha ducked. The next moment, another salvo came. This time, it swept the square low and hit the very midst of the mob. There was a strange silence. People fell without uttering a sound. Fire at such a close range left no time for the victims to scream.

The next salvo followed closely and with a deadly aim. Agonised shrieks rose in the air, accompanied by moans and sounds of running feet.

The fourth salvo hit the Senate, tearing metal sheets off the roof and ripping holes in the walls. Tongues of flame shot through the broken windows and acrid smoke drifted over the square. In the glare of the fire, Masha saw the rank of rebels still standing, black against the snow. She screamed 'Sergei!' and began to run when something sharp and burning hit her left shoulder. She fell on her knees, struggled to get up and fell again. The stampeding mob trampled her underfoot.

The cannon fire pursued the fleeing crowd down the side streets. Fugitives knocked frantically at the locked doors of the nearby houses only to collapse dead before the inhabitants had time to open. The rebel troops retreated towards Neva and tried to form ranks on the frozen surface. But the cannon-balls broke the ice and many victims went down into the dark waters.

A red fog in front of her eyes, Masha crawled under the steady rain of fire. The pain in her shoulder was becoming unbearable, her last reserves of strength were giving out. She tried to get on her feet as another salvo boomed, but someone grasped her around the waist, pulling her down. The screams around her grew faint and the darkness became complete.

22

Afterwards

Masha whispered, 'Please take that light away,' and shielded her eyes. To her amazement she heard Michael's voice. 'Are you feeling better?' it said and added anxiously, 'No, don't move.'

'Michael?' Dimly, Masha could make out dark arches above her. 'Where are we? How did you find me?'

Now she could see Michael's face in the lantern-light. He was kneeling beside her. 'We are under the portals of somebody's house,' he said. 'The owners must be away. I knocked but no one answered. Two of my men came running to me about an hour ago, shouting that a lady was lying dead near the cathedral. It turned out to be you. Thank God you were alive, only grazed by a shell. I made a bandage of my handkerchief and carried you here. This house is just around the corner from Senate Square. It seemed the best thing to do.'

Memory was slowly coming back to Masha. The cannon-balls-flying, the screams, the darkness… 'Is it over then?' she asked. 'I don't remember. The cannons opened fire and I was crawling…on the ground, trying to hide…' She rubbed her forehead and let her hand fall.

Michael nodded. 'Everything is over. The rebels resisted to the last minute. Of course, they had no chance.'

The light flickered on the arches behind his head. Surely, if something had happened to Sergei he would have…said. 'Is it very late?' she asked.

As if in answer, the Admiralty chimes struck seven.

Michael stood up. 'Do you think you can walk?' he asked. 'There are no carriages. The town is in a state of siege. But you must get back to the palace somehow.'

'I am sure I can walk,' Masha assured him. 'There is really nothing wrong with me except my shoulder. At least I don't think so,' she whispered fearfully. Her eyes were becoming used to the light and she saw that her cloak was dark with blood.

Michael said quickly, 'Most of that blood is not yours. A young rebel's body was lying almost on top of you. That is what may have saved your life. It looked as if he were shielding you. Do you remember anything about it.'

'Someone pulled me down when the salvo came. I...I think I know... Oh, Michael, yes, yes, I must get back to the palace.' She sat up and a wave of giddiness and nausea swept over her, then mercifully ebbed away.

'Lean on me.' Michael bent over Masha and began to lift her, but she flinched from his gentle touch.

'Wait! Michael, I must tell you something first. It is about Sergei. We are not going to be married. We... He wanted me to...'

Michael interrupted her. 'Masha,' he said gravely, 'whatever happened between you and Sergei, I know that from where he is now, he knows all and forgives all, if there was anything to forgive.'

For a moment she stared at him, her eyes enormous. 'Sergei...' she said painfully. 'Sergei...'

Michael bent his head. 'He was killed in Senate Square.'

Staring over Michael's shoulder, Masha saw the flame of the lantern grow higher and higher, become giant, lick the stone arches of the portals, then become a flickering light again. The grey flagstones swayed.

Michael said gently, 'If you cried, it would be easier.'

'I...I can't.' Masha's voice sounded as if she was speaking in her sleep. She shuddered. 'Please take me away from here.'

They walked slowly, stopping every few minutes to let Masha rest. Michael wanted to avoid the Senate Square, but Masha insisted they pass through it. 'I want to see the place where you found me,' she said.

St. Petersburg did look like a besieged city. Big fires burnt on street corners. Soldiers gathered around them, stamping their feet and holding their hands to the blaze. Horses were tied to the lamp-posts. The ground was littered with straw and manure. Mounted policemen patrolled the streets. In the darkness, the gleam of lanterns came and went. From the opposite end of the square came a sound of spades scraping against the cobblestones.

Michael said, 'Order has been given to remove all traces of blood and cover the places with clean snow. Don't look,' he added as several sleighs loaded with dead bodies passed them.

Masha did not seem to hear him. She was looking at the fence by the cathedral. 'That is the place, isn't it?' she asked. 'I seem to remember touching the planks just before… everything went blank.'

Michael stopped. 'Yes, that is where we found you. He peered at something dark, barely visible in the faint glow of the street lamp. 'No, don't come near. The body of that man is still there.'

'The man who…who saved me?'

Michael nodded and made as if to move on, but Masha stood firm.

'I must see him. I must know, if I can, who he is.'

Michael sighed 'Very well, if you wish it.'

The man was lying on his back, his rifle still over his shoulder. Even in the dim light, Masha could see that it was indeed Mitia, met so long ago. She stood quietly, looking at the dead face.

Michael asked, 'Is it someone you know?'

Masha whispered 'Yes,' and tried to cross herself, winced with pain and stopped. Michael said, 'I will do it for you.' He reverently made a sign of the cross, then gently urged her on across the new-strewn snow. He could feel her trembling.

They found Winter Palace surrounded by a double line of artillery, every entrance guarded, but luckily one of the sentries recognised Masha and let her pass. When she had vanished safely within the massive portals, reluctantly but resolutely Michael turned back to the stricken city.

Inside, the palace was ablaze with lights and filled with people. A solemn mass of thanksgiving for the crushing of the rebellion was about to start.

Using back passages, Masha managed to reach her room unobserved. Faint and breathless, she sat down heavily on her bed and closed her eyes. Her shoulder throbbed and burned, but the pain in her heart was almost unendurable.

Slowly, the dizziness ebbed. She forced her heavy eye lids open and glanced around. Nastia must have been in the room recently for a candle was burning in a sconce on the wall and the curtains were drawn.

Setting her teeth, she stood up and untied her cape, then sat down again, almost crying with pain.

There was a light step behind the door and she thought with relief, 'Nastia!' But instead Sashette's voice called, 'Masha, are you in?'

Masha managed a feeble 'Yes,' and moved a little so that she was half-hidden by the bed-curtain.

Sashette entered and looked with surprise at Masha's huddled figure. 'When did you get back?' she asked. 'I've been here over and over to see if you had returned. Her Majesty is most anxious about you. I told her that you were undoubtedly with Sophie for I was sure you wouldn't really go near the rebels. That is where you have been, isn't it? There is no need for you to worry about Sergei; most of the victims were among the mob.'

Masha made a movement with her head and hoped that Sashette would accept it as a nod of acquiescence.

Without paying attention to Masha's silence, Sashette chattered on. 'Did you see any of it? Wasn't it frightening? We watched through that bow-window in the small boudoir from which one can see part of Senate Square. Empress Maria Feodorovna kept running around, lamenting in German, but your empress kept very quiet, only praying. When the cannons began to fire, she fell on her knees and stayed that way until it was all over. The fright must have affected her though, because... Well, you will see for yourself. But you must hurry. The service begins any minute now.'

Masha said shakily, 'I...I can't go. I'm too tired.'

'You must go. Empress Alexandra has been asking for you,' Sashette insisted. 'I will call Nastia and tell her to bring you something hot to drink. I must hurry and...' She stopped abruptly and stared at Masha's cloak lying on the floor. 'Why, it's covered with blood!' she exclaimed. 'You *were* there after all.' She came closer to Masha and gasped, 'It is you who is bleeding! Your shoulder...'

Masha got out, 'It is nothing, just a scratch,' but as Sashette touched her shoulder a whirling roaring blackness came out of nowhere and engulfed her utterly.

What Masha remembered most strikingly of the week that followed was the design on her room's ceiling. Sometimes she lay for hours, looking at the fat pink cupids throwing long blue ribbons to each other. It was restful to trace the ribbons through the intricate design of fruit and flowers. At other times nightmares and fantasies possessed her as the fever came and went. Only in a lucid moment she was aware of Alexandra standing beside her bed. From the expression in her eyes and from the way she said, 'My poor child,' Masha understood that the empress knew that Sergei was dead.

Alexandra herself seemed changed. Small bitter lines had appeared at the corners of her mouth and the beautiful blonde head was constantly shaking in a slight nervous tremor that was to remain for life, but at the time Masha was only aware of the current of love and sympathy that flowed from her beloved friend.

'She has suffered too,' Masha thought in her delirium, 'for the man she loves. She knows what it means.'

The empress did not come to see her again, but as the fever passed events began to catch up with Masha. Nastia was first with a gruesome story of how the chief of St. Petersburg police, anxious to obliterate every trace of the revolt, had ordered the bodies to be thrown through ice holes into Neva. 'They threw the wounded in with the dead,' Nastia whispered. 'His Majesty heard about it and the man was discharged, but what is done is done.'

The other ladies-in-waiting started to visit Masha. None of them mentioned Sergei's name, but they could not resist talking about the rebellion. It was so terrible! Carriages were ready to take the two empresses and the rest of the imperial family to Pavlovsk, in case the palace was attacked. Little Alexander did not realise the danger and was painting pictures while the cannons boomed. Such a sweet child! And the poor empress… Oh, dear! Oh, dear!

Masha answered 'Certainly,' and 'Yes, terrible,' sinking into her pillows. The only visitor she longed to see never came. She knew from Nastia that Mark was not among the victims of December fourteenth. Why then did Sophie not even write?

'I sent Sophie a note two days ago,' she told Sashette, who was sitting by her bed one morning, reading aloud a long letter from Herr Erhardt. 'She's never answered it. Do you suppose there is something wrong?'

Sashette appeared not to hear Masha's question, and

went on reading the four long pages in which Herr Erhardt apologised for having lost Masha in the Senate Square. He was knocked down, he explained, and broke his ankle. It took him hours to crawl home almost on all fours and he collapsed on his doorstep.

'Poor man,' Sashette said, putting the letter down. 'Do you remember how we used to tease him in Smolni?'

'I was talking about Sophie,' Masha interrupted her sharply. 'Why are you silent? What is the matter? Is Sophie ill?'

'Sophie is quite well,' said Sashette.

'And Mark?'

There was a brief silence and then Sashette said, 'Mark was wounded.'

'Wounded?' Masha exclaimed, 'Dangerously?'

'No. It is just a slight wound in the leg. It might have been better if he had been wounded more seriously.'

'What do you mean?'

Sashette lowered her voice. 'Her Majesty doesn't wish you to talk about it and maybe get upset, but you might as well know. All the members of the Freedom Society have been arrested. However, the wounded ones are not disturbed…yet.'

Masha sat up in bed. 'Who are they?'

'Goodness, at least half of the men we used to dance with, and many others as well,' Sashette clearly relished telling Masha the important news. 'Princess Volkonska is beside herself. Her son, General Volkonski has been arrested. I believe you know his wife.'

'Marie Volkonska!' Masha stared at Sashette. 'She has only just had a baby!'

'I saw prisoners brought to the palace for interrogation,' Sashette went on. 'They looked terrible. Haggard faces, no swords, soiled uniforms.'

'I must go to Sophie. Immediately!' Masha pushed back

the bedclothes. 'Will you fetch Nastia? I don't care what the doctor said. You should have told me before, Sashette. No wonder Sophie could not come. She can't leave Mark.'

'I'm not sure I'd go, if I was in your place,' Sashette said slowly. 'After all, you are…still sick.'

Masha noticed the slight pause, but chose to ignore it. Sophie was in trouble and she must go to her at once.

23

Smolni again

It was not easy to get away. The doctor had forbidden Masha to so much as leave her room, but with Nastia as accomplice, she managed it. She did not dare to ask for a palace carriage. Sitting in a hired cab, she winced every time the wheels hit a large cobblestone.

The day was clear and frosty. The streets were swept clean of snow, but the ledges and roofs were piled high and glistened in the mid-day sun. A police wagon with lowered window curtains rattled by. Masha realised there were prisoners inside and clasped her cold hands inside her muff.

Sophie's house was reached at last. 'Don't announce me,' Masha told the footman and ran up the stairway.

Sophie was in her bedroom, sitting at her dressing-table and rummaging in the drawers. Masha had never seen her friend look so pale; every feature was set in hard lines. Instead of the usual fashionable hairstyle, Sophie's bright hair was swept back and fell in waves on the white peignoir. At the sound of Masha's step, Sophie looked up and gave her a long cold stare. 'You are too late,' she said drily, 'Mark was arrested last night.'

Masha caught at the door jamb to steady herself. 'Arrested? But he was wounded and Sashette told me…'

'He was up these last two days,' Sophie interrupted bitterly, 'so he was considered well enough to be put in prison.'

'Oh, Sophie!' Masha made a movement to come closer, but Sophie stopped her with a sharp, 'No. Don't bother to come any further. Haven't I already told you that you are too late? There is nothing for you to do here.'

Masha murmured helplessly, 'I don't understand.'

'Don't you?' Sophie's voice was very low and Masha knew that this was a signal of coming anger. 'I can see through your plan, no matter how innocent you pretend to be. The government is trying to obtain the names of everyone even remotely connected with the Freedom Society; they want to know every detail of the conspiracy. They are using any method to obtain this information…promises, bribery, lies. So why not friendship? I must admit that the idea is clever. Mark would have been too honest, too upright to have guessed that you had come to get a few facts out of him.'

'But it is not true!' Masha cried wildly. 'I only came because you are my dearest friend. I also wanted to ask Mark if he had seen Sergei at…at the last hour. If there was anything he could tell me about…'

Sophie's cheeks flamed. 'About Sergei? How dare you even mention his name! Yes, Mark did see Sergei at the last hour. Sergei fell almost at his side.' Sophie stopped for a second then went on, stressing every word, 'But there was enough time for Sergei to tell Mark how you abandoned him just when he needed you the most.'

Masha stared at her friend, her face chalk-white, her lips dry.

'I had no choice. He was asking me to do something that was not right.'

'What was right for Sergei, was right for you,' Sophie clasped her hands and took a deep breath. 'If you loved Sergei as I love Mark, you would have been at his side.'

Masha bent her head under the onslaught, then again raised her eyes at Sophie. 'No,' she whispered, 'I couldn't do it. Your Aunt Daria was right. I ask more from love than you do.'

Sophie replied with scorn, 'And so you chose to remain faithful to Emperor Nicholas. In other words, you never really loved Sergei, or your career at court would not have been important to you than being his wife.'

'That is not true! Sophie, please stop! You have no idea how much you hurt.'

But Sophie did not relent. Getting up, she approached Masha and looked her full in the eyes. 'Oh, it hurts? But you did not care when your precious Emperor Nicholas was shooting people down with cannon-balls? All that blood meant nothing to you?'

'But they were going to kill him!' Masha exclaimed. 'What was the emperor supposed to do? Give up his life and his empire and the life of his little boy without even trying to save them?'

Sophie did not answer. She paced the room, picking up books and knick-knacks, looking at them with unseeing eyes and putting them down again. 'And now Nicholas is to be the supreme judge,' she said bitterly. 'Sergei has escaped into death, but Mark and the others are in his power. He can and will destroy them as easily as that!' She snatched a perfume bottle from the tray with the three golden monkeys and hurled it on the floor where it splintered into a thousand shards. Tinkling music filled the room.

Masha turned and fled. She ran blindly down the stairs, stumbling on her skirt, her eyes blurred with tears. The music seemed to chase her; it grew louder and louder, became the beating of drums in the Senate Square. Trembling, she collapsed on the cab seat and covered her face with her hands.

Several minutes passed before she became aware of a voice persistently asking something. Looking up, she saw the driver who wanted to know where to take her.

The answer came of itself. 'To the Smolni Institute.'

It was a long way, but at last the familiar white-pillared

portico came in sight. Masha paid the driver and got out of the cab. The uniformed doorman recognised her and greeted her with a wide smile. Old girls frequently visited the headmistress, so he did not ask any questions. Glancing over her shoulder, Masha saw his smile change into a surprised stare as he watched her turn in the opposite direction from Madame Adlerberg's apartments.

The long corridors were empty. From behind closed doors came the sounds of voices reciting the multiplication table, or stumbling over irregular French verbs. Somewhere, unsure fingers were playing scales to the sharp tic-tac of a metronome. It smelled of floor-polish, blackboard dusters and green soap.

A few pupils passed her and curtsied. All were wearing black aprons in mourning for the Emperor Alexander.

Another corridor, a glass door and Masha stepped into the garden.

Only the wide central avenue lined with century-old trees was cleared of snow and sanded. Masha followed it for a short way, then turned into a side path and headed For the clump of lilac bushes. The snow was deeper than she expected. She found herself ploughing heavily through the drifts. The bottom of her skirt was all wet. Unheeding, she pushed on. A flock of crows fighting over a crust of bread flew off at her approach and croaking hoarsely settled on the top of a statue. Masha started, caught her foot in the edging of a flower bed, invisible under the snow, and fell on her hands and knees. An agonising pain wrenched her shoulder. But it did not matter, she had almost reached her goal. If only the snow were not so deep. It was over her knees now.

Stumbling, picking herself up and falling again, Masha emerged at last on the well-remembered round lawn. The birch tree stood there, waiting, its bare branches loaded with snow, the black on the trunk sharply outlined against the dazzling whiteness of the snow banks. There was nothing to hinder Masha as she rushed forward with a low moan.

The cold bark felt warm as she laid her cheek against it. 'I came to tell you everything because you understand,' she began, and could not go on. Slipping on her knees, she crouched on the ground, sobbing, 'Sergei! Sergei! He said that I deserted him, but I had to do it, I *had* to. *You* will believe me. I know you will.'

All the anguish in her heart seemed to spill over in dreadful racking sobs, but by degrees her tears flowed easier, soothing, relieving.

A shadow fell on the snow. Masha raised her head. Sophie was standing beside her, a shawl thrown over her head, her fur jacket unbuttoned.

'I drove after you,' she said. 'I wanted to ask you to forgive me. When I saw that you were heading to Smolni, I knew exactly where to find you.' She swallowed hard and went on, 'If you could only realise how jealous I used to be of that tree sometimes. But it has proved to be your real friend after all. It is here, faithful and true, while I failed you.'

Still on her knees, Masha managed to sob out, 'It is not your fault. You only repeated Sergei's words.'

'Listen to me,' Sophie knelt beside Masha. 'Sergei never said you *deserted* him. His exact words were, "I *lost* her when I needed her the most," and Mark could see that Sergei admired you for living up to your ideals. I was miserable, angry, I wanted to hurt you or anyone who came from the palace. Masha, I am so sorry. Do you believe me? Can you forgive me?'

Masha breathed, 'Oh, I do. I do,' and the two girls held to each other tightly. Her cheek against Sophie's, Masha could feel her friend's tears mingling with her own.

In the Smolni building a bell rang announcing midmorning break, and soon, muffled-up figures, big and small, began to stream out of the doors to pace the central avenue, chattering and laughing.

24

By Peter and Paul Fortress

It was February when the body of the Emperor Alexander arrived in St. Petersburg. Thousands of his subjects came to say good-bye, filing in a steady stream past the closed casket.

All the same, strange rumours continued to circulate. The emperor was not dead. The casket was empty. He was wandering all over Russia, dressed like a peasant. People swore he had been recognised in a church, in a roadside inn, in a group of pilgrims walking to a faraway shrine. Police seized those who talked too much. When questioned, they denied everything, were released and talked again, only this time in whispers. 'The mystery of Alexander I' was slowly becoming part of history.

The Empress Elizaveta never returned. On the way back from Taganrogue, her health took a sudden turn for the worse and she died in the small town of Belev.

Immediately more rumours sprang up. The empress was not dead. She was a nun in a monastery somewhere in the north. She was fulfilling a promise made to her husband to die to the world, just as he did.

Masha was often tempted to ask Alexandra Feodorovna if there was any truth in these steadily-growing legends, but never gathered enough courage. The new empress had troubles enough.

Sashette was married at last and away on her wedding trip. Masha had acted as a bridesmaid, trying to ignore the gnawing, aching emptiness of her own heart, and her growing loneliness. She thought she would never forget the sarcastic note in Sashette's voice as she said just before leaving for church, 'So much ado for a business contract,' glancing down at her long white satin gown, all trimmed with old lace, the gift of the dowager empress.

Michael was in St. Petersburg, but Masha had seen him only once. It happened one afternoon, when she had come to visit Sophie and, finding her out, had settled down in the drawing-room to wait for her. When Michael suddenly walked in, Masha became so embarrassed, without really knowing why, that she could barely murmur a greeting. He looked ill at ease too. They tried to talk about Sophie, about Mark's fate, but the silences between each sentence became longer and longer. Masha was just wondering if she shouldn't leave, when Michael rose and, coming over, stood with one hand on the back of her chair. She looked up and met his eyes, blue and honest and anxious.

'Masha,' he said awkwardly, 'there is something I want you to know. During that night in the Senate Square, I wished many times, and I still wish, that I could change places with Sergei, so that I would be lying dead and he could be back with you.'

Bowing her head, Masha listened. She opened her lips to speak, but could not say a word, stunned by the storm of protest that was welling in her heart. Bewildered, she thought, 'But...I did not feel like that about Sergei.' Again she tried to speak, cry 'No, no!' but instead of words tears came. At the same moment, Sophie arrived.

Masha quickly dried her eyes, so that Sophie would not ask questions. A few minutes later, Michael left. He said good-bye to Masha in a strange abrupt way, as if he was anxious to get out of her sight.

She had not seen him since that day. She thought of asking Sophie: 'Is Michael avoiding me?' but all Sophie's thoughts were with Mark, in the Peter and Paul fortress with the rest of the rebels.

Lonely in the stately corridors of the Winter Palace, homesick for her cosy room in Anichkov, Masha brooded, read Sergei's old letters, looked at the pencilled notes on the margins of the books he gave her. Every night she dreamed she was in his arms, only to wake up in the morning and discover that his image had become a little paler in her remembrance. In spite of herself, she was beginning to realise that she was only trying to preserve a memory of love, while love itself ended in that small room in the Senate building. She could pity the man who had walked down the stairway into the Senate Square to meet his death, she could even grieve for him, but pity and grief were not love.

In those heart-breaking days, only the empress's silent compassion helped Masha not to give in to utter despair. She felt deeply grateful, especially as she knew that those were difficult times for Alexandra too. The new empress was constantly besieged by relatives of the rebels, pleading with her to intercede with the emperor on behalf of their loved ones. Alexandra read the long petitions, granted audiences and often talked to her husband in his study, the doors closed. But she always came out with lowered eyes, her face pale, and disappeared in her rooms. Her pleadings were in vain.

Knowing the Emperor Nicholas, Masha was not surprised. He had insisted on interrogating the rebels himself, sometimes patient and tolerant, sometimes harsh and violent. 'How can they understand each other?' Masha thought. 'He considers that every man's sacred duty is to obey his monarch and the laws of his country. They were ready to gamble their country to give it new life.' With a shudder, she remembered the mob in Senate Square, ready to destroy and murder. The gamble had been great… 'I don't know who is right,' she murmured.

Meanwhile, the 'Decembrists' trial' was getting closer and closer. The name was becoming almost official and the revolt was now called 'the Decembrists' rebellion.'

'And I have a new name too,' Sophie said bitterly, 'Decembrist's wife.' I am getting so accustomed to it, I will be soon signing my letters that way. Oh, Masha! I am so anxious. So many judges have been appointed. It is to be a court without mercy! There may be a death sentence for many of them.'

Masha sighed without answering. The aims of the Freedom Society were no longer a secret to anyone. Its members did have the highest ideals. Most of them rich and well-born, enjoying all the privileges of their class, they had been ready to renounce everything in order to secure equal rights for everybody, freedom of the press, liberty for serfs.

Arrest and the accusation of treason made many of them lose their nerve and make full confession, naming even those members of the Society who did not actually take part in the revolt. Several, however, refused to talk. Mark was one of them.

'They will make him pay for his silence,' Sophie said, restlessly pacing the floor of her boudoir. 'Oh, Masha. I am so frightened.'

'Don't,' Masha pleaded, 'Have hope. At least Mark is alive.'

'Alive?' Sophie shook her head. 'I wonder... When I look at the Peter and Paul fortress, it seems so dark and sinister, I simply don't know how anyone can be in those dungeons and live.'

Masha understood what Sophie meant. She found she too was avoiding the palace windows from which the black silhouette of the fortress could be seen.

Finally permission was given to the wives of the prisoners to visit their husbands once a week. Sophie asked Masha to come with her. 'You will not have long to wait,' she said, 'They will only allow us fifteen minutes.'

But it had seemed longer to Masha, as she sat in the

bare-walled waiting-room, sentries at the door and a greyish February sky behind the narrow windows. It seemed an eternity of anxiety and dread before Sophie reappeared. She was walking blindly, as if feeling her way. 'I am ready,' she told Masha. 'We can go.'

Frightened by her friend's deathly pale face, Masha took her arm. She could feel Sophie shaking uncontrollably and at the door she stumbled and had to be helped over the threshold. But she did not speak again until they were seated in the carriage and silence was becoming unbearable.

'How…how was Mark?' Masha faltered.

'He…was…well,' Sophie spoke with difficulty. 'Thinner. His clothes are so grey and baggy, he looks strange in them. But he said there was enough to eat, hot tea too, and that is important, the dungeons are so damp. He…' Suddenly, her mouth twisted and tears started to rain down. 'Masha, he is chained! I did not notice at first, but then I heard something clang. I looked down and saw chains on his feet. They were clanging.' She hid her face in Masha's shoulder, repeating, 'The chains were clanging.'

Masha tenderly caressed the bronze curls, tears welling to her own eyes. The carriage swayed, rain beat against the windows. Between sobs, Sophie choked out, 'We are going away from those we love, from happiness, from everything that made up our lives, going away with no coming back.'

Rocking Sophie as though she were a child, Masha forced herself to answer briskly, 'You mustn't talk like that. Mark may be set free. Let's keep hoping.'

But as days went by, it became more and more difficult not to lose hope. Accusations against the Decembrists were steadily growing. Their plan of killing the emperor was discovered and the word 'regicide' cast its dark shadow over the rebels.

Alexandra gave Masha permission to spend as much time with Sophie as she wanted. They went to the fortress every day. The prisoners were only allowed their one weekly visitor, but sometimes it was possible to catch sight of Mark being walked with the other Decembrist prisoners in a small fortress garden. Sophie found out from one of the sentries which of the narrow cell windows was Mark's and determined to send him a message. 'Dare I try to look in?' she whispered to Masha.

'Better not,' Masha cautioned. 'The sentries are watching you.'

'Then I have another plan.' Sophie bent down and started to fumble with her shoe-ribbons. 'Go on for a few steps, then turn around and call me,' she ordered. 'Speak French.'

Masha could not understand what Sophie intended to do, but obeyed. 'Are you coming?' she called over her shoulder.

Sophie's ringing voice answered, 'Just a minute,' and in the same breath, still in French, 'I am here! I love you!'

A faint sound came from Mark's window and something white flashed behind the bars. It was all, but Sophie smiled all the way home.

Other Decembrists' wives also wandered around the fortress, especially as the weather became milder. Ladies in fashionable gowns and lace shawls stood in small groups, or walked slowly, keeping as close to the fortress as the sentries allowed. From a distance it looked like a social gathering.

One day Sophie and Masha ran into Marie Volkonska, and stood for a long time talking to her.

'I've left the baby with my parents and came to St. Petersburg,' Marie explained, 'I want to be near my husband.' She glanced at Masha and abruptly changed the subject. 'Did you read in the papers about Glinka being arrested?' she asked. 'I was so glad it turned out to be another Glinka. Ours is in the country with his family and composing hard.'

'And Pushkin?' Masha asked. 'Is he still in exile?'

Unexpectedly, Marie smiled. 'Yes,' she answered, 'He is still in his estate and it is just as well. My brother has received a long letter from him and gave it to me to read. It seems that when Pushkin first heard about Emperor Alexander's death, he decided to go to St. Petersburg without asking permission, hoping that in those troubled days no one would care. He was on his way when a hare ran across the road, right in front of the carriage. It is considered a bad omen, and Pushkin is terribly superstitious. He decided to return home and put off his trip for a day or two. That is how he missed being in Senate Square... And now either in his grave, or in there,' she added sombrely nodding at the fortress.

Masha was listening with interest to Marie's story, but her attention became distracted by the sight of a small black-livened man, who kept running from group to group as if looking for someone. 'Sophie!' she exclaimed as the man came nearer. 'Just look! There is your father's butler Maksim.'

'Why, yes,' Sophie cried, changing colour. 'Could something have happened to Papa? Maksim! Maksim!' She ran towards the man.

Masha and Marie waited anxiously.

Sophie was back almost at once. 'Papa is all right. It's Aunt Daria. She died last Wednesday. She complained of not feeling well these last few days, but it did not seem serious. On Wednesday morning, Emma went into her bedroom and...and found her dead. Maksim says that a messenger has just arrived. He brought two letters. One is for Papa and the other is addressed to you, Masha! Aunt Daria must have written them when she first felt ill. There is also a note from Emma. We must return home immediately.'

25

For ever and ever

The letter to Masha from Daria Ivanovna was quite short and like Aunt Daria herself went straight to the point.

'My dear Masha,' she wrote. 'You like my house, Rodnoye, so I want you to have it after my death. Sophie doesn't need it. I am leaving her enough. Besides, she and Rodnoye are not suited to each other. She would want to change it and it is too set in its ways to stand changes. *You* will accept it as it is, with mice, mould and faded draperies. Be kind to it as you would to an old and faithful dog. Maybe it is only an old woman's fancy, but I believe that you will find happiness under this roof.'

'Happiness...' Masha said aloud. The word sounded hollow and strange. Yet at the same time the thought of Rodnoye seemed somehow to promise a kind of peace. 'Aunt Daria, Aunt Daria,' she thought, 'what thanks could I ever make for such a legacy?' Tears ran down her face and dripped on Daria Ivanovna's letter open in her hand, but why she was crying she could not say. Only a longing to see Rodnoye, dear Rodnoye, now so astonishingly her own house, her home, swept over her like a fever. At Rodnoye, deep in the tranquil countryside, there might be time for bruised hearts to mend...some day.

The trial of the Decembrists began a few days later. In July, the verdict was announced. Five of the Decembrists were sentenced to death, among them Pestel and Kahovski. The others were sentenced to hard labour in Siberian mines, a few for life, the rest for long terms.

When Sophie learned that Mark's sentence was twenty-five years of hard labour, she said simply, 'Thank God he is to live. We can be happy in Siberia too as long as we are together.'

Seeing Masha's movement of surprise, she said firmly, 'Yes, we will be together. I am going to Siberia after Mark.'

Many people hoped that Emperor Nicholas might pardon those condemned to die. Masha knew better. But he relented enough to shorten the terms of those who were to be sent to Siberia.

'Twenty years instead of twenty-five. How generous!' Sophie said ironically. She was frantic with worry about Mark's health. 'He looks thinner and more nervous every time I see him,' she kept saying. 'At least in Siberia he can breathe the air and see the sky. I hope he is going soon.

But summer and autumn slipped away while Mark still languished in the fortress. One foggy November morning, almost a year after the revolt, a sentry, bribed by Sophie, came running to her house to announce that Mark was about to leave.

Masha, who was spending the night at Sophie's, had barely time to throw a cloak around her friend's shoulders. They were just out of the house, when an open wagon flashed past, with Mark inside, sitting beside an armed guard. Mark saw his wife and sprang to his feet, but the heavy hand of the guard pushed him back into his seat.

Sophie turned back into the house. 'They did not even let me kiss him good-bye,' she said brokenly. 'But it doesn't really matter. I will be with him in a few weeks.'

As the months passed, Masha often recalled these words, thinking, 'Thank heaven Sophie did not know how long it would take her to join Mark. She would have died of despair.'

The government did not approve of Decembrists' wives going to Siberia. They were refused the necessary permits and were faced with almost impossible conditions, the hardest of which was that no other member of the family could go. This meant that any children had to be left behind.

'It is inhuman,' Sophie said. 'Poor Marie Volkonska has to leave her baby, and her father threatens to disown her if she does not come back within a year.'

'His Majesty feels that children should not be exposed to such a long journey and hard life,' Masha began, but Sophie cried, 'No, don't speak his name, not in this house!' She added immediately, 'I am sorry, Masha, I did not mean to scream at you, but all these delays are driving me out of my mind. I hear that Catasha Trubetzkoy has all her papers and is leaving soon. Marie is almost ready too. But I am still writing petitions and knocking at doors. Father doesn't do anything to help me. He can't forbid me to go to Mark, but he hopes that I will be prevented from going by the government.'

Catasha Trubetzkoy, wife of the leader of the Decembrists, did leave soon, the first one to go. She was closely followed by Marie Volkonska. Both wrote back long letters to their families and friends, describing the tribulations they had lived through on their way to Siberia. Apparently an order had been given to the authorities to put every obstacle in the way of Decembrists' wives in the hope that they might get so discouraged they would turn back. 'We were refused fresh horses,' Marie wrote, 'We had to sign a document in which we renounced our rights to nobility and our rights to our estates. Catasha was even threatened with the prospect of being sent with a party of criminals, on foot, if she still persisted in her decision. But we did not give in,' Marie ended her letter, 'and now it is all over, we are here, near our husbands.'

'When shall I be with Mark?' Sophie sighed.

Her turn came at last. She left early in the morning of a

mild September day, almost a year after Mark. There was just a faint breath of autumn in the air. Tearful servants filled the hall. Masha was making every effort not to break down. Michael was there. He seemed calm but Masha noticed that his hands were shaking. Sashette stood beside Masha. At the time of Mark's sentence she had written to Sophie a letter of unexpected sweetness and sympathy. 'How like Sashette,' Masha thought. 'She and Sophie have always been across each other, yet now that real trouble has come to Sophie, Sashette has put aside her own ambitions to be loyal and kind.' Smirnov was now governor of a province and did not approve of his wife's association with Decembrists. Sashette pretended she had come to St. Petersburg just to get away from the town of Kaluga. 'It is so nice to be back in civilisation even for a few days,' she told Masha.

Katish Muffle was there too, just back from a trip abroad. Her pink cheeks pale, with frightened eyes, she kept whispering to Masha, 'How can Sophie have such courage? I never could... Never.'

Good-byes were over quickly. Sophie slipped out of her father's arms and went down the front steps, a slender figure in her grey travelling gown, her bronze curls hidden under a tight-fitting grey bonnet.

A special carriage, light but sturdy, with luggage strapped to the roof, stood waiting. Michael helped Sophie in. The door slammed. The driver cried, 'Eh, now, God speed!' For a second Sophie's face appeared in the window, then became a mere blur as the horses picked up speed.

The small group stood frozen in front of the house, the servants lamenting in the door. Then Sophie's father ran to the edge of the pavement and raising his right hand made a sign of the cross in the wake of the disappearing carriage. When the last rumble of the wheels died away, he stumbled up the steps into the house, crossed the hall with unsteady steps and began to mount the stairway, his shoulders sagging. In one brief hour General Brozin had become an old man.

No one attempted to follow him as he went into his study and closed the door behind him. Katish left almost immediately, crying into her handkerchief. Sashette asked Masha, 'Can we sit somewhere quietly and talk just for a few moments? I am going back to Kaluga tomorrow and who knows when we shall see each other again?'

Masha longed to be alone to cry and cry, but she did not want to hurt Sashette's feelings and led the way to the library. Michael followed them, somewhat to Masha's surprise. He did not take part in the conversation, however. Muttering something about being very tired, he lowered himself into a deep armchair and covered his eyes with his hand.

Sashette did most of the talking. As if attempting to dispel their sorrow, she began to describe her new life. Masha could not help thinking of Pushkin. It was the same witty and rather merciless caricature of life in a province.

'And what about yourself?' Sashette asked at last, 'Are you planning to remain a lady-in-waiting?'

'I really don't know,' Masha confessed. 'Everything is so changed since the Emperor Alexander's death. It is not at all the family life we led in Anichkov. I am not complaining, really. Her Majesty is as kind and attentive to me as ever, but she has so many new obligations, she has hardly time for herself. The children's life is changed too. Young Alexander is being prepared to inherit the crown one day, so he is always at the lesson table. His little sisters have new governesses; they have to appear in public, conform to the etiquette much more than before. I would like to leave the court, but where could I go?'

'You could live in that old house Sophie's aunt left to you,' Sashette pointed out, 'Or are you going to sell it?'

'Oh, no,' Masha said quickly. 'I would never sell it. Yes, I would love to live in Rodnoye and there is enough income from the orchards and the dairy to take care of my own expenses and to maintain the house, but the empress says I cannot possibly live there alone.'

'Isn't there Daria Ivanovna's old companion?'

'Emma? She doesn't want to remain in Russia. Daria Ivanovna left her a handsome legacy and she is going back to Germany next month.'

Michael spoke for the first time. 'Would you consider Miss Alice?' he asked Masha. 'I happened to meet her a few days ago. She was walking two unruly little boys on Nevski. She told me that they were too much for her and that she was going to look for a new position. I am sure she would like to live with you. She is not really as old as she looks. She could take good care of the house and of you.'

There was warmth in the last words. The icy burden that was crushing Masha's heart since she parted with Sophie, became a little lighter.

'Miss Alice liked the house,' she said dreamily. 'What a good idea! Maybe, maybe, it could be arranged! She could rule the servants and I could take care of the garden. Sophie and I spent a few days with Emma last spring. The garden was very neglected. The old gardener can't do much. I suppose we could train two young lads from the village. The rose bush under the drawing-room window should be replaced and the bushes pruned. The summerhouse needs a new roof...'

Her eyes fell on the pale autumn sky behind the windows and the light that had kindled in them faded out. 'Those are only plans, after all,' she murmured. 'Winter is not the right time to move into the country, and well, I don't know yet just what I am going to decide.'

'Well, give a thought to that Miss Alice. It sounds like a good idea,' Sashette said rising, 'I must leave you now. I have still a lot of shopping to do and we are leaving the city tomorrow. Can I drop you off at the palace? My carriage is waiting for me.'

Masha shook her head, 'No. I will stay on for a while. There are some things of Sophie's she asked me to put away.'

Michael also rose. 'I must be going too. I don't think my uncle would be in a mood for talking.'

'Would you like a drive?' Sashette asked graciously.

Michael bowed. 'It is very kind of you. I let my cab go. If it is not too much trouble…'

He turned to Masha. 'I suppose that by the time I am back in St. Petersburg, you will be settled in the country,' he said, 'for I have a feeling you will find Miss Alice the answer to your problem. May I offer you now my best wishes for a happy life in your new home?'

Masha gave a start. 'Back in St. Petersburg? I didn't know you were leaving.'

'I have decided to ask for a discharge, I am going to travel abroad for a year or so, then…grow turnips somewhere.'

In a daze, Masha said, 'Sophie never mentioned it.'

'She did not know. It is a recent decision.'

Sophie's voice came back to her, desolately. 'We are going away from happiness, going away with no coming back.' Now Michael was going too. 'I must say something,' she thought, 'Wish him good luck, thank him for all he did for me that night in Senate Square…'

She remained silent. It was useless to talk to someone who seemed already so far away. Even Michael's voice sounded remote, as if coming from a distance. She could hardly hear him when he said good-bye. Sashette kissed her and she answered something, hoping it was the right thing to say. Now he and Sashette were going to the door. A pale sunbeam caught the gold of Michael's epaulettes. It was like watching someone on the other side of an abyss. A few more steps. They were gone.

Masha sat down beside the writing-desk, her chin in her cupped hands and vaguely glanced around.

The sun was gone, leaving the library filled with bleak light. The furniture was disarranged; a thin layer of dust covered the polished surface of the desk. In the turmoil of the last few days before Sophie's departure, servants had neglected the room.

'I must…' Masha said aloud and stopped, wondering what she was going to say. 'Oh, what is the difference?' she whispered to herself, letting her head drop on the desk. The door creaked and she quickly turned around. For a second she thought she saw Sashette's face, but no one came in. Getting up, Masha walked to the window and pressed her forehead against the glass.

'You wanted me? What can I do for you?' Michael's voice asked behind her.

'But it couldn't be. He is gone, gone forever,' Masha told herself, then turned around very slowly, because of course it was all a dream and if she moved fast she might wake up.

But it was Michael. He repeated, 'You wanted me?' Masha silently shook her head. Michael looked bewildered. 'I went to order Mademoiselle Rossett's carriage brought to the door,' he explained. 'When I came back, she told me, "Go to Masha. She needs you".'

Masha corrected mechanically, 'She is not Mademoiselle Rossett any more.'

But Michael was clearly not interested in Sashette's married name. 'The way she said it, I thought you really needed me,' he said slowly, 'Never mind, I must have misunderstood her.'

He turned to go, then stopped and looked back. 'Masha,' he asked softly his eyes on her face, 'Are you sure you don't need me?'

Masha never realised just how she had moved. She only knew that the next moment her head was resting on the gold epaulette and she was whispering frantically, 'Yes, I do need you, Michael! I do. I do.'

He whispered back, 'And I need you more than I can say. For years now you have been the centre of my dreams modest, everyday dreams, but they were all for you.'

'But you never told me,' Masha began.

He answered gravely, 'There was no need. I think that in your heart you always knew I loved you, but...there was Sergei.'

Masha tried to speak, but he wouldn't let her. 'No,' he said, 'You don't have to explain. You and Sergei were in opposite camps on December fourteenth. I can guess what happened. But I could also see how hard it was for you to see me alive when Sergei fell in the Senate Square. I have told you before, and I am repeating it now...if it depended on me to change places with my brother, I would do it to give him a chance to win you back and make you happy.'

In the stillness that followed Michael's last words, Masha was remembering. The dark garden...light falling from the drawing-room windows and forming squares on the flagstones of the terrace...music...Sergei's kiss, mingled with the taste of raindrops and the smell of wet earth. She asked herself, 'Could I ever forget?' and as if in answer, another remembrance came, Marie Volkonska's voice singing, *A moment I recall enchanted.* She knew then that she could not forget, but that her first love was now only 'an enchanted moment' in the past. But there was a new feeling in her heart now and she was ready to carry it into the future, without fear of disappointment, without misgivings ...

Suddenly calm, she looked into Michael's face. 'How could I let you give your life away?' she asked, 'when it is going to be my life too.'

He stared at her almost unbelievingly, then a look of such tenderness came into his face that she almost cried out. His arms tightened around her, their faces almost touched. He spoke low, 'Masha, you care, then… But I want you to be sure, darling. You have just lost Sophie; you are tired, upset. You need time to think. Suppose you went to the country with Miss Alice and in spring, when your flowers begin to bloom, I will come and ask you to be my wife? Then, if you still think you could be happy with me…'

Masha interrupted him. 'No,' she whispered, 'You don't have to wait till spring. I am sure. I want to be yours.'

'For ever and ever,' he said, and their lips met.

Sometime later they both remembered Sashette and went to look for her. Maksim, the butler, said she had left, and presented Masha with a note on a silver salver. She read it, with Michael looking over her shoulder. There was only one line, 'I want at least one of us three to be happy.'

26

The reunion

It was June 1829 when Masha saw Sophie again. By that time, the Decembrists had been transferred from the mines of Nerchinsk to a small settlement called Chita.

'Siberia scares me,' Masha confessed to Michael as they were discussing their long planned voyage. 'I can't imagine it otherwise than a wild tangle of woods, full of ferocious animals.'

'I will be with you,' he reminded her with a smile. 'We will brave the woods and the animals together.'

Masha blushed and smiled back, but still looked anxious. 'We will be away from home for almost three months,' she said frowning, 'I am worried about little Sophie. She is only a year and a half and this is the first time I will be leaving her.'

Michael stroked her hair, 'Don't worry, darling. Surely with Miss Alice ruling the house and Nastia in the nursery, little Sophie will be quite safe.'

'I suppose so,' Masha agreed. 'Aren't we lucky to have them both! Oh Michael, sometimes I think I have almost too much good fortune.'

Michael smiled, drew his wife close and kissed her. 'I am the luckiest one,' he said, 'So let's do some more planning. If we leave in the first week of May, we will be in Siberia by June, right in summer. And their summer is short, you know, only five weeks, but in those weeks everything is in bloom. We will have a wonderful trip, you will see.'

The voyage did turn out to be pleasant. The roads were

good and the horses swift. Masha was awed by the woods, even though she did not see any wild beasts. Michael was right. In every meadow, flowers were blooming, larger, more vivid than any flowers she had ever seen before. Fields of corn promised rich harvest. Nature was doing its utmost in the short spell of sun it was allowed to have.

Chita was not in the woods. It lay in a valley fringed by two small but clear-watered rivers. Mountains protected it from the cold northern winds. The whole settlement consisted of about twenty small log houses, an old church and a prison.

Sophie's house was a log cabin rented from a peasant. There were two big flower-beds in front of the porch and a vegetable garden behind.

'All planted by me,' Sophie said proudly, 'And we have poultry too. It is nice to have fresh eggs. Only I don't expect the hens to lay twice a day,' she added with a laugh.

Masha gave her friend a quick glance. Sophie had not changed much. Her face was thinner, but it was still Sophie's young, eager face. The bronze hair waved and curled. The eyes changed from blue to green. Only the laugh was different. There was a broken note in it that no gaiety could cover.

The first night of Masha's visit, the girls did not sleep at all, there was so much to talk about.

Sitting cross-legged on the bed, Sophie was telling Masha everything she could not write about because the Decembrists' mail was censored. 'This is paradise compared to our first year in Siberia,' she said. 'It was only once or maybe twice a month that we could visit our husbands and a guard was always present. The rest of the time we only got glimpses of them as they passed to and back from work surrounded by guards. Mark was ill and wretched. The prison was filthy.' She knitted her brows in painful recollection. 'The three of us, I mean Catasha, Marie and myself, rented a small room, so small we had to sleep on the floor; there was no place for beds. When the other wives came along, we were already in Chita and everything was easier. There are no mines here and this means no underground work for our husbands. Mark may spend a few hours with me every day. You will see him tomorrow.'

'Is he still...' Masha began and hesitated to finish the sentence.

Sophie understood her. 'No, he is not chained any more. The chains were taken off all the Decembrists last year. But Mark is taking his exile hard. Marie's husband shares his cell. Mark talks in his sleep every night and it is always about Otrada. He gives orders to saddle his horse, calls the dogs for a walk, asks about the fruit harvest. Masha, did Otrada really exist? Or did I fall asleep during a dull lesson in Smolni and dream it all up? I am not sure any more.'

Holding back her tears, Masha caressed the small hand roughened by work. 'Sophie, dearest, why feel so hopeless? You will be back in Otrada one day.'

'Back?' Sophie smiled sadly. 'You know, Masha, the first year, I used to pray for a miracle that would make it possible for us to return. Later, especially since Papa's death, I gave up praying and hoping. Anyway, even if we did return sometime...it would not be the same. When you see Mark, you will understand.'

To distract Sophie, Masha began telling her the latest news about their old Smolni classmates. Sophie listened eagerly and kept asking questions. 'So Sashette is travelling abroad again,' she said pensively, 'Does she ever live with her husband?'

'As little as possible,' Masha admitted. 'She is not happy with him, or rather more unhappy than she expected to be. I wrote to you about Stephanie. She is married to a Polish nobleman and lives in Paris. Sashette is with them now.'

'I never liked Sashette,' Sophie said, 'but she came the

day I left…and after you wrote to me how she straightened things out between you and Michael, I tried to think kindly of her. Only…I am probably not trying hard enough.'

Masha laughed and breathed easier. The last remark sounded more like old Sophie. They talked on…about Nadia Maslova, married to an Italian count and living in Rome, about the recent wedding of Katish Muffle. 'Her husband is an officer of the Imperial guard, and he is pink-cheeked and kindly, just like Katish herself,' Masha described.

'Marriages and marriages,' Sophie said, 'I suppose you will be telling me next that Lena Mandrika is engaged too.' Masha's face became serious. 'Lena? No, just the opposite. I met her at Katish' wedding and she told me… It is confidential, but I don't think she would mind my telling you.'

'She is going to be a nun after all?' Sophie gasped.

Masha nodded. 'Yes. She is quite decided. Sometime this year, she said.'

'And Anna Wulff?' Sophie suddenly remembered. 'Do you see her often? I can remember how you complained that she hardly ever wrote since we saw her in the country. But now that you are neighbours…I often wondered why you never mentioned her in your letters.'

Masha sighed. 'Because there is nothing much to say about Anna. She lives at home as before. Helps her mother to entertain guests, looks after the house. She seems just as usual, even happy. Only I know that she is…well, *empty* inside.'

'Pushkin is in St. Petersburg, I suppose?'

'Oh, yes! He is becoming more and more famous. Of course now that we live in the country I don't hear much St. Petersburg gossip, but Katish told me that Pushkin is courting a beautiful young girl, Nathalie Goncharov. I never mentioned it to Anna. Why make her suffer?'

'Do you miss the palace, and the grand duchess, I mean Empress Alexandra Feodorovna?' Sophie asked curiously.

'The palace life? No, not at all. Her Majesty I see every time we are in St. Petersburg. She is my little daughter's Godmother and I am afraid she expected me to call the child Alexandra, but I couldn't. Both Michael and I felt Sophie was the right name.'

'It is sweet of you,' Sophie said warmly. Her face became sad. 'I would have liked to have children, but it is better that we don't. What a future they would have exiled in Siberia, deprived of their birthrights...I had to sign a paper renouncing my rights. They wouldn't even bear our name. They would be called Markov; that is the regulation. Children born to the prisoners in Siberia are called by their father's first name. Oh, never mind. I am with Mark and that is all that matters. Poor Mark. I wonder if you are going to recognise him.'

'You exaggerate,' Masha protested. But when she saw Mark the next day, she stared at him, waiting to hear his voice, to make sure that this thin, tired-looking man, with slightly hunched shoulders and unsteady hands was really the gay, elegant master of Otrada. He and Michael spent a long time sitting on a bench outside the house and talking. Michael told Masha later that Mark wanted to know every bit of news about his old regiment and the friends left behind, but spoke very little about his prison life. As he talked, his eyes were constantly on Sophie who was showing her flower-beds to Masha. 'If she had not followed me here, I would have done away with myself, or gone out of my mind,' he said simply.

Other Decembrists' wives gathered at Sophie's in the evening to greet Masha. There were nine of them altogether. Masha found Marie Volkonska very changed, looking much older than her early twenties, with deep sadness in every feature. 'It is since her baby son died last year,' Sophie whispered to Masha.

The young women talked all at once, telling Masha how difficult it was for them to learn how to cook a simple meal or to put a patch on their clothes. 'Behold our teacher!' Catasha Trubetzkoy cried, introducing Masha to a thin, dark-haired woman with quick, bird like movements. 'This is Pauline Annenkova. She is French and she followed her fiancé, Captain Annenkov to Siberia like the rest of us. We had such a wonderful time at her wedding. Now she generously shares with us the secrets of French cookery.'

Pauline smiled and said, 'If I could only persuade all of you that cleaning a chicken is not such an heroic deed after all.'

'Masha has brought a big case of books with her,' Sophie announced. 'I am going to be the librarian and keep track of the borrowers.'

'You can't imagine how hungry we all are for something new to read,' one of the young women told Masha. 'Many of our relatives send us books and magazines, but they take so long coming. We know every book we have by heart now.'

'So we compromise by telling stories,' Sophie joined in. 'We all gather in someone's house and each one of us in turn tells a story she had read or made up, the more unusual the better. And lately we have had a real mystery to occupy our minds. There has been a lot of talk lately about a strange man called Feodor Kuzmich. He appeared in this region about a year ago and people consider him almost a saint. He lives in a hut in the woods and dresses like a peasant. Yet, it is rumoured that he speaks several languages and that he is highly educated. Nobody knows where he comes from. He never speaks about himself and if someone asks, he doesn't answer. But strangest of all; he looks just like the late Emperor Alexander.'

'Emperor Alexander!' Masha exclaimed. 'Could it be he?'

'Of course not,' Marie Volkonska shrugged her shoulders. 'Unfortunately, we can't really judge. The man lives several miles away from Chita, too far for us to visit him. As to the local people...who of them knows what the emperor really looked like? Most of his pictures show him when he was quite young.'

'It is not impossible,' Catasha Trubetzkoy said thoughtfully, 'There was talk, you remember...'

'There is bound to be talk when the ruler of Russia dies suddenly in a remote place like Taganrogue,' Marie insisted. 'The whole story was probably invented by someone. Now, would you like me to sing for you? Then Pauline can recite a French poem. Pity we have no piano!'

Singing and reciting, laughing and joking, the Decembrists' wives never let their husbands realise what a sacrifice they made in following them. But underneath the shield of courage, Masha could sense a desperate longing for the old brilliant life, the loved ones, the ancestral homes, the freedom.

Little things betrayed them... Tears in Marie Volkonska's eyes as she looked at a coloured illustration of a valley in Crimea, in one of the books Masha brought. 'I recognise it,' she whispered. 'We stayed in an inn nearby. It was the time when Pushkin travelled with us. He and I galloped along that very road. Just behind that bend, there was an old stone wall, the top all hung with wild roses. Pushkin picked one for me and almost broke his neck doing it.' Sophie's eyes following the flight of a flock of birds and her almost inaudible, 'They are free...free.'

She rallied fast, began to laugh and to tell Masha about a new kind of cake she had baked for tea. 'I really enjoy cooking you know,' she declared with her usual dauntless air. Marie too had smiled and said that of course Crimea was beautiful but she preferred Siberian landscapes because everything was so immense, so breathtaking.

The men were less good at pretence, but they spoke cheerfully about their new hobbies. Some were writing their memoirs, some turned mechanics, taking old clocks apart and making new ones out of them, a few painted. They did their best to sound enthusiastic but it was never wholly successful.

Masha tried to help in keeping up the illusion. She also laughed and talked, told every bit of news about common friends, the latest books, and fashions. But every night, when she found herself alone with Michael in the small two-roomed hut that was put at their disposal, she wept bitterly, and nestled close to him.

'It is so heart-breaking, so pitiful,' she whispered to him between sobs, 'They are all slowly dying, not so much from physical work, but from despair. Marie Volkonska is still in her twenties, but she looks forty. And Mark! Do you know that he is losing notion of time? We were talking about our little Sophie and he said, "She must be about twelve now, or is she older?" I did not know what to answer. Then I saw Sophie's face and the way she looked…it went right through my heart. Oh, Michael, maybe I should have thrown myself at His Majesty's feet at the time, and pleaded for his mercy. I lived in the palace then; I had access to the emperor.'

'It wouldn't have done any good,' Michael spoke heavily, 'His own wife tried to plead for the Decembrists, without success. You told me so yourself.'

'You think there is no hope!'

'Hope?' There was so much bitterness and grief in Michael's eyes, Masha could hardly recognise her always calm, even-tempered husband, 'Every time another child is born in the Imperial family, or a victory is celebrated, I hope. I keep saying to myself that maybe there will be an amnesty. Often an amnesty is given, but never to *them*. I don't know if *we* should hope any more, but *they* will, year after year, until they are too old to care any more.'

'Some have given up already,' Masha murmured, 'And yet,' she went on, 'several people told me that at least twice a year new instructions arrive from St. Petersburg, signed by Nicholas, and they always contain orders to make life a little more comfortable for the prisoners. Do you think it is a good sign?'

Michael sighed, 'No, I don't think so. On the contrary, I think it means that they are to stay in exile for a long time.' He clenched his hands so that the bones cracked. 'To think that all those high ideals, noble dreams, youth, intelligence, are all rendered useless, trodden into the ground. That is what is torturing these men, the feeling of uselessness.'

'And at the same time most of the prisoners speak about the emperor without hate, even with devotion,' Masha said wonderingly, 'Can you understand it?'

Instead of answering, Michael rose and, walking over to the window, stood looking at the dark night sky. 'How could we understand them?' he said. 'They were knights fighting for what was sacred to them, the way they understood it. Now they are martyrs.' He turned around and coming close to Masha leaned on the back of her chair. 'We are just two ordinary people,' he said softly, 'All we can do is to help them carry their burden of suffering for at least a few steps of the way.'

The burden of suffering...it seemed to Masha that she was feeling the full weight of it on her shoulders when the day came to leave Chita.

The carriage stood ready. The Decembrists' wives were all gathered around Michael and Masha. Their husbands had said their good-byes at dawn, before going off to work at some excavation at the other end of the settlement.

For several minutes no one spoke or moved. Then Marie Volkonska stepped forward and coming to Masha, embraced her. 'God speed,' she said, 'Thank you for bringing us a little of the world. Your visit had done us all good.'

She pressed a small packet of flower seeds into Masha's hand, saying, 'Plant these in your garden. They will remind you of us.'

The other young women followed Marie, kissing Masha, thanking her for coming, wishing her well. Their voices were calm, but the eyes were wistful.

'Next time you are abroad and visit France, think of me,' Pauline Annenkova begged Masha with a little catch in her voice.

Sophie was the last to say good-bye. Her cheek felt icy cold as she laid it against Masha's. 'If you only knew,' she whispered, 'how I thank God for letting us see each other once more in this life.'

'Sophie, darling,' Masha clung to her friend, 'Don't talk as this were the last time. We will be coming again. Michael promised…'

Sophie interrupted her. 'No,' she said, 'You will not come back. I feel it. Oh, I know you want to, but life is going on. Little Sophie will be needing you more and more; other children will come. Masha, if you have a son, will you call him Mark? So that there will be Sophie and Mark again?'

'Of course I will,' Masha assured her through tears, 'Oh, Sophie, you two were so happy and then… Why, why did all this have to happen!'

'You don't understand,' Sophie drew herself up, straight and slim in her plain calico dress, her blue-green eyes shining in her pale face. 'If on my wedding day,' she said clearly, 'someone had told me that I was going to be the wife of a prisoner in Siberia, I would still have married Mark. I am happy, in a different way, but I am, and I have no regrets.' She took a deep breath, murmured, 'Good-bye. Give my love to little Sophie,' kissed Masha almost vehemently, flung her arms around Michael, turned and ran up the porch steps into her house.

'Better leave her alone,' Pauline said. 'She does not like

to be seen crying.'

Masha only nodded. Through a haze of tears, she watched Michael saying good-bye to each of the young women, reverently touching with his lips their work-roughened hands.

It was all over at last. Masha was in the carriage beside Michael. A speck of white fluttered in Sophie's window. A chorus of voices called, 'Good-bye! God speed! Come back!'

Overcome by grief, Masha spent most of the day hunched in her seat, her face in her hands, memories crowding around her.

Smolni...Sophie in brown uniform...the Summer Garden...Otrada...Peter and Paul fortress...Sophie leaving for Siberia...

It was almost evening when Masha calmed down a little. She drew a long quivering breath, pushed back her hair and looked around.

The sun was low in the west. Woods and clearings rolled by. It smelled of earth and pines. Tired after crying, Masha leaned against Michael and fought drowsiness as the open carriage balanced softly in rhythm to the horses' steps.

A man appeared from a side road. Tall, with stooping shoulders, dressed in a long white shirt and white trousers, he walked slowly, leaning on a stick.

Masha felt pity for the man. He looked old and lonely. Please stop for a moment,' she called the coachman. 'Let this man sit with you. We will give him a lift.' Turning to her husband she said in French, 'It is going to be night soon. He is too old to wander alone on the roads.'

The man was now walking alongside the carriage. At the sound of Masha's voice, he started and lifted faded blue eyes. She saw a round face framed in white beard, high forehead and grey hair sparingly covering the head. But before she had time to say another word, the man turned and began to walk rapidly in the opposite direction. In another moment he had vanished behind a clump of trees.

'It was he!' Masha exclaimed, 'Didn't you recognise him?'

Michael answered, bewildered, 'I am afraid I was not really looking at him. Who is he?'

Masha whispered, 'I recognised him, and I think he recognised me. It was…Emperor Alexander.'

27

Home

'Should I tell Her Majesty about the emperor?' Masha asked Michael the next day, as the carriage was speeding along the Siberian roads.

His eyes on the far-away horizon, he answered. 'No, I don't think you should. First of all, you can't be really sure. It was twilight and you saw whoever it was only fleetingly.'

'But I *am* sure,' Masha insisted. 'It was the emperor; his face, his eyes, and when I began to speak, he looked at me and our eyes met. I am *sure* it was he.'

Michael would not be persuaded. 'I still think you should not mention it to anyone,' he said. 'The emperor is believed to be resting in peace. Let him rest. Maybe one day when he is just a figure in history you can tell the story to our children. But now, let's say that it was only a dream.'

'I suppose you are right,' Masha agreed pensively. 'Very well then, it was a dream.'

Animation faded from her face and it became serious and sad again. She kept silent most of the time, answering listlessly when her husband talked to her or pointed out some beautiful spot they passed.

'You are worn out,' Michael said anxiously as day after day Masha remained quiet and withdrawn. 'All this travelling has been too much for you. The best thing would be to get you home fast.'

But in spite of his generous tips to the coachmen to get the fastest horses, it was five weeks later that they reached Pskov. Once more horses were changed, but this time they were horses from Rodnoye and Daria Ivanovna's old coachman was in the driver's seat.

It was a warm day at the end of August, with a faint breath of autumn in the air. Here and there red and yellow leaves showed among the greenery. It had rained the night before. The wheels of the carriage left long traces on the beaten-down dust.

Masha sat with clasped hands, her bonnet hanging by the ribbons on her back, the light breeze ruffling the ringlets of her hair.

Michael looked at her with concern. 'We should have rested a little longer in Pskov,' he said, 'I did not expect the horses to arrive so quickly.'

The old coachman turned around. 'I had the horses out of the stable and harnessed the minute your messenger arrived from Pskov, barin,' he announced, well pleased with himself.

Masha murmured, 'I am not tired. I did not want to stay in Pskov,' and closed her eyes.

Michael bent over her. 'Masha, dearest, I haven't seen you smile once since we left Chita. Are you still grieving so much? Or is there something else? Couldn't you tell me?'

Masha opened her eyes and looked at Michael's face, so anxious, so loving and tender. Taking his hand she pressed it against her cheek. 'Don't worry about me,' she said softly. 'I will tell you. That month in Chita made me realise something... For *us* the Senate Square tragedy was like a passing storm. It came, crashed upon us, made everything around us dark, and then it passed. We saw that our world was still with us. We reached out for happiness. It was granted us and...we began to forget. For those in Siberia the storm is over too, but their world is in ruins. They can't forget because the nightmare is still with them. I can't forget either. They are in my thoughts always, their grief is my grief. I feel guilty because we are free and they are not.

Michael, how am I going to live with it?'

'I will tell you,' Michael's arms went around Masha, strong and reassuring. 'Yes,' he said, 'The exiles of Siberia are with us; they are part of our lives and it depends on us to make those lives worthy of them. Please God, we may have enough strength to do it. I will do my best to help the serfs, ease their living, prepare them for the freedom. And you will bring up our children, until one day our sons too will be ready to uphold their ideals, and our daughters will follow their husbands wherever fate might take them.'

Masha echoed, her face already clearing, more serene, 'Yes, please God, we will do our part.'

The carriage rolled up the lime avenue. The roof of the house came in sight, the attic windows gleaming in the sun.

Masha started. 'There is something in the attic! Something grey moved behind that window!' she exclaimed. 'Do you see it? No, now it is gone.'

'Perhaps it is the Domovoy,' Michael suggested seriously. 'Welcoming us home.'

'Yes, you promised me a Domovoy, that day in Yelagin, in the snow. 'Maybe it *was* a Domovoy,' Masha said smiling for the first time. Then her face clouded again and she said anxiously, 'Michael, I have just thought of something. We have been away so long, little Sophie may not recognise us.'

Michael looked into her eyes. 'Little Sophie will not have forgotten us,' he said earnestly. 'But you *have* changed. There is something new in your face, some new light in your eyes. You have grown up and you are even dearer to me than before.'

Another turn of the wheels and there was Rodnoye. Miss Alice stood on the porch steps in her best green gown, an imposing bunch of keys at her belt. Beside her stood Nastia, her pink calico dress stiff with starch, little Sophie in her arms. The child clasped Nastia's neck with both hands and stared at the approaching carriage with big grey eyes. Behind them servants were crowding. Everyone was present, from Maksim the butler, whom Michael had inherited after General Brozin's death, to the last kitchen maid.

Something warm, almost burning, stirred in Masha's breast. 'Here they are all,' she whispered to herself, 'waiting for us, loving us. Even the house itself is waiting and loving. How much, how very much God had given me.'

Little Sophie suddenly cried, 'Mamma!' and began to jump in Nastia's arms.

Masha opened her arms, her eyes shining, her heart overflowing with deep, humble thankfulness as the carriage drew to a halt.

ALSO AVAILABLE

Masha

Mara Kay

Masha Fredericks travels to St. Petersburg from her home in the country in 1815 to attend the Smolni Institute for Noble Girls. Girls are expected to study there for the full course of nine years and spend all their holidays at the school. Quiet, superstitious and very shy, she finds it difficult to adapt to boarding school life preferring to watch from the side-lines.

Mara Kay (1918-1990) provided little information about her own life avoiding interviews and publicity. Contemporary accounts indicate that she was of Russian origin, but lived in Yugoslavia before emigrating to the United States. She worked as a translator and a copywriter in New York in the 1960s and 1970s while also writing more than ten novels for young adults.

ALSO AVAILABLE

The Two Linties

Clare Mallory

> "We feel sure that the young people of Hillingdon will welcome a new feature in our columns, devoted exclusively to their interests. To-day we launch a children's page, and we want it to be reader-written. The first issues cannot be, but as soon as possible the results of literary competitions will provide the greater part of the material used. We are convinced that there is sufficient talent in this city to fill a weekly page with stories, poems, articles, and sketches of good standard. Prizes will be generous, and every encouragement given to the young writers and artists. Cousin Rosemary will be a friend to all of them, and she will, we know, receive a very warm welcome. All success to her and her Hillingdon Club!"

These are tempting words to an imaginative orphan and ones that inspire her to create a new identity for herself. Lintie Oliver, the most mischievous resident of St Anne's Orphanage, reinvents herself as Lynette Hope, prize-winning writer. Submitting stories, articles and plays under a nom de plume result in colour and excitement flooding into her drab life. *The Two Linties* is the story of her double life as she grapples with unhoped-for success and the chance to change her own life and help her friends realise their dreams. Out of print since the 1950s, Clare Mallory's rare novel is a gentle tale of childhood life in New Zealand.

ALSO AVAILABLE

Five Farthings
A London Story

Monica Redlich

A sudden change in circumstances forces the five members of the Farthing family to move from a quiet corner of Sussex to the noise and bustle of the City of London

The family rents a flat in the shadow of St Paul's in a City dominated by Wren churches, publishing houses and busy office workers.

Five Farthings is a family story and domestic adventure set in London. With her father in hospital, her mother returned to work, eldest daughter Vivien looks after the home. It is a story of a girl's first job and first love as well as the need for sharp eyes and sharp elbows when attempting to board the bus.

ALSO AVAILABLE

Candy Nevill

Clare Mallory

Some people have a gift for cooking and Candy Nevill is lucky enough to be one of those people. She's also the slowest and youngest member of a family of academic high-flyers who don't always value light scones or delicious suppers when compared to captaining sports teams or achieving the highest marks.

Candida Nevill, known to the family as Candy, is an ordinary schoolgirl with a habit of daydreaming and coming a very distant fourth to her three successful and confident elder siblings. Candy is content to drift through her schooldays, not even playing team games, and it's only the start of cooking lessons that show that she can be successful too.

Unpublished in her lifetime Clare Mallory's novel is a tale of childhood life in New Zealand.